'If Hunter S. Thompson [met someone] in a bar and offered him some very high quality drugs, the resulting conversation would not be half so strange as Nick Revell's *Night of the Toxic Ostrich* . . . There are shades of Kingsley Amis here, a ruthless anatomising of motive and delusion and an appreciation that, in the end, nothing is as absurd as human behaviour . . . Revell's first novel *House of the Spirit Levels*, drew frequent comparison with Ben Elton but he is better than that'
The Times

Nick Revell's extensive writing credits for radio and television include *Drop the Dead Donkey*, *The Million Pound Radio Show* and *Sunday Format*, which won the 1999 British Comedy Award for best radio comedy. He has also presented Radio 4's *Open Book*.

He lives in London and wherever else he happens to be at the time.

Also by Nick Revell

House of the Spirit Levels

Night of The Toxic Ostrich

Nick Revell

HEADLINE

Copyright © 2000 Nick Revell

The right of Nick Revell to be identified as the Author of
the Work has been asserted by him in accordance with
the Copyright, Designs and Patents Act 1988.

First published in Great Britain in 2000
by HEADLINE BOOK PUBLISHING

First published in paperback in 2001
by HEADLINE BOOK PUBLISHING

10 9 8 7 6 5 4 3 2 1

All rights reserved. No part of this publication may be reproduced,
stored in a retrieval system, or transmitted, in any form or by any
means without the prior written permission of the publisher, nor be
otherwise circulated in any form of binding or cover other than that
in which it is published and without a similar condition being
imposed on the subsequent purchaser.

ISBN 0 7472 6755 3

Typeset by Avon Dataset Ltd, Bidford-on-Avon, Warks

Printed and bound in Great Britain by
Mackays of Chatham plc, Chatham, Kent

HEADLINE BOOK PUBLISHING
A division of Hodder Headline
338 Euston Road
London NW1 3BH

www.headline.co.uk
www.hodderheadline.com

To Rosemary and Peter

CHAPTER ONE

There they are – at the table in the corner, by the window. (The seats by the window are the best seats in the restaurant; and getting any seat in this restaurant can take two months if you're not connected, even at Saturday brunch-time.) That's James, gazing out through the opaque glass diamonds in the leaded panes. The bloke in the suit sitting opposite him on the bench – sorry, the banquette – keeping one eye on James and one eye on the rest of the room – isn't a bloke. Not that the fact she isn't a bloke but appears to be one should necessarily be the first thing you notice about her, but it always is – 'Is that bloke a woman?' is a phrase you always hear in public around Cressida. Or Sid, as she prefers to be known. Yes, that bloke is a woman. Yes, the one with the moustache and sort of unisex Bruce Lee haircut. Yes, a moustache. Relax, it's just a moustache, what else did you think it was? A groomed, manicured, deliberate moustache – so what? This is London in the twenty-first century for heaven's sake.

Listen, if you're freaked out by a woman proudly sporting facial hair then that's your problem. It looks sick? Oh, really! You are stuck in totally outmoded conventions of gender distinction. You wouldn't get upset about a woman wearing trousers, would you? Well then, relax about the moustache.

Anyway, the thing with Sid's moustache is, she had it grafted on specially. She had some piece of skin that supports hair growth removed from... wherever it was before... and grafted into her upper lip. She had it done at some clinic in New Mexico and it was very expensive and it's a Statement. Of some kind. Fashion, probably, with a little bit of Political thrown in. In eight months the fashion will have passed and Sid will go back to the clinic in New Mexico to have the hair-bearing skin re-replaced with ordinary non-hair-bearing skin. She's already trying to sell an idea to ITV featuring one of her ex-stand-up comedian clients as the presenter of a wacky TV series – a sort of gardening-DIY-cookery-nostalgia-costume-drama quiz show, apparently – just to pay for it.

So they're sitting there, James with a Bloody Mary, Sid with a Virgin, and studying the brunch menu and you won't be surprised to know this is a showbiz restaurant. Which is how come Sid is wearing an extremely well-cut grey Prada suit – while James is slouching in jeans and a sweater that would make Bob Geldof look like Beau Brummell. Well, judge for yourself – there's Bob Geldof over there.

James being the client – Sid's top client – he has at his right hand a tin of rolling tobacco. Sid being the agent has at her right hand – that little silver case – her mobile phone.

They both like this restaurant. James likes it because people don't bother him for autographs and occasionally he'll get a cheery wave or matey nod of recognition from someone more famous than himself which secretly still gives him a bit of a thrill. (Although of course at the same time he also hates anyone more famous than he is.) He likes being a member of the Famous Club. Not that he can admit to this of course, he's too cool. Moody, iconoclastic. A full-blown Scourge of the Establishment. This is why he sits with his back to the room. It implies he's not interested. His slouched posture as he reads the menu is meant to convey he's only there under sufferance, that he'd just as happily be in a greasy spoon. In fact, he's only reading the menu to give the impression he doesn't know it off by heart but he does, and he knows exactly what he wants, which is the Eggs Benedict.

Sid, on the other hand, likes to sit facing the room because she is never off duty, never missing a trick, never failing to absorb and assimilate the subtle information around her, to read the latest shifts in the showbiz power structure: which agent is dining with which producer, which actor is dining with which journalist, inferring from tiny clues in body language who has fallen out with whom, who has made up with or started sleeping with whom; who is getting the best table, the most attentive service, who is on nodding terms with minor royalty (is there any other kind these days?) or a major TV executive. Oh, and the food is very good. Very good indeed, although they're long past noticing that, if they ever did. But it's OK, because if they do occasionally remember, they can go home and, in their hardback copies of the restaurant's very own cookbook, look up the meal they've just had, and know what to think of it.

Cressida has never been known to eat any of the food set before her in public anyway. This is *not* because she uses coke, OK, if that's what you're thinking. She spent six weeks in Cold Turkey dealing with all that. Not cold turkey, but Cold Turkey™, the new Post-Modernist Rehab Clinic For The Post-Ironic New Millennium©. And now she's completely clean. Completely. Just the occasional social line or two when it would be rude to refuse. She's certainly not anorexic, either; she's an agile ten stone and works out in the gym every day. Her fitness is a mystery which has provoked hushed conversations about pacts with the Devil from even the most notoriously materialist of commentators.

Sid has been James's agent for over ten years now. They met – where else? – in Edinburgh, at the Festival, when James was a skinny little would-be iconoclast and budding Scourge of the Establishment (although already moody), performing in a nondescript venue way off the main vein of the Fringe, and Sid was a theatrical agent with a second-rate client list reinventing herself as a manager for the new rock and roll, which apparently comedy was at that time (although much harder to dance to). Agents and managers were swarming all over the Edinburgh Festival in those days looking for an Elvis to play Colonel Parker to. Sid had never expected anything could cause her to go as far north as Edinburgh, but she took a deep breath, joined the gold rush and started panning. She sacrificed her designer suits and six pairs of kitten-heeled Manolos to the harsh climate and conditions of the Edinburgh Festival – trudging up and down hills by day, negotiating weather that lurched in minutes from Mediterranean to Arctic, and by night hanging out in bars full of chain-smoking hard-drinking drug-taking rubber-necking egomaniacs with barely a genuine smile between them and only one thing on their minds: they all wanted to fuck each other. Either metaphorically, or literally. Indeed she got the impression that the ideal was both ways simultaneously. She felt so at home.

James's show had created a bit of a buzz that year by being controversial ('controversial' in comedy terms means giving your audience stuff they agree with but which they think would upset the kind of people who would never go to see the show anyway) and several agents and managers had been chasing him. Sid saw his show, saw potential, and hatched a plan. She eavesdropped on his conversations in late night bars for a couple of evenings whenever he was persuaded (such a difficult task) to talk about his act. Then when she 'bumped' into him a couple of days later and proceeded to repeat his own opinions back to him, James was beguiled. It was as if this woman was a part of him. She understood him. Her favourite parts of his act were his favourite parts of his act.

She was pretty too, he realised. At first she had seemed severe and less approachable than most of the women he knew. It was the suit. But now he realised she was younger than she'd first appeared. Her hair in those days had been cut in a short crop, and at first accentuated the hardness of her face. But four or five Jack Daniels later James decided it wasn't hardness, it was fine bones. She probably wasn't much older than him. And she kept herself fit; you could tell from how she moved. And the freckles across her nose, which he now decided was quite snubby and cute, actually gave her a flirtatious edge if you paid attention. Especially when she gave that little . . . look. He was sure she'd just given him a little . . . look. Hadn't she?

For a male feminist comedian, he didn't half have a surprisingly consistent slant on women. Not that he realised it. Of course, this came as no surprise to Sid, who had been playing him like a fish. In fact, he was standing there gaping as if he'd already been gaffed and slung in the bottom of the boat. But Sid was in no hurry, wanting to be certain, happy to bide her time. Whenever other people joined them, she happily conceded the conversation to them and stood there smiling and listening and forgetting nothing. During the evening of course, dozens of James's friends and acquaintances – many of whom he didn't know – came tumbling, staggering and strutting into the room and greeted him. James was popular because his show was going very well. (Oh, and because he was such a nice guy.) Strangely enough, none of his mates had seen any of the many good reviews his show had had, but most of them were able – with much anguish and sympathetic outrage – to quote the one single unkind review repeating word for word – in scandalised tones – its barbed phrases and hurtful comments before supportively dismissing them.

Despite all these interruptions and distractions,

James refused to let Sid leave his side, except when either of them went to the bar. He found her company absolutely captivating. He couldn't put his finger on it . . . (but in fact it was the way she listened so attentively to everything he said). So they had a couple more drinks, she gave him the look – definitely, this time – and asked him another question about his act. About an hour later, when he had finished answering it, she invited him back to her hotel room for a quick line. In the taxi he made a mental note to ask her something, when she came out with another question about his ambitions and it somehow slipped his mind. He was still talking as they stepped through the doors of the George Hotel and all the way up in the lift.

'You producing a show up here then?'

'No. I'm an agent. I've come to Edinburgh because I want to sign the most talented young comedian in the country. And that's you, isn't it?'

Before he could disagree she told him she wanted to represent him, that she thought he was a genius, that she was a lesbian, that she would do anything for her clients and to prove it, handing him another Jack Daniels, knelt down in front of him and gave him a spectacular blow-job, even reaching up in the middle of it to pass him a little pinch of coke to rub on his gums. (No doubt this is a squalid picture to some but, for comedians, life does not get any better.)

It was only as he was crouching over the glass table with a rolled $50 bill in his left hand that the mental note he'd made in the taxi came back to him.

He called over his shoulder to the bathroom, where Sid was gargling with mouthwash and flossing her teeth. 'By the way... what's your name?'

'Cressida. But most people call me Sid.'

'Nice to meet you, Sid.'

Two days later, James signed.

In the restaurant Something Serious must be happening because Sid has actually turned off her mobile phone. This is not at all common, and signifies a high-level emergency. She has done it with virtually no discernible movement of her hand or finger. She does not want to give away to anyone that she is confronting a crisis.

James has just told her that he has decided to come out and tell the world, proudly, that he is straight.

Sid's eyes are going beady. She's not shocked that he's straight, she knew that all along. But for the past four years, pretending that James was gay – celibate gay, he had insisted – had been a brilliant career move. It had generated a great hook for publicity – the rough tough street-credible white hip-hop comedian with the Doctor Marten's and the beany was gay?! It was very cool. It had opened doors to all the highest profile charity gigs in town – AIDS Benefits, Amnesty International, Romanian Orphans . . . it got him newspaper articles and magazine interviews, TV appearances and, ultimately, his own hard-hitting satirical series.

His image as the macho rough-trade gay has been invaluable, the distinguishing feature that has set him apart from his contemporaries and got him the attention. In conversation Sid has always of course, promoted James's natural talent, but it has been the image that's given him the edge over a pack of equally talented performers. She suddenly wonders whether James knows this, or if, now that the publicity stunt had got him this far, he is beginning to believe he'd be fine without one.

She drums her fingers for an instant on the pink table cloth, before regaining control. But James has clocked it and is concerned.

'Sid, are you OK?'

'Course I'm OK.' She's smiling. That's always a menacing sign.

'Well, what's wrong?'

'What's wrong? I can't . . . believe what you're telling me, that's what's wrong.'

'Look. I've just done the series, I've just done the tour, I want some time to relax, chill out, see some friends . . .' Sid looks at him suspiciously – it's not a concept she's familiar with '. . . just generally have a life for a while. And part of that is being able to get laid.'

'You can have a heterosexual shag every once in a while, for God's sake. No one would care about the odd aberration.'

'Look, I've been totally celibate for three years now – that's how devoted to my career I am. I'm established now and I'm sick of being hit on all the time by people I don't fancy. The people I do fancy never thinking I'm interested. Or if they do think I'm interested they think I'm a disgusting pervert who's just using them as a kinky sex toy for a bit of variety. It's not easy to build a lasting relationship on that basis.' Sid narrows her eyes.

'You want a lasting relationship?'

'Well, yes. In the sense that I'm in control enough to be the one who finishes it.' He swigs his Chablis in a huge gulp which makes the sommelier wince, raps his glass back down on the table, continues, animated, with a spark in his gestures which grows as the idea expands. 'Who knows? Maybe I will settle down. The new image could be Mr Cutting Edge becomes Family Man but without losing his radical credentials . . . yeah, yeah . . . you know, starts seeing the world in terms of what the future holds for his wife and kids . . . building a world safe for children to live in . . . it's got a good "new millennium" kind of feel to it . . . whole new angle . . . not bad, you know . . . I reckon Four would really like it . . . and hey – wouldn't it be fantastic if the Republicans win the election and start tearing up Nixon's nuclear treaties! – everyone will start getting paranoid about bombs again, and I'll already be voicing their fears – it would fit in perfectly. Shit! I'd be massive! Go Bush!'

'Does it have to be now?'

'Good a time as ever.' He looks up, looks her straight in the eye. 'I'm going to do this, Sid.' Sid knows when to pretend that she knows she is beaten. She leans back with a little smile, raising her palms.

'OK, OK, I respect your decision.'

'You do?' James has expected more of a scene.

'Yes, of course. We can get some mileage out of it, you know, "The day I knew I was hetero . . .", "the woman who changed my sexuality" – there isn't a particular woman in the frame at all? Pity . . .'

'This isn't just a cheap publicity stunt you know, Sid.'

'Of course it isn't, darling. But who's to say the papers might not see it that way? Or they might start looking at the past four years as a cheap publicity stunt. Might undermine your integrity.'

'I don't care. I'm coming out and that's that.'

'Anyway, how do you know you're *not* gay? You've never actually tried it.' James glares at her. 'Come on, there's a lot of people who would love to pluck the word "celibate" from the phrase "celibate gay comedian James Randall." I was just idly ruminating. It's such an alluring image, that's all I'm saying. It might not be the right time to let it go.'

'I've made up my mind.'

'OK.'

Sid beckons the waiter and they order. The waiter smiles, takes the menus, withdraws, gestures to another waiter who rushes over to pour them more water. The ice cubes tinkle as they rise in the glass. Sid makes a point of smiling up at the boy. James stares at her. She never smiles at staff.

Sid smiles at James.

'I haven't had kedgeree for years.'

'OK, what?'

'What what?'

'What's all this "this might not be the right time" number?'

'Just idle speculation. Nothing more.'

She finger-waves to Maggie Smith, who pretends to recognise her. James retaliates by lighting a roll-up.

James waits. Sid counters by ignoring him and asking the maitre d' for a new ashtray. James inhales deeply and breathes it out through his nose. The heavy pewter ashtray is placed on the table with just enough of a cushioned thud to discreetly alert James to its presence.

'Well? What?'

'Forget it, James, I shouldn't have mentioned it.'

'OK, fine. Doesn't make any difference. I'm coming out.'

'I respect that.'

'And there's nothing you can say to stop me.'

'I know.'

'Good.'

Sid casually says: 'I was talking to Stride Boswell last week.'

'Uh huh.' James will not bite easily. He knows her.

'He has an interesting proposition for us.'

'What?'

'Well, it sounded quite exciting to me. He's planning this big charity gala, from a space station.'

'From a space station?'

'Yes. Sounds wild, doesn't it? Some billionaire in LA is going to be opening this hotel made up of old NASA space stations, and they plan to publicise it with a grand charity gala. Not sure which charity yet but all the biggies are pitching – anyway, global TV coverage, it's going to be huge. Mainly American acts of course – Billy Crystal was mentioned, Robin Williams . . . but he's looking for a couple of international acts and, as you know, he's been a huge fan of yours ever since Montreal.'

'Are you serious?'

Sid smiles, inwardly this time and jerks the hook a little.

'Absolutely. Of course, your profile's not big enough in the States yet but we're talking three years off at least, by which time you could be just right – provided we keep the momentum going.'

'They'll use Eddie. No question.'

'I wouldn't be too sure. And we have a trump card.'

'What?'

'Stride's a huge fan of *you* . . . as well as your work. He's in town next week – we should arrange a meeting. I'm sure if the two of you got on well enough there'd be no question of you not getting the gig. But, of course, if you're going to come out as straight . . . well, your personal life is much more important.'

James takes in her full meaning, says nothing for a while.

'Yes. It is.'

'All right,' says Sid, pretending to be beaten. 'Just thought I'd mention it.'

'Well, you can forget it.'

'OK.' But *you* won't, she thinks – give him some slack for now.

Without looking down, she furtively switches on her mobile phone.

CHAPTER TWO

Earlier that day, Stevie, before he leaves for his shift at the supermarket, is scraping out a few take-away cartons into the bottom of the hedge. Les and Stevie's flat backs on to the disused railway line and Stevie's well pleased because there's loads of wildlife – birds – blackbirds, thrushes, sparrows, blue tits, wrens, robins. He's seen a hedgehog, and sometimes, when he comes home late, he gets a glimpse of a fox. Not unusual in London these days he knows, but it gives him a buzz. There's a whole family he reckons, living somewhere nearby, and their appearances are becoming more and more frequent since he's been leaving scraps out for them at the end of the garden. He has to be discreet because the neighbours complain it'll attract rats, which it does, but he manages to knock off quite a few with his airgun. Which again he has to be discreet about but he saved up and got a night-sight. In Stevie's opinion it's worth a few rats slithering about in the hedge to see a beautiful creature like a fox every once in a while.

And, if the neighbours get too lippy, it'll be them in the night-sight.

Stevie hears wheezing, and turns round to see his dad waddling down the overgrown lawn like a flabby Space Hopper in a string vest.

'What the bloody hell you up to?'

'I'm leaving some food out for the foxes, aren't I?'

Les does not seem to take the answer in, just stares out from vacant, obtunded eyes, pursuing his own concerns – 'I hope you ain't slung none of my mince pies.'

'You're not meant to be eating mince pies. You're not meant to have any mince pies.'

'Mind your own fucking business.'

'It is my fucking business. They ain't good for you,' says Stevie, heading back to the house.

Les now carefully undertakes the difficult manoeuvre of turning round. If he shouts at the same time he knows he runs the risk of falling over, but he needs to know where his mince pies are, so he risks it anyway. Food is the issue and food is important: 'Fuck off. Where's me pies?' He's shouting the length of the garden.

'Maybe you ate them all, you fat bastard,' suggests an unseen voice from a few gardens down, in a witty allusion to the song. 'Fuck off,' Les shouts back, equally wittily.

By the time Les, red-faced, sweating and panting, like a flesh steam-engine, makes it back to the kitchen, Stevie has finished the tricky task of wiping the sweet-and-sour sauce from his metal hands with a damp cloth and put on his gloves. (It tends to make people nervous when they see he has metal hands, especially the passengers, when he's minicabbing.)

'Right, Dad, I got to go. Remember, we're eating together tonight, all right, and we're having salad. OK? If you bear with me today and hold out, I'll do you a sausage sandwich tomorrow, OK?'

Les is too out of breath to put up a fight.

'Got no choice, have I? There's nothing in the house.'

'It's for your own good, Dad.'

'At least leave me the money for a Mars Bar.'

'No.'

'Well, will you pull a cracker with me before you go?'

'Go on then.'

Les holds the cracker out while Stevie carefully uses his left hand to close the right around the other end.

The cracker cracks, Stevie gets the fat end, drops it on the coffee table, and puts on his denim jacket.

'Don't you want your present?'

'You have it.'

'At least read the joke out.'

'Later, yeah?'

Stevie is out the door.

Les slowly opens the cracker, as if he has to make this little burst of pleasure last as long as possible, delicately unfolds the pink paper hat, holds it against his grubby vest to see how the colours match, slides it gently over what remains of his greasy hair – nowadays just a wispy horseshoe sprawled around the edge of his shiny red pate like a month old dead cat in a gutter – examines the toy, holding it up close, scrutinising it from every angle, lifting it to the light; a diamond dealer would not have displayed more time and interest on a spectacular gem than Les does in this tiny plastic mouth organ, which he now reverentially brings to his lips and blows. A timid squeak comes out. He removes the mouth organ from his lips, looks at it with surprise, as if it had made the sound of its own accord, unexpectedly, and sets it down on the table. Next, he reads the joke, and is (rather tragically) disappointed that he's heard it, screws it into a ball and chucks it in the direction of the fireplace. When the ball hits the floor, it is lost, indistinguishable amongst all the other bits of paper, crushed and crumpled ends of crackers, bits of wrapping paper and tinsel.

A look of fearless resolve now crosses Les's face. He drops his hands on to the surface of the table, braces himself, inhales deeply, and slowly, painfully, grunting and groaning, pushes himself on to his feet and walks in what seems like slow motion, like an astronaut on the moon, to the video recorder where, using the wall, he lowers himself slowly on to his knees, picks a video from the pile next to the machine and inserts it. Two or three minutes later he has managed to get back to his feet, adding fresh greasy palm-prints to the wall in the process and dislodging a couple of Christmas cards from their blue-tacked mountings. It is September.

He wades over to the table, finds the remote control, recalls with apparent difficulty how to operate it, starts the video – a *Mike Yarwood Christmas Special* – and collapses on to the sofa to recover from the exertion of it all. His guts rumble dully, causing him pain from the look on his face, he shifts position, waits eagerly before emitting a long, low fart. This does not bring the relief he hoped for. His face registers disappointment. Twenty minutes later, when he is certain that Stevie is not going to come back and surprise him, and has regained enough strength to struggle to his feet once more he begins raiding his secret stash-holes for spare change and take-away menus.

Les started eating severely about two years ago, when he ran into an old friend who said he'd heard that Les's ex-wife had won a few thousand on the lottery.

Until that point Les had forced all thoughts of Pam way down into that little bit of consciousness that only gets opened up by bad luck – the smell of frying chips, hearing their special song – 'Son of my Father' by Chicory Tipp – or the chance sighting of an Austin Maxi, the car they'd owned when they first got married. Many's the time Les has tried to make the best of it and remind himself how much worse it would have been if they'd bought an ordinary car. Thank God they hadn't gone for a Golf. Or a Nissan – he'd never have been able to take a mini cab. (Not that he can take that many these days, unless they're people-carriers with the extra-wide sliding doors.) You don't see Maxis around that often. On those occasions he just used to drink himself stupid for a couple of days and then get on as best he could. But when he heard Pam had won the lottery it all changed. The bitterness and regret came out of their hiding places and wouldn't go back, no matter what he did. He was burning, he was sick, he couldn't breathe . . . he'd known she'd met someone else shortly after she'd gone but blanked it out. Now the thought of someone else having his woman and her fortune was just too much. He hit the bottle and when he came round in the middle of the night he found himself, as he knelt vomiting before his toilet, recalling in great and poignant detail the last time he had felt happy: Christmas Day, 1974.

In the morning it had been just the three of them opening presents; pub at lunchtime, little Stevie really well behaved except when he pushed the table over scattering glasses and bottles all over the floor, but they'd all laughed because it was the notoriously tight-fisted McCarthy who had actually for once just got the round in and was so pissed off to see it seeping into the carpet; then Pam's parents came round for dinner, turkey done to a turn, with all the trimmings. They had crackers, more presents for the boy, sang a few songs, told a few stories and none of the old bones of contention got dug up for long. It all went very well. They were doing it for the boy; he was three and he'd been very upset the year before with all the shouting and fighting and weeping. In fact, when in mid-December they'd brought the Christmas tree out of the box and set it up, Stevie had been in a state of terror for days – crying, hiding in corners, banging his head against the wall. So they'd decided to make a special effort to try and show him that Christmas Day could be a good thing.

After dinner the women had done the washing up. While Les and his father-in-law had played with the boy and his presents. The two men were of course hoping to set up the Scalextrix, but for Stevie the really exciting present, head and shoulders above everything else, was the gerbil. Stevie loved the little rodent the moment he set eyes on it. He was amazed, overwhelmed, he jigged up and down, he yelled, he ran around in circles, he gaped, he laughed, he yelped. The others were all touched by this demonstration of sheer innocent childish joy. All except Pam's mum, whose mouth had puckered up tight like a cat's arse as soon as she saw the cage; she sighed and remarked caustically that she couldn't see the point of spending money on food for a bleedin' rat to live in a cage in your house and how all through her childhood they'd been plagued by the bloody things. But Les explained it wasn't a rat and Pam had backed him up and then got her out of the room to make the tea and begged her not to go on about it and Pam's mum had taken a long stare through the window shaking her head asking herself out loud what the world was coming to but she got no reply and Pam made her promise not to mention it for the sake of the boy and then they'd all sat round afterwards and fallen asleep in front of *The Great Escape*.

Les had been a bit pissed, but it *was* Christmas Day.

Christmas night some of Les's pals came round because Les had to stay in and babysit while Pam went back with her mum and dad and probably was going to stay and have a couple of drinks . . . Well, the boys come round and there's an argument going on, an intense debate about physiology and psychology and behaviour in extreme situations, and the whole general relationship between the mind and the body. Although, not in those words. Specifically, the psychosomatic phenomena under enquiry related to fear – namely, do people really shit themselves if they're really really frightened? Has anyone ever seen someone so scared they've done it? Do animals shit themselves?

Then someone thought it might be in the interests of science to see how the gerbil reacted if you lit a fart in its direction. So someone lit a fart, someone else lit a bigger one, and pretty soon Les was lying on his back while two of his mates held the cage above his arse. Les lit the match and there were bets placed on whether the gerbil would shit itself or not. Instead the poor little thing was enveloped in a fireball and turned to ash before it could even think about voiding its bowel, even supposing it wanted to. Some of Les's mates pissed themselves (although not literally). Others were horrified. Les took a little while to get upright and work out what had happened. (He was a little portly even then.)

Les's pals had decided they ought not to stick around and, after seeing them out, Les had foolishly had another glass of vodka to calm his nerves before disposing of the body, which he then failed to do because the vodka made him pass out head down on the coffee table.

When Pam came home and saw what had

happened she went up the wall, came down, bashed Les around until he woke up, then bashed him around till he passed out again, packed her bags, and left.

Stevie lived with his mother until he was fourteen when he was allowed to make a choice and, to everyone's surprise, chose to move in with his father. Stevie's reasoning was that nothing could be worse than being with his mother, who resented him for making her fat, and had never hidden from Stevie her attitude that he was just a hindrance to her living a decent life and only tolerated at all for the child benefit.

The memory of that fateful day ran around in Les's head all the time, tormenting him, mocking him, until in a moment of inspiration he saw a way of capturing the memory and possessing it rather than being tortured by it. It was June, and he went out Christmas shopping. He got the tree out of the cupboard where it had lain for twenty-odd years, poured himself a lager, put a tape of Christmas hits on his 1974-model music centre, and ran a tape of *The Great Escape* with the sound down. He'd whacked some turkey legs and sprouts in the microwave and some roast potatoes in the oven, which filled the house with the bitter smell of burning dust as the long-dormant elements heated up, poured himself a few cans and, by half five that evening, he was weeping and throwing furniture around in alternating bursts. But, for a couple of hours in the afternoon, he'd managed to get the combination of lager and gluttony just right and reached a point of mental blankness where he drifted out of time and tasted for a precious while the feeling of contentment he'd had that day so long ago, with his paper hat on and Steve McQueen on the bike and his little boy crawling around happily on the floor amidst a scattered mess of presents and wrapping paper.

With every bite of the economy-sized pack of deep-frozen drumsticks, every roast potato (he burnt them, just as Pam always had) and every overcooked sprout, the sensation of that happy, distant day grew more real within him. Les was delighted by the way the totemistic recreation had soothed him. As soon as he realised he was experiencing it, of course, he was out of the moment and back to miserable reality. He lit a fart for old time's sake and then dragged himself out of the chair to occupy his mind with washing up. But the out-of-time feeling had been real enough for him to believe in the therapy and so, whenever the rage and pining came over him again, he would go out for turkey drumsticks and the rest and recreate his Christmas Day again. He kept an eye out for bargain sales of decorations, old singles and videos of the period and soon the flat looked like Santa's grotto as run by a drunken bear. The next real Christmas to come along, he had actually got a job as Santa in a department store, but it had all turned ugly when he refused to stop turning up for work when the season was over, and in the end the store had had to send bailiffs round to make him hand back the outfit.

Soon moments of release became harder to find and more difficult to hold on to, and the memories of the pain became stronger. So, like any addict, he increased the dose in size and frequency. By the time Stevie came out of prison a year ago, Les was on Christmas dinner seven days a week – and twice, even three times a day.

He was delighted by Stevie's greeting of 'Fuck me, Dad, you ain't half put on weight.' Les explains with relish that that is the whole point. That's his plan.

Les has decided that he needs to get a message to Pam to show her what she's done to him. It will not be a written message, or a phone call, or something passed on from intermediaries – although he knows if he puts his mind to it he could find out where to write. No, it will be more dramatic. Les will carry on down the path he is on. He will eat and eat. And eat and eat and eat and eat until he is the fattest man in the borough of Islington. Then he will get into the local papers, be a novelty item for local press photographers to snap as he attends the opening of a new take-away, or hands over a charity cheque. He might – with dedication and a bit of luck – become London's Fattest Man and get on Vanessa or Gilda or Richard and Judy with his own caption: Eats Christmas Dinner Every Day Because His Wife Left Him. And somewhere down the line, she'll see him, she'll know, and she'll see his huge bloated form pointing like an accusing finger, shouting silently, 'Look what you done to me, you slag!' and she'll never be able to live with herself despite her thousands and a bungalow near Walton-on-the-Naze, he heard.

Now that Stevie has left for work, Les can get on with his day and with his mission – eating for victory.

CHAPTER THREE

Henry Randall was in the bath, staring at the ceiling, motionless, consumed with dread. A terrible challenge lay before him: in a few minutes he would have to rise from the warm, comforting water and go shopping.

Henry's meditation was broken when his wife, Elizabeth, rapped briskly on the bathroom door. 'Henry, it's half past eight.'

'Right.'

Another day had dawned and like it or not, he was going to have to deal with all the horrors it might throw at him. His stomach burned with anxiety and, even under the water, he could feel his palms were sweating. His breathing quickened. His stomach tightened and the dull ache got stronger. No getting round it, he was afraid. And ashamed: going to the supermarket was not exactly the most hazardous undertaking that has ever been asked of an Englishman, and Henry would be the first to admit it.

But Henry is afflicted. He sees potential and imminent disaster everywhere. He is unable to rid himself of the constant awareness of all the terrible, random misfortunes that can befall any of us going about our mundane everyday business. Road accidents, terrorist outrages, lone psychotics with axes or knives, planes falling out of the sky, buildings collapsing, gas mains exploding, getting caught in the crossfire of a gangster shoot-out, being struck by lightning ... Henry's psychic immune system is breaking down. He has lost the ability that we all need, to live in the illusion that nothing is ever going to rip through the fabric of our everyday lives and shred it.

It had all been triggered by a bit of bad luck he'd had one afternoon early that summer. Elizabeth had gone to a yoga workshop and Henry had decided to enjoy the rare appearance of the sun to wander over to Clissold Park. He was sitting on a bench, doing the crossword, and had one clue left: 'Honesty destroyed when he leaves for legendary English paceman (5).' After thirty minutes frustration he had suddenly seen it: Tyson. In his delight he had punched the air and triumphantly yelled the answer out loud. 'Tyson! Tyson!'

Within seconds he was surrounded by several ferocious pit-bulls and rottweilers who had all obediently responded to the call of their name. Henry had managed to get up a small tree before any of them bit him, but it had been a close thing and the memory of all the snarling fangs leaping and snapping around the trunk only inches from his ankles had henceforth plagued his dreams and his waking life.

It became more than just an incident, it seemed to be a lesson. Terrifying monsters could suddenly appear to violate any moment of idyllic tranquillity. Security was an illusion. However hard he tried, he couldn't shake off the knowledge of how vulnerable we all are. He knew Elizabeth was right when she'd said it was just bad luck, but it didn't help. He tried various ways of dealing with it. He told himself not to be stupid, to pull himself together. He even thought about trying some kind of therapy but rejected this on the grounds that, as an Englishman, it would compromise his whole identity and sense of self-respect. He tried martial arts but, on the way home from his second lesson, had been mugged by three teenagers.

They had not initially been muggers at all; one had innocently asked him if he had the time. Because it was late and dark and Henry was afraid, and – though he hates to admit this – because the boys were black, Henry's liberal attitudes had deserted him for what he realised later was a shameful underlying prejudice, and he had adopted a fighting stance and told them in an unconvincing voice to fuck off. The boys had not done so. In fact, they had laughed, and then identified from his stance what style of karate he was practising and proceeded to comment on its strengths and weaknesses, with practical demonstrations. They had not hurt him badly, but they'd run off with his kit bag, which had totally humiliated him. As if the incident had not fuelled Henry's self-loathing enough, he'd told the story to his brother who adapted it into a routine in his stand-up act.

He sat up in the bath. Come on, Henry, get a grip will you? It wasn't as if he was a refugee or being hunted by death squads or selling the *Big Issue*, for God's sake. He didn't have any life-threatening diseases, why couldn't he just get on with his life? Live in the moment, take everything as it comes, and not until it does. But he just couldn't, and he sank back into the water, despising himself.

He must get that crack in the ceiling seen to. One day it would collapse and it would be while he was lying here; it would knock him unconscious and he would drown, in his own bathtub. If he tried to share his anxiety, Elizabeth would never understand. She would just listen to him patiently and then, in curt dismissive tones, tell him he should pull himself together and jolly well count his blessings. Unfeeling middle-class English bitch, he thought.

'Henry, hurry up!'

With unthinking Pavlovian obedience to the voice of authority, Henry leapt out of the bath – 'Coming! Sorry!' – and before he knew it was shaved, dressed, breakfasted and ready to go.

They were going to the new supermarket just up the road in Holloway, and they were going, of course, in the Volvo.

Henry was wearing his Saturday morning outfit, stylish olive-green hiking trousers and French-made cross-trainers, check shirt and grey waterproof fleece. He hoped the casual properties of the clothes would inform his mood like a magic cloak. It wasn't working. He tried to relax his shoulders, breathe deeply and banish the thoughts. It was all unlikely, he kept telling himself. He was being ridiculous. Unlikely is not impossible though, said the other voice, and he sighed, agonised. Elizabeth raised her eyebrows but carried on looking straight ahead.

He looked at people in the other cars, people walking along the pavement with their backs to the traffic, clearly unconcerned by the possibility of an airliner dropping out of the sky and snuffing out their lives in an instant, or a pack of hungry rats, fresh from the Continent via the Channel Tunnel, falling upon them with sharp, rabid fangs. He envied them in their denial of the dangers all around them, yet he knew at the same time that if – as he often now wanted to – he stopped and asked them how they managed to go about their everyday business so easily, ignoring the perils of being alive, that they would consider him mad. Recognising they would be right didn't help. He let out another long and anguished sigh.

This time Elizabeth gave in and turned towards him.

'What's the matter?'

'Nothing. Nothing at all.'

'You're sweating. What is it?'

'I'm fine. Just a bit fluey, that's all.'

Bad choice of fib. It immediately set him thinking of all these weird new viruses that were floating around nowadays – who knew when you were inhaling something that would have you sneezing one minute and writhing around in mortal agony with a death rattle in your throat the next? One careless cheeseburger and they're discovering a new fatal disease with your name on it. It hadn't helped that while he was in the bath he'd seen an article in the *Guardian* about the Ministry of Defence leaking 'controlled doses' of various warlike germs into the atmosphere to test them. Not to mention stories of horrible freak accidents involving cable cars and fires in tunnels and someone electrocuted in a Superloo.

'No cable cars in Islington anyway, for God's sake,' he said to himself contemptuously.

Elizabeth looked at him, perplexed. 'What?'

'Nothing. Just thinking out loud. Clue in the crossword.'

He smiled feebly and Elizabeth noticed he had begun humming the twenty-third psalm. She declined to think anything of it. Henry had been behaving strangely for weeks now. She could tell there was something troubling him that he probably wanted to talk about. But now was not the time. She wanted to enjoy the simple everyday process of shopping, and if there was to be conversation it should be undemanding and banal, not emotionally charged and personal. She worked hard all week and Saturday morning shopping was a time to relax and regroup.

Elizabeth got a special pleasure out of going to the Aldingtons' Store in Holloway. She liked not only the convenience of the place, the sheer size and range of choice, but also the wider cultural significance of shopping there. She'd read in the Sunday supplements of how the man who built the place, the celebrated French visionary architect Antoine Barjoles, considered the Aldingtons' contract saved his life, pulling him out of the terrible depression he suffered after his pitch for the new Guggenheim in Bilbao was turned down. Elizabeth had read how

Antoine vowed to put Holloway on the map with a building that would be one of the new wonders of the world, not a mere supermarket but, in Antoine's words, 'a veritable Cathedral of Retail'.

You couldn't really call it a supermarket. Supermarkets are one thing, this place was something else. It was huge. You came up the long hill from the station and, where it crested just past the tube, you looked to your right to where there used to be a big patch of waste land behind the old overground station with some broken-down buildings — dirty red-brick, turn-of-the-century probably, with the roofs caved in and the odd bit of glass still clinging to a frame here and there, abandoned to the rats and the graffiti artists and the glue-sniffers. All that was completely gone. In its place stood a startling, enormous, extraordinary structure — an imperious crowded mass of post-modern domes and spires, a bewildering mixture of brick and concrete and super-tensile steel-cabled flying buttresses, huge panes of tinted glass and shining aluminium tubes and ducts, incorporating allusions to every architectural style of the last thousand years, but 'all pointing to the future, reflecting the traditional yet modern, homogenous yet diverse, cultural reality of the new millennium' as Antoine had explained to the *Observer*.

Aldingtons claimed it had been conceived as a symbol of regeneration for the whole area and, as a marketing ploy, it certainly worked on Elizabeth. She liked the feeling that, simply by going shopping, she was helping the Third World develop and prosper. It might seem patronising, but when all was said and done, that's what the north end of the borough was. And now, the Badlands of Islington North had a landmark building with an international reputation! In Elizabeth's opinion, Antoine was a bit like that chap who built the opera house in the middle of the Brazilian jungle. It was more than shopping to shop there. It said something about you. That you cared. About style and aesthetics and putting something back into your community just by buying things. Which was her favourite method of doing anything, really.

How did they describe it in the special feature in the *Independent*? 'The cutting edge of supermarket conceptuality.' She wasn't going to spoil a major lifestyle experience by asking Henry what was on his mind.

Fearing the car could be involved in a collision, Henry, in complete contradiction of all London traffic conventions, braked sharply at the sight of a red light instead of accelerating through it. Elizabeth was jerked forward towards the windscreen until the seatbelt snapped taut. Before she could yell at him, there was a screech of brakes and an angry blast on the horn from the car behind. Henry could see the driver, a large greasy-haired man in an Arsenal shirt leaning out of the window of his aged lime-green Nissan. His obscenities could be heard faintly over their four-speaker stereo system, which was playing Schubert's string quintet.

'Yes, what the fuck *are* you doing?' said Elizabeth, pushing a strand of blonde hair away from her face.

'Light was changing.' He knew it sounded feeble. He didn't dare look in the rear-view mirror again in case the man was striding towards him with a large knife, and merely checked that the doors were locked.

Elizabeth rolled her eyes and said nothing. Henry was trembling, trying to breathe deeply, just about keeping it under control. The lights changed back to green and Henry moved off carefully, braking again almost immediately as the lime-green Nissan careered past and cut in in front of them, just missing the Keep Left sign, the driver leaning over to stare at Henry and shake his head. The three small children in the back, also in Arsenal shirts, had even deigned to stop picking their noses for a few moments to jab V-signs at him and pull faces.

They were within sight of their destination. Through the gaps between the terraced houses on the right of the road you could catch glimpses of the huge structure. Of course, if Antoine Barjoles had been allowed to have his way, it would have been a lot more than glimpses. His building would have dominated the entire steady climb from the very beginning of the gradient two or three miles away, for he had originally conceived an awe-inspiring first sight of the place akin to the effect created by the great French cathedrals, where the towers and flying buttresses stamp the omnipresence and mightiness of God on the landscape and eyeballs of the approaching traveller even while still several hours distant. The local council, however, had felt that the aesthetic gain of his proposal to pull down several square miles of residential property for the sake of a nice view had to be sacrificed to the pragmatic questions of rehousing tens of thousands of people. Antoine had sulked for a while; what were homeless people when compared to the eternal greatness of true art? Ultimately he accepted that the Philistines he was dealing with had to be indulged from time to time. Especially as he was, at that time, in acute danger of being declared bankrupt.

A large overhead road sign told drivers for the Superstore Car Park to get into the right-hand lane. Henry painstakingly checked his mirrors, indicated, slowed down, turned and looked over his shoulder, turned back and only then very cautiously changed lanes to join the long stationary queue of shopping pilgrims. Elizabeth watched this conscientious process out of the corner of her eye with discomfort. It was like driving with her parents, who came to London once every two years and believed that the same Highway Code that pertained to a gentle market town in the south west had some resemblance to the traffic conventions of the metropolis. They could spend twenty or thirty minutes stuck at a T-junction in the misguided belief that eventually someone would politely stop and let them out, and that they could avoid the anxiety and inherent bad manners of forcing their own way out into the incessant flow. Henry seemed to be losing the front you needed in order to be a Londoner.

They turned into the entrance. Huge landscaped car parks with electric carts to take you from your car to the door of the store surrounded the building. Electronic signboards announced special offers and promotions, also flashing up information about the air temperature, the local air quality, humidity, wind chill factor, the time, the date. News headlines, ticket offers and traffic and transport updates. Shopping trolleys were being collected by an army of pimply youths in long green plastic coats.

The Schubert was interrupted after the third movement by a man who, in an unctuous Anglo-Irish accent, announced that after the commercial break they would be hearing the Autumn section of *The Four Seasons* and Elizabeth realised to her horror that they were listening to Classic FM. In *their* car? It was like being acquainted with Shakespeare solely from the cinema. Even though the windows were closed and the traffic to their left was moving, Elizabeth found herself reflexively looking round to check that no one they knew was in an adjacent car to overhear. She then turned to look at Henry. Classic FM? Really! Whatever next? A CD of *The Three Tenors' Greatest Hits*? The smirk in her thought dissolved into disgust: it was not so far-fetched. After all, Henry had been referring to films as 'the movies' for some time now.

A bland three-part harmony of Lieber and Stoller's 'On Broadway' was now coming out of the speakers.

'They say the shopping never stops

In Holloway

They say there's always magic in the air...

In Holloway'

A chirpy urgent manic cockney voice broke in. 'And they're absolutely right! The new Aldingtons' Superstore in Holloway is now open ... twenty-four hours a day ...' Elizabeth dimly recognised the voice as belonging to an alternative comedian they had seen from time to time in the late eighties, when they used to go to that kind of thing. Then he had been known for his coruscating satires on the Thatcher government.

'It's that friend of James's ... you know, the fat

one who's in that TV show now. Doing the voice-over.'

But Henry was too busy concentrating on feeding the ticket machine as quickly as humanly possible, to minimise the chance of the raised barrier coming down prematurely and slicing through the roof of the car, forcing shredded blades of sharp metal into both their skulls, their last memories of their time on earth the sound of cutting equipment and a blurred perception of flashing blue lights.

But it didn't happen! They were through! Now all he had to do was find a parking space and get into it unscathed and he could relax for a while... a youth in a large fluorescent yellow jacket was waving them off to the left. Elizabeth protested.

'He can't possibly mean down here – we're still about a mile from the shop.'

'I think he did – they do seem awfully busy today.'

'It's raining now as well.' She managed to say it in a tone that made Henry feel it was his fault.

They reached the end of the next row of cars without finding a space. Another fluorescent teenager motioned them left again.

'We're further away now than when we came in,' observed Elizabeth indignantly. They found a space and to his relief Henry was equal to the challenge of reversing in. This made him a little more cheerful as they locked up, even though you could hardly see the shop at all now through the mist. It was that kind of dejected London rain that can't be bothered to go up to proper cloud height and then fall down again, and instead just oozes out of the atmosphere horizontally.

Another fluorescent coat approached them.

'Welcome to the Aldingtons' Superstore,' it said in a monotone. 'The nearest shuttle stop is at the end of Row K.' It pointed, robotically.

They followed the direction of his finger and about fifty yards further on saw a group of people huddled in and around a plexiglass bus shelter. A few moments later a high-pitched humming noise announced the arrival of a trolley bus from out of the mist. To his horror Henry noticed there was no driver. It was all too much like a cable car and he felt a tightening in his chest. He couldn't turn round and get off though, there were already too many people behind him. He took a deep breath and told himself once more to fight it.

The carriage doors closed and the shuttle moved off again. The Winter movement of Vivaldi's *Four Seasons* started playing, quite loudly, before fading down to accommodate a vocal track.

'Welcome to the Aldingtons' SuperNovaStore,' said the trolley in a rich, enthusiastic, classic English thespian voice. 'The SuperNovaStore! Europe's foremost staple-shopping experience – staple-shopping and much much more.' Elizabeth imagined a middle-aged English actor with a bow-tie huddled in front of a microphone in a studio somewhere in Soho oozing with excitement as he recorded this announcement, having to be hosed down between takes such was the level of his commitment to Europe's foremost staple-shopping experience.

'Over eight hundred and ten thousand square feet of floorspace! Offering not only the finest quality produce at the most competitive prices, but much much more! Leave your children to enjoy themselves in the crèche, supervised by our fully qualified staff who are regularly checked for any kind of psychological disorder! Stressed out? Visit our Customer Well-Being Department for full details of stress-relief programmes: Massage! Hypnotherapy! Acupuncture! Cholesterol Analysis! Holidays! Instant credit! Just ask any member of staff!'

The trolley appeared to have reached the building but then swerved off in an unexpected arc to prolong the journey just long enough for the bow-tie voice to give full details of that week's special offers.

Vivaldi came back and, as a novel diminuendo faded it away to nothing in the middle of the climax of the Summer movement, the trolley finally drew to a halt and the doors slid quietly open to disgorge the passengers into the Cathedral of Retail.

There were gasps of wonder as those here for the

first time surveyed the arrival point. Henry and Elizabeth were making sure they looked utterly blasé to imply they had been here before. The passengers stepped out into a huge atrium. Coloured water danced into the air from half a dozen fountains, cascading down from the roof, nourishing tier upon tier of flowerbeds full of exotic plants before disappearing into an underground river to begin its cycle again.

A task force of young women wearing bright uniforms in the company colours – red, white and green – and made up in accordance with the unique aesthetic that exists on the other side of cosmetics counters were handing out leaflets like a regiment of corporate pantomime fairies.

People in ostrich costumes, a whole flock, strutted about, handing out more flyers. Henry took one. It was promoting the virtues of ostrich meat. He looked at the ostriches again with fascination. Their movements were so realistic and convincing as they strutted around promoting their own destruction that it made him feel uncomfortable, even though he knew they were just human beings inside the costumes. Another bird approached him and offered a tray of ostrich meat canapés. He felt unable to take one. Elizabeth took two and made sounds of pleasant surprise – 'Mm, a bit like beef' – before striding on purposefully towards the entrance to the store proper with Henry, still amazed at the ostriches, following a pace or two behind.

They were brought to another halt a few yards further on. In the centre of the atrium a sumptuous stand bedecked with luscious arrangements of white roses – Anne-Marie, Biancas, pale pink Bianca Candy, off-white Champagnes, Escimos – and Casablanca lilies, Longiflora, Lilies of the Valley flown in from Holland (and Kenya) surrounded and entwined with a dazzling array of foliage: the tiny white flowers of Philadelphus; lime green Achemilla Mollis and Angellica; pink and white Hydrangea and wispy fronds of dill; blue, pink and even – Elizabeth noticed – the rarer white Delphinium. A plastic banner suspended across the top proudly proclaimed: The Aldingtons' Blind Date Wedding of the Year! From loudspeakers came the sound of pealing church bells, followed by an excited voice: 'Next Saturday! is a very special! day. Hundreds of young single people have entered the Aldingtons' Blind Date Wedding Quest and next Saturday! is when it's all happening! Amanda and Lawrence' – their photographs beamed down from hoardings – 'have never met! but have been chosen out of hundreds of hopeful entrants, brought together by the computerised matching of their Aldingtons' till-receipts. Next Saturday! at twelve-thirty they are to be married in the car park. Everyone is invited!'

'How bizarre,' remarked Elizabeth needlessly and strode on, leaving Henry to take a trolley from the rank. It was a state-of-the-art trolley, with a soft rubber coating on the handles instead of the usual hard plastic and a brake. For a moment Henry felt comfortable and safe, then ticked himself off for not being fully alert to the potential perils that surrounded him. A collision could trigger an incident of trolley rage. The most unlikely people were being had up for assault and manslaughter these days – *pay attention*.

They worked the aisles in their customary manner, Elizabeth picking items off the shelves and bringing them back to Henry who stood obediently with the trolley at a convenient distance. He occupied his time reading more of the sheaf of promotional leaflets that had been thrust upon him, leaflets which explained how the shop had been designed in a synergy of post-modern neo-classical traditional and ancient Feng Shui principles for optimal customer and employee convenience and well-being.

'We're going to need another trolley,' said Elizabeth. 'Perhaps you'd like to take care of this list, while I do the rest and we'll meet at the wine section in what? Fifteen minutes?'

'Sounds good.'

'Is your brother still a vegetarian?'

'Yes, I think so.'

'Pity. They have a special offer on organic lamb. Oh well never mind. I expect I'll think of something.'

'I don't mind cooking, if you want me to take care of lunch.'

Elizabeth considered the offer briefly.

'No, it would mean transferring too many general headings from my list on to yours, and vice versa.'

'All right then. See you in a quarter of an hour.'

But she had already turned away, heading for Vegetables and Fruit.

CHAPTER FOUR

Loretta and her flatmate Yvette were drinking tea and amphetamine-strength coffee respectively at a table in the Aldingtons' staff canteen. Yvette was skimming a newspaper, denouncing the 'fucking wankers' and 'fucking capitalist bastards' and 'fucking hypocrites' in every story, sometimes in French, sometimes in English, before angrily turning the page.

When they had first started sharing a flat, Loretta had tried to share Yvette's interest in current affairs and develop the discussion of whatever topic was under review, but quickly learnt that Yvette felt no need to look beyond her initial abusive exclamations. Indeed she seemed suspicious that Loretta felt there was anything more to be said, that to explore the issues in a greater depth was to challenge the infallibility of Yvette's wisdom. Sometimes Loretta wondered if she had been so lucky after all to be offered the room in Yvette's flat so quickly after following up the advert. Yvette had described herself as New Age, vegetarian, female, mid-twenties, seeking similar. Loretta, not having met a French person before did not realise that French vegetarian cuisine included fish, chicken and bacon, and Loretta also found Yvette a little more aggressive than other New Age people she'd encountered. For example, Yvette had physically assaulted someone in a cinema queue for laughing. Yvette found the idea of giggling while waiting to see *Schindler's List* clear evidence of Nazi sympathies. Still, Loretta had come to Europe to assimilate new experiences, go with the flow and fully embrace the learning experience opportunity, so she decided to give Yvette the benefit of the doubt and see her assault on the laugher (a trainee rabbi) as proof that she was passionate about her convictions rather than mad.

Right now Loretta ignored Yvette and stared into her tea, concentrating on the memories of her recurrent dream. It concerned a magnificent lover, handsome and caring, who whisked her away from some kind of depressing bar or maybe a party, full of ugly unkind men who were all staring at her hungrily and a small dog lay on its back and urinated into the air and then this dashing . . . guy carried her off on a white horse — or was it a silver jet-plane? — while a fat vicious rat with an erection yapped and snapped vainly at their heels as they rose into the sky. Then they were on some kind of tropical island making love to the sound of the waves.

It made her guilty to realise she always called her brown-skinned hero Prince Charming – it was such a non-feminist stereotype. But she tempered her self-recrimination by remembering that he first appeared in the dream as a dolphin. And not just any dolphin, but Cochise, the dolphin with whom she had swum daily for almost two months in the Bahamas. It was clear to Loretta that Cochise had given her the dream, she knew that – for had she not first had it the night after their last swim? Swimming with dolphins had been the most successful therapy she had ever experienced, and she had experienced many kinds. In fact, she would probably still be there now if her affair with the Welsh didgeridoo player had not ended so messily. That he had left her so suddenly, and for a female dolphin . . . Cochise would never have countenanced such a venal relationship with Loretta . . . well, it was all in the past now, and she had decided it was just nature's harsh way of telling her it was time to move on; the Dream had been Cochise's parting gift, an amulet to ward off the perils of the wide world.

'Another tea?' said Yvette, somehow in a tone that implied whatever answer Loretta gave would be the wrong one.

'Sure. Thanks.'

They were working two shifts today, morning in

addition to their normal evening one so that they wouldn't have to be in the store at all the following Saturday for 'the fucking bullshit publicity stunt', as Yvette so accurately described the Wedding.

They normally worked evenings, eight till two in the morning. Today they were on the checkouts, although usually, because they were young and attractive and athletic, they had one of the more glamorous jobs in the store, shooting around the shop floor on roller skates, offering exotic food samples to the younger and more bohemian customers who shopped late on their way to or from a night on the town. It was slightly better paid but still, in Yvette's opinion, 'a fucking rip-off'.

Loretta didn't mind. She was in England precisely to do menial jobs. She felt it would be spiritually cleansing and hoped it might lead to enlightenment. She was from Beverly Hills, you see, and all her family had more money than sense.

One of the storemen came into the kitchen. He was a spindly youth of about twenty-eight with enough acne to pass for sixteen at a distance, and metal bars through both eyebrows and a ring through his nose.

He approached them gingerly, a video cassette in his outstretched hands, and when they noticed him he got what he always got in greeting, a dark scowling pout from Yvette, her grey eyes glaring out from under her jet black fringe, and a smile from the blonde Loretta.

Stevie was in awe of them both. 'I've brought that video you wanted to lend. The one on the monkeys.' He handed it to Loretta, head down. She noticed that, as always, he was wearing gloves. He dared to look up as she took the cassette and, as he'd hoped, Loretta smiled again. 'Thanks, Stevie. I'll look forward to watching it.'

Stevie loved it when Loretta smiled. It went right through him, like an electric shock, except nice. He dropped his head again, and shuffled from foot to foot, then addressed the skirting board behind his right shoulder. 'I got loads more if you like that one.'

'Great. Want some tea, Stevie? Kettle's just boiled.'

Yvette shook her head in disgust and went back to the paper.

'Oh, yeah, OK.' Loretta got up and flicked on the kettle again. Stevie clumsily pulled one of the chairs out and sat on it a good five feet away from the table, still looking at the floor. Loretta made tea in a mug and put it on the table.

'Do you like ostriches?' he asked.

Yvette rolled her eyes.

'I guess so. Sure Stevie, I like all wildlife, you know that,' said Loretta. Yvette scowled to herself. Why was Loretta always so patient with this weirdo?

'I'd like to show you something.' He stood up and

moved to the doorway. 'If you got a minute.'

'What, now?'

'Yeah. Only if you want.'

'Sure.'

Yvette got up and poured the dregs of her coffee into the sink. 'It's an original chat-up,' she murmured sarcastically into Loretta's ear. Unfortunately, Stevie caught the comment. It angered him deeply. Yvette was accusing him of showing affection. What's more, she was right, which made it worse. His shyness was forgotten, he straightened up and glared at her.

'I meant you as well.'

Even Yvette was scared to argue. She was a connoisseur of the psychotic stare and could tell this one was up at the Manson-Thatcher end of the scale. Gently she put down her mug and, with only the merest hint of a recalcitrant shrug, gestured she couldn't wait, really she couldn't. Lead on Stevie, lead on . . .

CHAPTER FIVE

Henry had got everything on his list except for coffee. He had time in hand, and so he was taking a little break to read more about ostriches. Apparently Aldingtons had their own free-range ostrich farm in the Highlands of Scotland. Henry was interested to learn that this was not a problem for the ostrich, which is a hardy bird and, despite being native to Africa, is farmed and survives happily as far north as Alaska. The leaflet went on to explain that in the Highlands the birds could roam free over thousands of acres to guarantee that they kept fit and strong, so that the meat they supplied was not only low in fat and cholesterol (like all ostrich meat) but of a very high quality.

Henry read further. In order to offer Aldingtons' customers protection from the thousands of new viruses in the world the birds were transported to London and slaughtered on these very premises, which contained huge underground pens and boning rooms. The leaflet guaranteed that all Aldingtons' meat was 'As Fresh As Fresh Can Be, As Safe As Safe Can Be.'

What the leaflet didn't say was that to make their meat As Safe As Safe Can Be, and less susceptible to salmonella and e-coli, Aldingtons had introduced a new technique – giving the ostriches a therapeutic dose of microwave radiation to zap any bugs.

'Perhaps we should try some sometime,' thought Henry.

Stevie led Loretta and Yvette around the corridors to a goods lift and pressed the button for the basement. Another corridor took them to a locked set of double doors. Stevie keyed in the code and beckoned the girls through. They stood on a metal walkway. Below them, on the other side of a high wire-mesh cage, were perhaps four dozen ostriches, cramped together in a space that made a complete mockery of the company's much vaunted free-range claim.

'Jeez . . . how come there's so many of them in there?'

'Dunno. They've had some kind of problem with the slaughtermen.' This was correct. Aldingtons engaged outside contractors to come in and slaughter the birds every week or so. The details were not clear, but twelve of the slaughtermen had suddenly become devout vegetarians. Something to with a stag-night in Amsterdam with lots of mescaline and a quasi-religious Naked Lunch experience aboard a cross-channel ferry, when, collectively and simultaneously, all twelve beefy third-generation Smithfield slaughtermen became life-changingly aware of the origins of their quarter-pounders-with-crispy-bacon as gentle-eyed cows and happy smiling piggies. Consequently the contractors were short-staffed, over-booked and frantic, and Aldingtons' ostrich pen was fuller than it should have been.

'It ain't right,' said Stevie. 'I wanna let them go or something. But I can't afford to get sacked, cos, well . . . I can't, innit? But it ain't right, is it, innit?'

'Everything happens for a reason,' said Loretta, solemnly. Among the people she generally hung out with, this was a useful little phrase with which you could wrap up a discussion of anything disconcerting and which left you feeling satisfied you had explored the issue to the very limits of human wisdom.

'Well, what's the reason for this then?' asked Stevie, diffidently.

'I don't know,' said Loretta. 'Yet,' she added, hoping to sound less feeble.

'Well, I fucking do,' said Yvette. 'We wait till next Saturday and let them go in the middle of that fucking stupid wedding.'

Loretta could tell Yvette was serious. 'They might be gone by next week,' she said, trying not to sound timid.

'They might be. They might not be. And if they're still here, then that's the reason this happened, isn't it? We've got time to plan it so that none of us get caught.'

'Just how exactly?'

'I don't know yet, do I? That's what we 'ave to plan, you know?'

Independently, they all turned to look at one of the ostriches, who was staring at them with an unsettling look in its imperious eye. They all had the same feeling, so ridiculous that none of them even thought to mention it. The feeling was that the ostrich had understood what they had been talking about.

'We'd better get back,' said Loretta.

CHAPTER SIX

The malevolent-looking ostrich was called Spartacus.

How to tell the tale of mighty Spartacus, a giant among ostriches, most cunning and resourceful of all ratites?

Even the choice of name, proud and noble Spartacus, slave, gladiator and glorious fighter for freedom – a name he bestowed upon himself – implies a considerable knowledge of European culture and civilisation (as far back as early Kubrick at least) and thus, even if through the second-hand conduit of cinema, some basic awareness of Classical history. Whether or not he was also aware of the inspiring legacy of Rosa Luxemburg when he took that *nom de guerre* is not revealed. Maybe he was just a big Kirk Douglas fan. But one thing is clear – it's an impressive achievement for a creature so stupid it is known to drown in rainstorms by looking up to the heavens in amazement without sufficient sense to close its mouth.

Make no mistake, Spartacus is planning to escape. And, make no mistake, this is one mean ostrich.

There are other theories offered to account for Spartacus's unnatural intelligence. One is that he was descended from a mythical species of super-ostrich wily enough to have lived far from men – either in the Mountains of the Moon or the jungles of the Congo, depending on which legend you prefer – who were tempted on to the savannah to breed with an inferior species by the irresistible pulchritude of its females.

Others say the reason is the fault of modern science. One problem Aldingtons found when first rearing the ostrich herds in the Scottish Highlands was the large number of birds being lost to predators such as foxes and wildcats, and also to human poachers. Ostriches can disembowel you with a kick but they're not the most intellectually powerful of creatures. Under attack they are just as likely to run round in a circle or lie down with their necks flat on the ground and hope you mistake them for a rock. (The head in the sand thing is just a myth.)

Scientists at Aldingtons' research establishment addressed the problem and came up with a novel solution. They took as their starting point the flatworm MRNA experiments of the late seventies, in which flatworms were trained to negotiate a maze and then – rather an unkind reward for their achievement – were mashed up and fed to untrained flatworms. Result: the untrained flatworm could negotiate the maze. They had absorbed the relevant information from the MRNA of their unfortunate predecessors (just think, they might even have been related). So, and this is pretty sick – the exact details are still under wraps somewhere in a top secret file in the Aldingtons' Research and Development mainframe – some twisted boffin goes into a meeting with his moneymen, tells them what he's going to suggest is going to sound far-fetched but – and he actually uses this phrase – but, he says, 'It might just work . . .'

'OK,' he says, 'we know the birds have the physical ability to defend themselves, they just need the right mental attitude. So here's what we do. We talk to the Chinese who, being good Communists, are well known for being prepared to do anything provided the money's right, and we arrange to purchase the corpses of any and every recently demised martial arts master we can persuade them to sell. We freeze them, we ship them to the labs here, we extract the limbic nerve – the Deep Brain, where functions of the memory are stored once they have become automatic – then we mash up the limbic nerve and feed it to our ostriches who will become expert in ancient Chinese arts of self-defence, and be able to look after themselves out on the hills.'

The money men sit silently for a while, feeling a little bit uncomfortable, not making any sudden moves, trying to see if the boffin (who, they are suddenly very aware, is sitting between them and the door) is within reach of any sharp objects, look at each other, wonder if it's April the First, ask to be left alone to think it over, and come to the conclusion they'd better say yes, largely on the basis that it's safer to have someone like that on your team rather than playing for the opposition, or unemployed, alone, bitter and scheming with lots of time on his hands, and off goes a delegation to Beijing.

To cut a long story short – and please don't sling the book across the room at this point – six years later there are herds of ostriches roaming the bens and glens who can land a roundhouse kick on a poacher quicker than you can blink.

(There's also a rumour they can speak Pu Tong Hua and Cantonese and have a passion for gambling, but in my opinion that sounds a little bit implausible.)

Still others claim that Spartacus's cunning is not his own, but is in fact being beamed into him telepathically by a dolphin called Cochise, who is determined that his protégée Loretta shall fall in love and live happily ever after.

CHAPTER SEVEN

As he walked back to the canteen with the girls, Stevie plucked up his courage to ask Loretta the favour.

'Loretta, there was something I wanted to ask you. You know you're into organic food and Chinese medicine and all that? Well it's about my dad. He ain't well.'

'What's the problem?'

'Well, he eats shit food all the time, and he's putting on loads of weight and . . . well, he won't go to the doctor, but, well, he's like, bunged up.'

'Bunged up.'

'Yeah. To be truthful with you he ain't had a shit in weeks and I'm really worried about him. I was wondering if there was anything you could do.'

'Look, I'd need to get more details from you . . . we gotta go on shift now . . . why don't we meet up tomorrow lunchtime? . . . I really have to run now. But try, you know, to get him to eat fresh fruit and drink lotsa water for now, yeah? Let's say . . . you know the Prince of Wales Feathers? At what, one-thirty?'

'All right, thanks.'

Stevie pondered briefly the strangeness of life. Here he was, fancying Loretta like crazy, and he knew he would never be able to summon up the courage to ask her out on a date, but had no trouble at all arranging to meet her to discuss his father's bowels.

When Elizabeth reached the wine section Henry was not there. There was no real rush she told herself, but couldn't help checking her watch and feeling a little irritated when she saw it was not fifteen but eighteen minutes since they had split up. Oh well, it *was* an unfamiliar layout – perhaps he was having trouble finding his way around. She was naturally more talented at this kind of thing. In fact if he'd been there first it would have challenged her unquestioned status as the superior one. Wait a minute though – he had had a much smaller list. He must be dithering somewhere. Or possibly buying items that weren't on the list. In which case he would probably duplicate some of the things on her list . . . really! It was like living with a delinquent child. She couldn't leave him alone for a moment . . . She checked her watch. He was now five minutes late. This really was too much. She marched briskly in the direction of washing-powder.

Henry, however, was not at washing-powder. He was standing before the massive array of coffees. The choice was paralysing. He had narrowed it down to organic whole beans of course, but it was still not easy. Which of the many Third World coffee-producing countries was in greatest need of his money? As if that was the only question. There were straightforward organic beans, arabica, blended, medium roast, dark roast, French after-dinner roast, Continental breakfast roast, Italian midmorning special blend ... there were brands from autonomous co-operatives that promised a greater share of the profits went to the actual farmers, but there were also beans from plantations that went out of their way to preserve natural vegetation which was the habitat of many tropical creatures, including several endangered species, others that guaranteed sanctuary for migrating birds, others still that channelled funds into various local community projects – fresh water schemes, education, solar power, children's homes ...

He eliminated anything to do with Church-run missionary projects on the basis that however well-intentioned and beneficial these contained nonetheless an element of post-colonial cultural imperialism, but this still left a good dozen which he was trying to put into order of merit when Elizabeth found him.

'Hello,' she said, casually, but clearly inviting an explanation. She got one – long, involved and, as far as she could make out, only unintentionally facetious.

'So basically I reckon it comes down to a straight choice between this one, the Nicaraguan profit-sharing collective, and this one – the Colombian wildlife sanctuary.' He showed her the label on the Colombian packet. There was a map on the back. 'That's where it comes from – I just can't remember who controls this part of Colombia . . . is it the Liberation Army or the drug cartels? On the other hand, the Costa Rican organic is packed in one hundred per cent recycled banana paper . . .'

Elizabeth was staring at him with that half-concerned half-withering contempt look which he'd seen so much over the last few weeks.

He threw both packets into the trolley. 'I'm sorry; I don't know what's wrong with me at the moment.'

They stood in the check-out queue not speaking. Henry was forlorn. His indecision at the coffee shelf continued to appal him. But surely everyone had moments like that, which they might reflect on and be so distressed they wished they were someone else? He turned to Elizabeth with a pleading look.

'Do you ever wish you were someone else?' he said quietly enough for only her to hear.

Elizabeth took her credit card back from the

check-out girl and replaced it in her purse without even giving Henry the sympathy of a glance.

'Do I ever wish I were someone else?' she repeated, loud enough for the rest of the queue to hear, in the tone you would use on an irritating toddler. 'No. But I often wish you were. Just help me pack these carrier bags, would you?' She closed her purse with a contemptuous snap. Someone behind them sniggered. Henry swooned inside, bit his lip, and packed the carrier bags with his head hung low, preparing to cope with whatever terrors life might throw at him on the journey home.

Strangely, whatever incredible misfortunes his imagination might torment him with, none came close to what was really going to happen.

CHAPTER EIGHT

Raschid wakes from a pleasant dream about an attractive blonde Caucasian girl to discover he is not on the beach of a tropical island but still on the PIA flight from Karachi to London and considers the strange ways fate works. Ten days earlier he had been staring vacantly at the mountains that surround the isolated Taliban outpost he commanded near the Uzbeki border, when two soldiers had arrived on an ancient Bedford three-tonner and told him he was going to Kabul.

Raschid spent the entire journey trying to look unconcerned. Either the two mujahiddin didn't know why he'd been summoned or they weren't telling. Raschid knew he'd never been entirely accepted by his comrades. However well he fought the Russians and in the civil war that followed the Russian withdrawal, he knew that because he was born in Birmingham – of a Pakistani father and an Afghan mother – a faint cloud of untrustworthiness clung to him in his brothers' eyes. He had returned to Britain once, for his sister's wedding, and was absent for three months. It was during a lull in the fighting but some people still considered it a demonstration of divided loyalties. Although he had kept it quiet, some knew he had renewed his British passport. He had been encouraged to by Commander Abu, but that did not seem to be so commonly understood. Nor that it was held in safe-keeping for him in Kabul.

What really made him nervous was that his loyalties were indeed suspect. He was sure he had kept his Walkman and beloved collection of heavy metal tapes totally secret – but maybe not. If anyone at headquarters had found out about them, he could be in big trouble – considering this was a country where you could be executed for 'having an English-style haircut'.[1] When the Taliban had first emerged he believed them to be a cleansing force for good. Now he wished – a wish he had never dared express to anyone – that he had stayed in England after his sister's wedding. At that time he had still believed in the Taliban cause. Now, even though he was officially one of them, he saw them as hideous and twisted perverters of the creed of Islam and wanted out. But 'out' was not an easy option.

---

[1] For the benefit of any Taliban leader reading this book, the Author wishes to make it plain he is in no way implying any criticism or satirical portrayal of the Taliban either here or elsewhere in the work.

Raschid had been told only that he was to meet Commander Omer – a man who had personally executed at least seventeen men for homosexual activity and used petty criminals and untrustworthy elements (such as men with no beards) as mine detectors.

Raschid hops out of the cab clutching his Kalashnikov, even though he knows that for once it cannot really help him. Two foot-soldiers he doesn't recognise are standing by the door and stare at him silently. He enters, and the eight regional commanders pack up their games of bridge. Raschid knows that means it's a serious meeting. He tries to remain calm. He hangs his rifle on an empty coat-hook and sits on the rug cross-legged. Green tea is prepared and brief opening banalities are exchanged before Omer quickly gets down to business.

He gestures to a rack of television and video equipment in the corner. 'We were taping CNN the other night.' Generally the Taliban do not approve of television. And if the Taliban do not approve of something, it doesn't happen. But, of course, exceptions are made for senior commanders purely because they need to keep tabs on what is being said about them by the Great Satan and his mendacious acolytes in the rest of the world. And that is all they'd use it for. You'd never find them gaping at Italian variety shows for hours on end, with all the teeth and tits and tinsel and people winning luxury cars and singing and dancing. And even if they did, it would only be so that they could experience firsthand the depths of corruption and depravity to which the Western World had slumped.

'They were showing a special report on us,' says Omer. 'Unfortunately, the video recorder is a new model and the instruction book is bloody impenetrable. Even to my nephew,' he adds icily, and gestures to a beardless teenage boy who is standing sheepishly in a dark corner, 'who is here with his knowledge of infernal infidel electronics to penetrate the impenetrable, and yet still he tapes the wrong channel off the satellite.' There is complete silence in the room now. The boy hangs his head. Enjoying the boy's discomfort, Omer pauses before continuing in a flat tone from which you could possibly infer a hint of menace. (And, if you knew Omer, you'd bet on the menace being there.) 'Which means we failed to learn what new lies are being peddled about us by the mendacious scribes of Washington.' (Translated literally, he says 'by the lying, dog-marrying serpents, vassals of the Great Satan.') He pauses again, and then his tone brightens. 'However, it transpires that benign Providence must have been guiding the hand of my nephew as he struggled with the infernal new Toshiba.'

The nephew looks up, clearly amazed that his uncle is hinting that he may be forgiven for his error. He's been losing sleep over this for two days. 'We wish you to translate this programme which appeared on the video tape instead.' Omer calls for someone outside to start the generator, and several pairs of urgently scuttling feet emphasise the fear and respect in which he is held.

He doesn't show it, but Raschid is relieved. So relieved. He feels like leaping around the room screaming and shouting and laughing – all they want him to do is translate a TV show! And he thought they might have found out about his tapes – the AC-DC and Black Sabbath albums he cannot do without. He thought they might have read his mind somehow, and logged the thoughts he has been having about how the extreme policies and pronouncements of the movement have very little to do with Islam as he understands it. He thought he might be coming here to stand trial for thought crimes and all they want him to do is watch TV! He could jump through the roof. But he doesn't. He is impassive and merely inclines his head minutely. And he silently thanks God for repaying his trust and prayers. Truly He is compassionate and merciful and great.

'As you will see, one infidel on the sinful and depraved programme we are about to see utters the word Taliban, and I would like to know what he is saying about us.' Raschid nods solemnly and minutely once more. There is a shout from outside that the generator is up to speed and Omer reaches forward, searching the low table in front of him.

'Where's that bloody infernal remote control got to now?' Everyone in the room begins looking under furniture and behind cushions, before nephew finds the remote sitting on top of the television, holds it triumphantly aloft and runs to Omer who snatches it from him and rolls his eyes.

'How many times do I have to say this? What is the point of leaving the infernal infidel remote control on top of the infernal infidel television when the whole point of having an infernal infidel remote control is that one doesn't have to get up and walk over to the infernal infidel television in order to turn it on? It should always remain on the table. Is that understood?'

The others all mumble that they have understood. Generously they are taking collective responsibility, to lessen the chance of a reprisal. Although it is a relatively minor domestic transgression, Omer has been known from time to time to be capriciously vindictive — or stern but fair, depending on your point of view, and whether or not he knows where you live — but today he's obviously in a good mood. Outside, one of his hunting dogs lets out a long moan and everyone else in the room has the same thought:

the dog is registering its disappointment at Omer's mellowness. No tasty extra rations today.

Omer presses the buttons. Nothing happens. His nephew deferentially advances and humbly begs to suggest... Omer hands him back the remote, the boy presses a couple of buttons and the video clicks and whirrs, the screen has a picture and they all sit down to watch. Impatiently Omer turns to his nephew again: 'Fast forward!' – a cascade of adverts hurtle past – 'Fast forward... stop! Here! Here!'

The boy presses 'play'.

The video runs. A stand-up comedian in a double-breasted suit is introducing another stand-up comedian. Raschid begins to translate.

'Ladies and gentlemen, give it up right now for Mr... James... Randall!' The crowd cheer and a thin dark-haired man dressed all in black slouches moodily on to the set. He nods to the MC, reaches the mike, stares at it Columbo-style, hunched over, head cocked sideways. Stays that way long enough for the audience to go quiet and then let out a nervous laugh. James takes the mike from the stand with a quick, sudden movement and grins at the audience. Feet fixed he leans back, taking a deep breath, holds it, then lurches forward again with the release of his opening phrase.

'Un-fucking-believable what is going on in Afghanistan at the moment, un-fucking-believable.'

The accent is cockney street-credible, choppy, confident (and actually completely false, but we needn't go into that now). He pauses again, smiles, parodies the audience's thoughts back at them, adopts a mock terrified expression. ' "Afghanistan? Why should I give a shit about Afghanistan? (*mock indignant*) I'm supposed to know what's going on in Afghanistan? ... (*pointing to an imaginary ticket*) Stand-up comedy! That's what it said on the ticket! ... A laugh, a drink, and maybe a shag – that was basically the shape of my evening when I left the house, and very nice too thank you very much – I get here and (*growing outrage*) some spindly git is doing a documentary at me! Afghanistan? I can't even spell it. And why should I? It's Friday night for God's sake! What is this, the fucking Learning Zone? I'll sue!" ' He picks out a couple of blokes in the front row, clearly there on their own. 'Relax, guys, it's going to be OK.' He smiles. Audience laugh – at nothing, just the timing of the pause he holds after the breakneck pace of the opening bit. 'I'll take you through it, and next week you'll be able to impress that prospective sexual partner whose intellect has always intimidated you by saying casually: (*mock cool*) "Of course, it really is unbelievable what's going on in Afghanistan at the moment ... Afghanistan ... that's (*mock smugly*) A.F.G.H.A.N.I.S.T.A.N." ' Audience laugh. They trust him. He starts again, himself now, on the move, downstage left, then back along the front edge of the performing area to the opposite corner. He picks up the pace again, punching out the facts in an urgent staccato rhythm.

'Twenty-five years ago, Afghanistan was famous for three things: Afghan coats, Afghan hounds, Afghani black. Afghan coats . . . Afghan coats (*getting a laugh of anticipation just from the contemptuous tone*) – an uncured sheepskin with wool round the edges. Originally worn by fierce mountain tribesmen in Central Asia, adopted by European hippies whose fashion sense had been cruelly distorted by the legendary power of Afghani black. Hippies loved them for their one unique quality; whatever the weather, whatever the time of year, if you wore an Afghan coat you would automatically look as if you had been caught out in a heavy rainstorm. Or pissed on by big dogs. Hippies for some reason thought this was cool. Anyway, in the seventies, they were pretty much cultural icons; now they've almost totally disappeared. What a lot of people don't realise is that the three things were all connected. Afghan coats eventually disappeared when the effect of the Afghani black wore off and people realised they looked stupid in them. All on the same day, all over the country, thousands of hippies ran out of dope simultaneously, looked in the mirror and thought – oh no, look at the state of me! I'd better replace this stupid article of clothing immediately with something a little more stylish. I know! This really cool-looking army-surplus greatcoat!

'I don't know what happened to Afghan hounds but my guess is they were on the Afghani black as well, realised *they* looked stupid too, got straight down the poodle parlour for a short back and sides and they're still around but we think they're greyhounds. The crucial thing is why did the Afghani black disappear? People looked stupid but they were happy, then the drugs disappeared and they got a reality check. Basically the drugs disappeared because the Russians invaded Afghanistan and the supply routes got cut off.' Addresses someone near the front. 'Don't write this down mate it might not be entirely accurate . . . and I don't want to be responsible for you failing your modern history A-level, OK? Why the Russians invaded I don't really know. Because one thing about the Afghans, they are seriously hard bastards. Imagine Millwall with Kalashnikovs. No one has ever beaten the Afghans since Alexander the Great. All the Afghans do is fight. Presumably they're so aggressive because they're really angry at having to walk around all the time in Afghan coats, looking stupid. Anyway the Russians invade, because they're frightened that their Muslim populations in Tazhbekistan and Uzbekistan and Tajikistan – don't ask me to spell any of these –

and Kazakhstan and Kyrgyzstan – sounds like the lyrics of a Eurovision entry – (*sings, inanely bopping his head around from side to side*) "(Tazhbekistan Uzbekistan Tajikistan Kazakhstan Kyrgyzstan)" . . . were all going to become Islamic fundamentalists and rebel against Soviet rule. So they attack the Afghanis. Which is a bit like sticking a red hot poker into a hornets' nest because you don't want to be stung by a swarm of angry hornets. So the Russians invade, and they're in this country where basically you've got hundreds of different tribes who herd a few goats, worship Allah, sell a bit of dope, and pass the rest of the time indulging in their hobbies. They have two main hobbies. One, fighting with each other; two, fighting other people. Well, for the first few years, the Russians seem to be doing all right, one, because they've got better equipment like tanks and helicopters, but, two, because with so much fighting going on anyway, it takes the Afghanis about four years to notice that someone else has joined in. And when they do notice, they are seriously pissed off – here are these foreigners, invading their country, and trying to take the Afghanis on at their national sport. So the Afghanis stop fighting each other, get together and fight the Russians. And within a couple of years the Russians are getting their arses kicked all the way back to Moscow. So, the Russians leave, the Afghans have a big party, and go back home for a rest and to get on with herding goats and worshipping Allah in peace. After about two weeks they're bored. They start going into other tribes' territories and staring. Just stand there, on a mountain, staring. Pretty soon, somebody says to somebody else, "What you staring at?" The other bloke goes, "Who you talking to?" and within seconds they're off again, fighting each other. And now they've all got tanks and helicopters and rockets they stole off the Russians, so it's very noisy, and much nastier than it ever was before.

'One or two clergymen say to each other, "Look, all this fighting – it's madness, we are all brothers. Isn't there some way we can stop the civil war?" They ask the Russians if they'll consider coming back, but the Russians say they're broke and anyway it wouldn't be fair because the Afghanis have captured all their equipment, so the clergymen have to find another plan. They try saying to all the various different armies, "This is madness, we should live in peace" but they just get laughed at. In fact, I doubt there's even a word in Afghani for peace. Nearest to it is probably a phrase that translates as "just getting my breath back and reloading". So, to cut a long story short, the clergymen start recruiting their own army. What they do is tell the warriors that if they join the new army, which they're calling the Taliban and is severely fundamentalist, they'll not just be fighting for their own clan against whichever clan that clan is fighting against, they'll be fighting against all the other clans who aren't in the Taliban, at the same time. They'll be outnumbered, it'll be a serious fight. Afghanis love those kind of odds. So immediately, just about everybody joins the Taliban and at present the Taliban control about eighty per cent of the country.

'The Taliban leaders meanwhile, like anyone anywhere who has any power, are starting to get off on it. And they're sitting around looking for ways to control and frighten people and generally shove them around. They start making up loads of stuff which has nothing to do with Islam – but pretending it's all coming fresh from God. They're oppressing women; executing people for not doing as they're told, for transgressing the law, for looking at them funny. They must be terrified of women, because women have no rights. Example. Women cannot be attended by male doctors. And women are not allowed to be educated, so there are no women doctors. They have to walk around the whole time completely covered up in these great long veils, they're completely subservient to men. Women are not allowed jobs of any kind. None of this is prescribed in the Qu'ran. "Men shall have a benefit from what they earn, and women shall have a benefit from what they earn." Qu'ran, shura four, line thirty-two. They're just making it up. Probably when they were kids these Taliban clergymen were the really nerdy spotty geeks who could never pull at the local disco – or whatever the equivalent was – and all the girls their age used to laugh at them and say, "You're crap at fighting, you are." And so they're getting their own back.

'And I reckon a lot of them are probably repressed homosexuals, 'cos you can get executed for that in Afghanistan. They're so deep in denial about their true nature they have to destroy it. They're a bunch of sick twisted manipulative megalomaniacs. As you all know, I'm gay myself. And so, if any of those sick sad twisted manipulative closet gay megalomaniac distorters of the noble words of the great prophet, sallalLahu, if they're watching this when it goes out on satellite' – not for a minute did James really believe this would happen – 'here is my challenge to the Taliban.'

He turns to look straight down the barrel of the camera. 'Girls of the Taliban, it's OK to want another man's body. So, come to London, I'll meet you at the airport in a car from Ladycabs. We'll relax, chill out, we'll do a few poppers, 'cos I know you don't drink alcohol, we'll go to Heaven, we'll pick a Seventies Night where everybody's going a bit daft anyway, we'll have a dance to Village People, we'll go back to my place, me, you and a few close friends, we'll have a lovely little coming-out party, all get our kit off, there'll be candles, romantic music, soothing essential oils, we'll massage each other tenderly. We'll take our time – I know you're going be nervous – and finally, even though I don't normally go for blokes with beards, but this is for me not you, finally, I'll slip on a heavy-duty condom and give you the quality hammering you've been secretly dreaming of ever since you first played with your little wing-wang. You'll chill out and go back home full of peace and love and really do your best to create a better world, OK? You've got some of the best spliff on the planet, yeah? Why don't you use it to mellow out, innit? Alternatively, girls of the Taliban, if you find this offer offensive, why don't you come over here and chop me into little bits, you uptight psychotic arseholes?'

James takes the applause and turns back to the studio audience. 'In the production box the director's doing his nut now. "Take my name off credits – studio! Red alert – we will not be running any credits at the end of this show is that understood?" Well, my name's James Randall. Good night.'

He stands there, bold, defiant, loving the applause. He is a stormer of barricades, a voice of the downtrodden, a thorn in the side of authority wherever it may raise its ugly head and he gets off on it. He loves being adored for being altruistic. Whether he would feel quite so cool and fearless if he knew his performance was being watched by members of the Taliban is not so certain.

Raschid can't believe what he's just heard. Omer clicks his fingers and his nephew stops the tape, rewinds it to the beginning of James's set. Raschid is still staring, stunned. Now he has to translate for the assembled dignitaries, and remembers the old adage about what often happens to the messenger who brings bad news.

To begin with it's not too bad. They like all the stuff about fighting prowess and beating the Russians. They even like the first bit about the Taliban as a unifying force. Then, it all goes very quiet towards the end and Raschid offers up the words with a sense of reluctance and indeed, dread. Omer's nephew turns off infernal infidel video and infernal infidel television. It stays quiet. It feels like there is a low dark cloud in the room. Raschid stares straight ahead. He keeps hearing the last section, the invitation, going over and over in his head. To his horror, as the cold chill which has numbed his nervous system begins to thaw out, he realises he has found it very funny, and in essence, possibly rather plausible. He also knows that if he indicates this, he will die. Which somehow, appallingly, makes it even funnier. But he keeps control.

Finally, Omer speaks.

'That is what he said?'

'Yes.'

Another long pause.

'This show was from England?'

'He spoke in an English accent. And the nightclub to which he referred, Heaven, is in London. As far as I recall,' he added carefully. 'A depraved den of corruption and foul perverted decadence.'

'There are elements within our movement which seek rapprochement with the West. We do not subscribe to this opinion. Raschid, Allah in his ineffable way has provided in you the means of furthering His Will and ours. We will return your passport to you, Raschid. You will protect our movement from the adulterating compromise with the Great Satan. You will go to London and bring this Kaffaar's balls back to us in a little bag.'

The room murmured vehemently in agreement.

'Yes, oh Holy One. With pleasure. I am honoured and blessed to be the conduit of the will of Allah who speaks through you.'

CHAPTER NINE

It is two o'clock when Sid and James leave the restaurant. James knew an hour ago he was going to be late but, given that Sid is paying, he hasn't been shy at going through the Armagnac menu. Sid is happy to let him drink it and forget that there is no such thing as a free lunch.

They get up and sway elegantly like young giraffes in a stiff breeze and the gaps between the tables seem much narrower than they were on the way in.

Sid waves across to Fiona Shaw with a look on her face that suggests the two of them are sole keepers of an amusing but terrible secret and mimes speaking into a mobile phone, crooking her fingers in a wonderfully expressive although totally unnecessary manner, given that in her other hand she holds a mobile phone. Fiona Shaw has looked away.

James is almost excited to see Tom Cruise and Nicole Kidman in a corner table but then remembers just in time he is a moody iconoclast and sneers.

'Where are you heading?'

'Up to Islington, to my brother's.'

'I'll give you a lift.'

James is at first not keen to take the lift, then realises that the risk of a fatal accident is minimal – Sid's megalomaniac faith that nothing bad can happen to her means she's used to driving half-cut. On the day that she does meet her comeuppance, she'll be so deeply in denial that she'll probably proceed to win a sprinting medal in the next Olympics just to prove that the double amputation was just a vicious rumour being put about by enemies. More importantly, James accepts the lift because it suddenly occurs to him that the risk of an accident is far outweighed by the way it will save him having to pay for a taxi.

The lunch sits ready for eating on Henry and Elizabeth's American oak table. Henry has changed into his match clothes – black leather shoes, chinos, grey sweater and overcoat – which he always wears now in silent defiance since James derisively told him it looked like an anally-retentive accountant's idea of casual dress.

Henry grabs the cafetière and pours himself another mug of the Costa Rican bird-defending coffee. Elizabeth feels he's had quite enough already but decides not to make things worse by mentioning it.

'Where the hell is he?' mutters Henry. 'He should have been here an hour ago.'

'When is he ever on time?' says Elizabeth simply. 'Oh well, this will all keep.' She takes cling film from a drawer.

'I'm sure he'll have a good reason and a fulsome apology, darling.'

'That's all right, it's not your fault.'

'He's my brother.'

She reaches her hand across the newspapers and strokes Henry's wrist.

Henry is unusually agitated. Elizabeth finds this most unbecoming in a man, but decides she must make an effort. He was her husband. Surely her judgement couldn't have been that bad.

'Henry, he'll be here in time. Now just relax. We've got all next week off, remember.'

'At my mother's.'

'Well, yes, that's true.' She drinks from Henry's mug. 'But it won't be too terrible. We'll be able to take some long walks.'

'Yes. It won't be too terrible,' he agrees, equally unconvincingly.

There is the sound of feet stomping up the front steps.

'About bloody time too,' says Henry.

'He's got someone with him,' says Elizabeth, craning her neck to look up to the door from the basement window.

'Well, I've only got two tickets. He knows that.'

James has invited Sid in because he reckons she could do with another coffee before she sits behind a wheel again, because he's hoping she'll run him and Henry up to the football ground and, possibly most importantly, because Elizabeth will hate it.

Elizabeth and James don't really get on that well. Their relationship got off to a bad start.

James was at a party in Notting Hill, before either was trendy and famous. James had drunk just enough to give him the Dutch courage to get talking to this tall, slim girl with short dark hair and actually keep the conversation going, which somehow turned to comedy. James had just done his first TV and, when Elizabeth remarked that she didn't know how someone could stand up there in front of hundreds of strangers and try to get laughs, James was delighted. He replied with the classic comedian's gambit of pretending to be very humble and self-effacing, expecting to generate more praise and admiration which he could once more gracefully pretend to dismiss before following up with the disarming 'And what do you do?' manoeuvre, which generally flattered the recipient to the extent where physical intimacy was just a matter of patience.

But instead, from Elizabeth's next comment, James realised that she did not know he was a comedian.

'It's not exactly something to be proud of is it, making a living out of making people laugh? I find it rather creepy,' she said.

James was stumped.

'Yes. Nonetheless, it's quite a respected profession on Planet Earth.'

'I find that even more creepy.'

'Why?'

'Oh come on. Could you ever trust a person conceited enough to stand up and show off in front of hundreds of people? It's sick, frankly.'

'It's a sick society,' said James pompously – although his intention was gravitas.

From the way he said it, Elizabeth got the impression that James thought he was the first person to have noticed this. She also deduced from his disgruntlement that he must be a comedian himself. She felt a little embarrassed; it was not in her nature to cause direct offence, so she laughed in an awkward attempt at apology. James took the chance to regain some ground by agreeing that the majority of stand-ups were indeed frivolous self-obsessed creatures, while subtly attempting to imply he was different, when he realised she was not really listening, but looking over his shoulder. When he turned round he saw she was looking at Henry. James tried to keep his suffering internal – he'd had enough practice. It was the same when James and Henry were teenagers – James would be desperate to pull and Henry would be the one the girls went for. James's short, hunched body and strange bony face with its big curved nose was never any competition for Henry, tall and powerful, with curly brown hair and that unfailingly kind look in his big blue eyes. James often hated him, especially as Henry never exploited his blessings for nefarious ends. Since James's celebrity of course, it's been different – at least until he cooked up the notion of pretending to be gay.

But James's humiliation that evening had been complete when, at the end of the party, Elizabeth offered Henry a lift home and, at Henry's request, she very generously dropped James off first. They were still sharing a flat at that stage, although after that night Henry was rarely in it.

Things had not improved when, after sustained wheedling, Henry persuaded Elizabeth to come to one of James's gigs and they discovered that a long routine in James's act – about a posh country wedding – was clearly based on Elizabeth and several members of her large middle-class family. They'd all had a drink afterwards but it had left a nasty taste. Especially when James had done it on television.

Elizabeth opens the door and is hit by the alcohol haze. She recoils automatically and if James hadn't been virtually seeing double he'd have noted her welcoming smile wrestling for an instant with an involuntary look of alarm and disgust – which would have been enough to give him satisfaction.

'Liz, hello, good to see you again.' James always calls Elizabeth Liz, because he knows it annoys her. 'This is my agent, Sid'.

'Hello – Liz?'

'Elizabeth. Hello, do come in'

'Sid gave me a lift up so I thought you wouldn't mind if she came in for a coffee.'

'Hope I'm not imposing.'

'Not at all, we're downstairs.'

'This is such a fantastic house,' is Sid's greeting to Henry as she trips on the last step and heaves into the kitchen like a top-heavy galleon. 'Hello, I'm Sid, James's agent. I can't believe we haven't met before.'

'We have actually. Several times.' Sid never remembers anyone who isn't materially important to her clients' careers.

'No, I mean at your house. It really is beautiful.'

'Thank you. Would you like some coffee?'

'Love some . . . what nice cups, Elizabeth. What lovely paint – Jocasta Innes, isn't it?'

Elizabeth is dead-weighted. 'Yes, as a matter of fact it is . . . ' So the girls are off on a tour of the house.

Henry is still twitchy.

'What time do you call this?'

'I was with my agent.'

'We won't have time for a pint.'

'Sorry.'

'Have you spoken to Mum recently?'

'No. Should I have?'

'Never mind.' Henry hoped that James would work it out for himself.

'Think they'll win today?'

Henry gives up. 'Two-nil.'

'Without Petit?'

'Even without Petit.'

Sid is genuinely impressed with the house, and rightly so. They've got taste, Henry and Elizabeth. It's a typical mid-nineteenth century Islington townhouse – in Barnsbury, my dear. It's huge, and since they bought it, which was just at the right time, prices have gone sky high. Even if they fall back now – and let's face it the bubble's got to burst again some time, hasn't it? – they're still going to make a massive profit when they sell. Not that they would consider it at the moment – though maybe they'd leave London if they had kids but . . . that's another story.

It's one of those places you walk into and it's got a good feel to it. And it's nothing to do with hanging Ba Gua mirrors over a goldfish bowl or covering your toilet seat with red silk. It's got a good feel because somehow they've hit a balance between tasteful and lived-in. Some friends recently came by with their two-year-old who, according to her mother, showed none of her usual shyness in new places; this was intended as a compliment to the atmosphere in the house, and was taken as such with genuine delight by both Henry and Elizabeth, though it was a happiness mixed with a rueful twinge of regret that the only children ever in the house were visitors. Although they both separately had this same thought, they didn't share it.

The house has a pair of stone lions on the gateposts and a big basement kitchen with halogen lights concealed within and behind ash hand-made kitchen units designed by Scandinavians and so expensive the Scandinavians were all able to retire at forty-five. There's a Welsh slate floor, a Smeg cooker with six hotplates and lots of Hockney prints and sketches of sixteenth-century fruits, and pans and utensils hanging around gleaming and generally making a quiet statement about how seriously Elizabeth and Henry take their food – although the wok hasn't been used since 1989, and the Alessi fish kettle only once. The dining area is defined by the huge oblong table, in American white oak, which can comfortably seat twelve. Today it is bare save for some freesias in an asymmetrical silver Indian vase and the scattered sections of two Saturday papers – the *Guardian* and the *Independent*.

Upstairs on the raised ground floor is a minimalist reception room with an oriental feel (Elizabeth taught English for a year in Japan) and a Bang and Olufsen television and stereo.

On the second floor is another reception room, always referred to as the drawing-room, which is very English and where they both like to retreat into some kind of middle-class haven from reality and pretend they're in a Jane Austen novel. Quite a lot of furniture has been inherited through Elizabeth's family – polished mahogany and rosewood and stuff and a chiming clock and a barometer and antique port glasses in a tantalus and old maps. Sid is impressed, says so again when she returns to the kitchen and forces James to agree, although truthfully he just resents the feeling of stability and belonging.

'Yeah well, anyway, we've got to get going. You don't fancy giving us a lift, do you, Sid?'

Henry grabs his coat, pecks Elizabeth on the cheek

and promises they won't be massively late. James has not apologised for failing to turn up in time for lunch.

CHAPTER TEN

Henry would have spent the whole journey screaming to be let out of the car if he had realised Sid was drunk, but he never notices because he is still too stunned at meeting a woman with a full moustache. As we know, he craves certainty in his life, and seeing a woman with deliberate, groomed facial hair doesn't fit his sense of normality. To cap it all, this experience has happened just before the football – the one constant in his life. Whatever other chaos might be happening, he has always been able to count on Saturday afternoons to be the same. But getting a lift to Highbury from a woman with groomed facial hair? Nothing makes sense now. Anything is possible. He is seized by a sickening vision that he will take his seat in the stand and Arsenal will come out on to the pitch playing a racing pigeon in the back four.

Sid remarks on the difference in the way the two brothers speak and James sourly changes the subject. Henry has never made any attempt to hide his accent and this infuriates James because it undermines his street-cred image. 'Social climber, innee, innit?' James explains, and changes the subject. Sid drops them at Finsbury Park tube and James offers to give her directions back to Fulham.

'I know my way around my city, thank you, darling.'

She lets them out with a curt 'Have a nice time,' and drives away confidently. As soon as she is out of sight she will pull over and consult the A–Z, not entirely certain that this distant part of the metropolis lies within its pages.

Henry needs some explanation.

'So, she's your agent.'

'Yes, she is. You've met her before.'

'But . . . she's got a moustache now.'

'Yeah. And?'

'And . . . she's a woman.'

'Yeah. So?'

Henry is silent, decides he doesn't understand show business at all. Still, what the hell, it's over now. He's going to watch the Arsenal with his brother. They've been going together for years. But this is not a book about football, so let's not go into detail. Basically they enjoy the opportunity to have man-to-man conversations every couple of weeks and occasionally to shout 'cunt' out loud with impunity. From the moment he crosses Seven Sisters Road,

NIGHT OF THE TOXIC OSTRICH

Henry is just a boy going to the football with his brother, nothing else. In fact, Henry feels so relaxed he's decided he's going to confide in James, tell James about his terrors, maybe get some help from his younger brother. He'll wait till later though.

At the end of his last TV series James shaved off his goatee beard and had his bleached hair dyed back to pretty near its natural colour so this week he doesn't get recognised and no one shouts 'Lefty poof' at him. For fifteen minutes or so they talk about the team and recent form and make knowledgeable predictions about the other games being played that weekend, before James realises he hasn't had any abuse and feels inadequate, as if something is missing.

He asks Henry how things are going with a transparent lack of conviction which Henry ignores, and says 'Fine' with an equally transparent lack of conviction which James ignores in turn. Henry hesitates, begins again, gingerly: 'Although having said that . . .'

'Wish I could say the same. It's terrible, man. I mean, pretending to be gay was a great career move but now I'm just fed up of not getting laid.'

'Wait. You . . . you *pretend* to be gay?'

'Keep your voice down, Henry.'

'But, I thought you *were* gay.'

'Do me a favour.'

'Why would you pretend to be something you're not. For four years?'

'Image of course. It's a great mixture – street-wise, iconoclastic, macho . . . gay. Nobody else in comedy has ever put that combination together. Apparently one of the lads, actually a member of an oppressed minority.'

'Well, I never knew that. That you were making it up.'

'That's 'cos I never told you, did I? It was a secret.'

'But I'm your brother.'

'So?'

'So?'

'So! It was a secret.'

'Oh great. Well next time I have a secret, don't expect me to share it with you, that's all . . . and see how you feel.' Henry is furious at how childish he sounds.

James shrugs. 'OK. Cool.'

Henry is breathing deeply to control his anger and humiliation. He feels he must be blushing horribly and stares straight ahead, trying to become invisible, concentrating on the pitch, trying to enjoy the way that, week in week out, it is always so much brighter and radiantly green than he expects it to be.

James picks up pretty much from where he left off.

'Yeah, it's been terrible, you know, trying to get

laid. I'm sick of it. And sick of living a lie of course; it's more the personal integrity side of it than the . . .'

'Sexual frustration?'

'Yeah,' says James, unconvincingly.

Henry is surprised by this. 'Surely there must be enough people in your business who'd sleep with someone just because they're famous? Unless they're a complete arsehole.'

James hadn't thought of this, Henry realises.

'It's not that I *can't* get laid, obviously. It's just that I've got to be so careful – if I start seeing someone in the business they might talk, if it's someone not in the business they might sell it to the papers; either way, if it gets out that I'm straight I could be in real trouble. I mean, all I want, all I need . . . I just want to be with someone I can trust implicitly, have sex with when I feel like it and who I don't have to see otherwise. Is that too much to ask?'

Henry takes another deep breath and looks towards the pitch. Thankfully the players are coming out. And he is relieved to see, on this day, when he has been in a car driven by a woman with groomed facial hair, that neither of Arsenal's centre-halves have feathers or beaks.

CHAPTER ELEVEN

The plane has landed. Raschid is excited. He's back in England. Or the Depraved Whore of the Great Satan, as it's known in Taliban circles. But Raschid can live with that. Yes, there is depravity and injustice here but also a far better selection of heavy metal albums in the shops and more motorbikes. That's what he wants: to be able to worship Allah the Great the Merciful without having to chop people up into pieces to prove his commitment, to be able to repair motorbikes all day with AC-DC on the stereo. Get a wife and have kids, go biking at weekends . . .

Raschid has bought a sober grey suit in Karachi and in his suitcase are two pairs of denim jeans, a couple of shirts, a pair of Nike trainers, a towel, some complimentary airline toiletries, a London A–Z and his copy of the Qur'an. He looks like a typical Asian-British businessman. He has just confounded the prejudices of an extended family from Norfolk, back from a fortnight's bargain package in Florida at the other end of the tube carriage, by giving up his seat to an old lady.

At Earls Court, half a dozen drunken white teenagers come yobbing on to the train at separate doors, yelling to each other and tripping over their own feet. You can feel everyone else in the compartment shrinking, trying to become invisible. Suddenly no one is conversing any more. Not that you could really hear any difference over the noise of the train, but the little gestures of communication have all disappeared, no smiling or nodding, no one half turned towards their neighbour, everyone rigid now in their own space behind the sanctuary of the newspaper, children furtively watching their parents, parents with their heads full of every bloodcurdling anecdote they have ever heard about violence in the Big City. The drunks stumble towards the space by the central double doors and begin a football chant informing the rest of the carriage that Chelsea are the greatest football team the world has ever seen.

They applaud themselves, then two of them notice a girl of about twenty-two who got on at Barons Court. (Raschid has noticed her as well. She is slim, with long shiny brown hair and a short leather skirt. Raschid has been captivated. It's a long time since he's seen a woman's face, let alone long, flowing hair and most of a woman's legs. Apart from victims of shell-fire.) They stare at her, look at each other, grin, make lascivious gestures, look back at the girl, grunt. It's Quentin Tarantino directing the chimps in a PG Tips advert.

One of the boys leans over and says, 'All right, darling?' She has recoiled even before he speaks, jerked out of her paperback by the alcohol fumes. The gang, watching their star charmer doing his party piece roar out sarcastic amusement and horse-shoe in closer behind him. The girl looks up, she's frightened.

'What's your name?'

She turns back to her book.

'I'm Dave. What's your name?'

She doesn't look up, gives a nonchalant grimace to show she can handle this, she's used to it, she's a Londoner. Raschid wonders if she might. Perhaps this is what happens all the time to women who dress so. Perhaps this is how young people court in London these days. Otherwise, surely someone in the compartment would have bidden the drunkards to behave and leave her in peace. They are easily outnumbered by the able-bodied men in the carriage, none of whom seems particularly concerned with what is going on.

Dave has had no reply, looks around to his mates, appealing to them – she's being rude, what can I do? Suddenly he leans in and bellows right in her face.

'What's! Your! Name!!'

The girl gasps involuntarily and presses against

the window. Even the man sitting next to her on the outside seat has reacted to this. He looks up at Dave and gives him an impatient look. Dave looks him right in the eye and the man, not much more than forty, shrinks into his leather jacket and once more gives his undivided attention to his yachting magazine.

'My name's Dave, what's yours?'

The girl replies, quickly and quietly, without looking. 'Susie.'

Dave, hanging from the ceiling rail by his left hand extends his right. 'Pleased to meet you, Susie.'

Raschid is baffled. Surely the boy is due a reprimand from his elders, but no one seems to object.

Dave nudges Susie with his outstretched hand. She shrinks back as much as she can but looks up defiantly.

'Leave me alone, will you?'

Another sarcastic mocking cheer from Dave's mates.

'Don't be like that, darling . . .'

'Leave me alone.'

'How can I? I'm in love wiv yer!'

Dave's courtiers laugh at this laser-sharp riposte.

Raschid has been telling himself it's too risky to get involved, that either the girl or the boys will be getting off soon and nothing will happen apart from her being terrified for a few stops, but suddenly, in a process he knows from experience, his restraint has gone and he's in action.

'Excuse me, the young lady clearly does not wish to talk to you. Leave her alone please.'

The boys turn round as one to face the voice. Dave steps through his acolytes and stares at Raschid who is about two yards away from him.

'What's it got to do with you?'

Everyone is looking at Raschid now.

'Just leave her alone. You are frightening her.'

'I said, what's it got to do with you?'

There are eight of them in the space by the doors. With the way the compartment narrows when the seats start, Raschid calculates that they will find it difficult to all reach him at once.

Dave is staring at Raschid. Raschid is staring back. Sadly, Dave is too drunk to see the look in Raschid's eyes which, if Dave could focus on them, would tell Dave he was out of his depth. A couple of the chorus line have read the look, and gone quiet, but Dave still thinks it's eight to one.

Dave takes another step towards Raschid and repeats his question. Only four of the others step with him initially. The three stragglers belatedly shuffle up a half pace and then try and look hard again.

Raschid can smell Dave's breath now even though he's still out of range.

'I said, what's it got to do with you, Paki?'

Raschid would love to mash the boy now but he really doesn't want to risk an encounter with the police so he remains silent, staring, and hopes that Dave will deflate of his own accord. But sadly, for Dave that is, so in a sense not sadly at all, Dave interprets Raschid's silence as a lack of bottle. With a yell he rushes forwards and swings his right foot towards Raschid's groin. Raschid slides diagonally forwards a half step, pivots side-on on his rear foot, helps Dave's swinging boot on its upwards arc with a delicate stroke of his left hand, hooks it in the crook of his elbow and simultaneously smashes his right foot into the knee of Dave's standing leg which bends and folds with a loud crack. Dave collapses back into his friends, groaning. Raschid closes the gap now between him and the group, rushing in on the momentum of Dave's fall. One kid, to his right, is separated from the rest and still off-balance. Raschid's not really thinking now but, if he talked you through it in slow motion, he'd tell you he had to make an example of this one for the rest of the group. Raschid slams him into the carriage doors and catches him in the head with a hook and two fast straight punches before the boy can get his guard up. The boy hits the floor of the carriage as the doors open at Hyde Park Corner.

'Now leave the train,' Raschid says quietly. And

the yobs obey. There's a few astonished looks from the passengers getting on as Dave and the other injured boy hobble from the train supported by their friends. The girl looks at Raschid and timidly says, 'Thank you.' Those in the carriage who have witnessed the whole thing suddenly burst into spontaneous applause and Raschid smiles meekly. The applause continues for a few seconds more, stops as spontaneously as it started and everyone starts reading again.

A couple of people offer shy smiles of congratulation to Raschid as they get off, but that's all. Raschid is baffled: none of the other men offered any assistance. 'And this is the nation that once nearly conquered Afghanistan?' he asks himself. He notices that in their haste to leave the train, one of the gang has dropped a carrier bag on the floor of the compartment. Raschid stoops to pick it up, mainly to break the eye contact with the other passengers. He looks inside and to his delight discovers it contains about a dozen CDs. Black Sabbath, Iron Maiden, Def Leppard. He puts the bag under his arm, and smiles. Surely God is generous and great.

CHAPTER TWELVE

As they leave the stand at the end of the game, Henry looks out into the dark beyond the floodlights with dread, like a Neolithic hunter forced to leave the safety of the campfire and the cave. It will not be for a couple of hours – there is still Sports Report to overhear in fragments on other people's transistors as the crowd flows along and subsequent discussion of the rest of the day's results over a few pints and then maybe a curry. But the first advanced parties of anxiety are already infiltrating Henry's mind. When they stop at the same kebab shop as they have done for years, Henry orders only chips. He says it's because he's watching his red meat intake, but he knows it's because he's afraid of salmonella and e-coli and all the other bacteria which he was never afraid of until they started making the front pages. He finds himself walking at least a yard in from the kerb to give himself that extra second if a juggernaut does suddenly career off the road.

They cut down and across Highbury Fields,

coming out on to the very beginning of Holloway Road at Highbury Corner.

'They don't do any comedy there these days,' says James, pointing back at the little rock venue behind them.

'The Town and Country Club 2 wasn't it?'

'That's right, the T and C 2. Always had a great night down there. Happy days.' James uses precisely the same nostalgic tone he used to ridicule when he heard it from old comics reminiscing about music hall or the Windmill Club in his early days on the alternative comedy circuit. But he doesn't notice. Henry does, but lets it go. He's still hoping to get a sympathetic ear from James at some point in the evening, and besides, he has happy memories of that period too – he wasn't scared the whole time. He realises they're cutting through the station forecourt and about to turn into Highbury Station Road, a quiet, twisty, badly lit street. He stops.

'Shall we get a cab?'

'What for? We're nearly there now.'

Henry breathes deep. Yes, quite right. Get a grip. You're going to be fine.

'I tell you one thing which has been bothering me recently – sounds ridiculous but . . .'

James stops dead and turns round with an excited little jump to face Henry, grabbing him by the shoulders. 'I tell you what we should do later on! We should check out that new supermarket up the road.'

'The new Aldingtons? Why?'

'Yeah! It's open all night, right? Someone was telling me it's a real pick-up joint after midnight. A cross between the all-night bagel shop on Ridley Road and a singles bar. Oh excellent! Bound to find some stoned little babe with the munchies who'll do it for a couple of KitKats.' James hears this uncensored little burst from his subconscious with embarrassment. 'I'm being ironic, obviously.' They walk on. 'But we should go. I mean, it'll be interesting research, see what's going on on the street, you know. It's important for me.'

'Well, I don't know,' says Henry. 'Let's see how the evening goes.'

'You mean Liz'll be expecting you back after closing time.'

'No, that's not what I mean at all.'

But from the way Henry snapped it out, James knew he'd hit a nerve and felt content. Winding people up was what he'd been put on earth to do.

Raschid decides it might be a good idea to leave the train a couple of stations later just in case, to avoid being followed or someone getting too good a look at him. He emerges from Leicester Square underground and is thrilled to be back in the big city. He's only been to London a couple of times before. Once on a school trip when he was about twelve, when they'd done the Houses of Parliament and the Tower of London and all that, and then, when he was a bit older, a couple of rock concerts. It feels good to be back.

As he walks up the road he realises every other shop is a bookshop. Passing a large one which is still open a sudden wicked impulse shoots through him. He goes in and looks for books by Salman Rushdie. There they are, five different ones just on the shelf, just there! He picks one up at random and takes it to the counter. The young man on the till doesn't bat an eye. Raschid can't help grinning. He checks his watch and hurries back to the tube. Not because he's worried about being late, but because he can't wait to sit down and start reading his new book.

James and Henry settle down in a quiet corner with their pints. 'Have you spoken to Mum recently?' asks Henry.

'Not for a while. You know what it's like. They played well today, I thought . . . told you they wouldn't miss Petit.'

'You do know it's her sixtieth next Saturday.'

'Yeah, I knew that, yeah.'

'Elizabeth and I are going up.'

'Right.'

'You going to come up for the day?'

'When is it exactly? Her birthday.'

Henry tries to keep patient and polite. 'Next Saturday.'

'Great.'

'It'll be nice. Get out of the city for a couple of days...'

'Yeah.' James is holding his glass up to the light. 'Look at that. Lovely colour. It's always a good pint in here.'

'Yes...'

'Like a country pub really. A country pub slap in the middle of London.'

'Mm. Should come more often really.'

'Why don't you?'

'Well, Elizabeth isn't really much of a pub-goer. Actually I should phone her in a minute.'

'Ready for another then?'

'Blimey, you got through that quick.'

'Told you it's a good pint. Come on, it's your round.'

Two hours and two pubs later, the alcohol is just doing the trick for Henry. He's gone on to lager in the hope it might temporarily bestow upon him the more superficial, hedonistic mindset of the typical lager drinker, and it seems to be working. They are in a conversational lull, and while James is slyly checking himself out in a huge gilt mirror, Henry is contemplating his affliction in something like calm detachment. He decides there is a positive aspect to his fear – namely that his sensitivity to the fragile nature of existence is at least a deeper appreciation of what reality is really like. A sort of Buddhist thing, stripping away the walls of illusion. Then with a sudden anger it occurs to him that if this is the kind of understanding of reality Buddhists have, how come they are always so calm?

'Bastards!' he says out loud.

'Who?' asks James.

'Buddhists. Fucking Buddhists.'

'Who are you calling a fucking Buddhist?' says a large man behind them.

'Nobody,' says James. 'He wasn't calling nobody a Buddhist. He's just had a bad day, that's all. Come on mate, time to go.'

Before Henry can react, James has hustled him outside. It infuriates Henry, this ability of James's to talk and charm his way out of explosive situations.

'What d'you do that for? You think I can't look after myself?'

'Course you can, but what's the point of getting in a stupid scrap with someone twice your size?'

'I hadn't finished my drink.'

'We can go and have another drink.'

'But I wanted to talk to you about something.'

'Let's go and find another pub then. What you got

against Buddhists all of a sudden?'

'I'm hungry.'

'One more then a curry, yeah? Beat the rush.'

In the next pub, when Henry goes to the bar for the second time, he asks for change for the phone. Then he comes back to the table and James asks if he remembered the nuts.

By way of reply Henry says, 'Can I tell you something?'

'You left the beers on the bar.'

'Don't you fucking start. You haven't been to see Mum for fucking ages, you selfish bastard.'

'All right, Henry. Calm down.'

'Calm down? She's your mother. You – I bet you don't even know what colour her eyes are. I mean, when was the last time you were there? Even for Christmas? It's always, "Oh I've got to go to Los Angeles or New York for business... can't turn it down man, it's like contacts I can't afford not to cultivate. Later, yeah?" ' Henry is mimicking James's accent surprisingly well. 'And where did you learn to talk like that, you fucking poser? Like some black teenager from Hackney when you're a thirty-year-old ex-public schoolboy. Who doesn't even visit his mother. Call yourself a radical crusading comedian? You don't give a shit about anyone but yourself. You fucking wanker.'

'What's brought this on?'
'What's brought this on? You never listen to me, that's what brought this on.'
'What then?'

CHAPTER THIRTEEN

At first, when they were planning the mission, Raschid had assumed he would be able to stay with his family in Birmingham but he was persuaded that this involved too much risk of exposure. They had given him the address of a safe house which was in far less danger of detection. The safe house would be notified of his arrival well in advance.

Raschid found it easily enough with the A–Z. It was a quiet street, with cars double-parked almost all the way along. He rehearsed the password dialogue in his head once more before pressing the buzzer. 'Hello, is that Steve?' If the voice said yes, he was to say, 'I am a friend of Ali's from the firm.' If the voice said no, he was to say, 'I am a friend of Steve's, from the firm.' Then the other voice would say, 'It's a bit late to be working, isn't it?' And Raschid would say, 'Yeah. I could murder a cup of tea,' and he would be let in. He found the complexity of the exchange reassuring – it meant he was dealing with people who knew what they were doing.

* * *

Inside the flat that Raschid is seeking, Les was looking out of the window, impatient and salivating. There was no food in the house and so Les had ordered a pizza. The delivery was late – it should have been here an hour ago and Les was anxious because now Stevie was back. Les knew it was going to be touch and go as to whether he got his hands on the pizza now. He had to get to the door first, pay the guy and wolf the pizza down before Stevie found out what was going on.

Stevie handed him a mug.

'What's this?' snapped Les.

'It's peppermint tea, Dad, it'll help your digestion.'

'There ain't nothing wrong with my digestion. How many times do I have to tell you?'

'You ain't had a shit for three weeks, Dad.'

'That don't mean there's nothing wrong. I'll have a shit when I'm good and ready. Haven't you heard of metabolism? Everybody's is different. That's all.'

'You're farting all the time. Makes me want to throw up. I'm frightened of lighting a fag when I come in here.'

'Fuck off then,' said Les, and waved a lighter in Stevie's face before using it on an Embassy.

'Dad, I'm worried about you.'

This open declaration of concern made Les feel uncomfortable. He tried to hit Stevie, but of course, he was too slow. 'Well, don't be! Don't you worry about me boy! I'm all right. I'm going to be on TV soon. That's how much trouble I'm in. I'm up to thirty-eight stone now. They'll be having me on Vanessa soon, or Trisha. I'm sending a new load of letters off next week.'

'Dad, will you come away from the window and listen to me.'

'I can hear you and look out the window at the same time! What do you think I am? A fucking cripple.'

It can't be because they don't know the address, Les thought, it was his fourth pizza of the day. He heard a moped park in the street, and yes! Here was a man carrying a pizza walking up to Les's door. And, as luck would have it, Stevie was in the toilet!

As Raschid walked down the street checking the numbers, a moped pulled up and parked just ahead of him. Raschid slowed down. Was he being tailed? No, the boy got off the bike and went into a house, not looking round. Raschid continued a few yards further, found the number he was looking for and pressed the buzzer for the ground floor flat. Presently he heard a scrabbling through the intercom and some muffled cursing which then turned into heavy breathing being directed into the handset. There was also music in the background. Raschid recognised it. 'I Wish It Could Be Christmas Every Day' by Wizzard. A pause. The music had changed. It was now something Raschid could not make out, with sleighbells. The door was buzzed open and he walked into the narrow hallway, which was strewn with free newspapers and junk mail. A dull light spilt out from a door to his right. No one appeared, so Raschid tapped on the open door and walked in.

Raschid had experienced a few strange things in his time, but nothing to prepare him for what he saw when he entered the flat. First, there was the musty smell of stale methane. Then there was Les, in string vest and underpants, leaning against the wall, out of breath from the effort of walking to the entryphone. At first, Raschid thought he had interrupted one of the perverted sexual bondage games the English were famous for in the lore of the Taliban. Surely there had to be six or seven people tied up in that string vest? It was impossible that so much flesh could belong to one person. It was moving and writhing in at least four separate directions. But Raschid could only see one head however hard he tried.

Surveying the room, he was confused to see a Christmas tree in the corner, tinsel hanging from the centre light, bits of dead holly and a wizened bit of mistletoe skewered by a drawing pin above the door to the kitchenette. Five or six Christmas cards were bluetacked haphazardly around the walls, most of them faded and curling. Raschid remembered that the English celebrated Christmas earlier and earlier every year, but it was only mid-September – surely this was extreme even by the standards of this consumption-mad society? He didn't like to mention it for fear of unintentionally sounding disrespectful.

Les gulped air until he could speak.

'Turkey pizza?'

Raschid looked confused.

Les gestured at the carrier bag, and repeats:

'Turkey pizza? With extra sprouts?'

The huge man was trying to force money into Raschid's hand.

'I am here to see Stevie.'

With a surprising burst of speed, Les stepped round Raschid and collapsed against the door, slamming it shut. He leant there, a desperate look in his eye, clearly not prepared to move. And he would take a lot of moving.

'Look, mate, don't muck about. Never mind what my boy's told you, I've ordered a turkey pizza and that's what I want.'

'I haven't got a turkey pizza.'

'What you come round for then? Don't tell me you're wasting people's time telling them you ain't bringing them a pizza 'cos their son's told you they're on a diet?'

Raschid was completely confused.

'There must be some mistake. I have come to see Stevie. I was told he lives at this address.'

'Look, mate, I don't care what he's told you, I want a turkey pizza, and you ain't going anywhere until I get one.'

'So he does live here?'

'Might do. Gimme the pizza.'

A skinny youth suddenly stepped into the room.

'Who's this, Dad?'

'No one.'

'I have no pizza.'

'Pizza! Dad, how many times do I have to tell you? Look, I'm working two bleeding jobs, trying to save up so we can go on holiday, get you better, and you're ordering fucking pizzas every time my back's turned. Sorry, mate, he don't want the pizza.'

'I have no pizza.'

'You ain't got no pizza? Then what's in the bag?'

Raschid was confused but tried to keep calm. The large man was leaning against the door, and the skinny boy looked volatile and appeared to have metal hands. Escape would be difficult. It was not the kind of contact Raschid had expected, but he knew the address was right and the boy's name was Stevie. Perhaps it was some kind of test.

'You are Stevie?' asks Raschid.

' 'oo are you?'

'I am Raschid. From the firm.'

'They never told me someone was coming.'

'A message was left. I was assured.'

Stevie looks daggers at his dad. 'Have you been hiding my mail?'

'Well, you've been hiding my food.'

Stevie counts to ten. 'Let's go through and sit down.'

'What's going on? Where's my pizza?'

'Shut up, Dad. Wait there.'

Stevie ushered Raschid through to the kitchen and closed the door.

Raschid tried to begin the password exchanges.

Stevie stopped him.

'It's no good, mate, he's obviously been hiding my mail again. Look, we've got a few problems round here at the moment. But don't worry. Whatever you're here for, it's cool. OK. We are brothers and this is your house now.'

'OK.'

'Really, no problem, you can stay as long as you like. Relax, I'll put the kettle on. That's me dad through there, he's a bit weird but we can trust him. Come through, I'll introduce you.'

They returned to the front room.

'Dad, this is Raschid. He's a mate of mine. Might be staying for a few days.'

'Why?'

'He's my mate.'

'And he's staying tonight?'

'Yeah.'

'We could have a game of Monopoly.'

'He's knackered, he don't want a game of Monopoly.'

'You always say there's no point playing with two of us – now there's three.'

'Not now. I told you, he's knackered.'

'Won't take long.'

'Won't take long? Give it a rest, will you? Anyhow, I gotta go minicabbing tonight.'

Les walked slowly and reluctantly out of the room.

'Raschid mate, I'll show you where everything is, then we'll talk tomorrow, yeah?'

'OK.'

Stevie gave him a tour of the premises – it took all of a minute.

'Bathroom's here. You'd better take my room. There you go.'

Raschid pointed at a poster on the wall. 'AC-DC?'

'Er, yeah, they're like a heavy metal band. You know, rock music.'

'Yeah, yeah, I know. "Highway to Hell" is my all-time favourite track.'

'You're into heavy metal?'

'Yeah.'

'So you're not from Iran then?'

'No. Afghanistan.'

'Afghanistan? You Taliban then?'

'Yeah.'

This was not the kind of safe house Raschid had expected. He did not want to insult his host by being too obviously suspicious of him, but needed to know more. Stevie read this in his face.

'Don't worry mate, I may be white, I may be born and bred in Hornsey but I'm kosher mujahiddin,' said Stevie.

'Kosher mujahiddin,' echoed Raschid flatly.

'Yeah. See these.' Stevie held up his hands, which Raschid saw were indeed made of metal. 'Lost the real ones blowing up a Zionist target. Got a metal plate in me head and all. Right here.' He taps his skull. 'Watch.'

He grabbed a grimy towel from the draining board, led Raschid out through the kitchen door, wrapped the towel round his head, knelt down and smashed his forehead into the concrete with incredible force. He came up smiling and led Raschid back inside.

'Did three years, met Ali Mustaffah and Yussuf Mansoul.'

Raschid knew the names. The situation was worse than he thought. Mustaffah and Mansoul were idiot relatives of a Taliban elder, and had been sent to Europe to disseminate literature and covertly recruit for the cause. Instead they had set up a business dealing hardcore pornography into Britain from the Continent. Mustaffah and Mansoul claimed they had been framed and set up by Interpol, but their sentence was well-deserved. Obviously they had taken Stevie in with their protective fictions, and it was an emphatic illustration of their own stupidity that they in turn had decided Stevie was a reliable contact. It must have been in their desperation to make amends with their powerful relatives back in the mountains. Raschid could only hope they had assumed the contact would never be activated. But now it had, and he was dependent on it. Well, at least he was out of Afghanistan. *Keep calm and play it as it comes*, he told himself. He wanted just to walk away and take his chances, but he could not be sure there was not another team watching him. *Know your ground before you make your move.*

Stevie beamed with pride. 'They checked me out. If you trust them you can trust me. So, what you here for?'

Raschid did not want to talk further with Les in the house.

'We will discuss it tomorrow. But, before you go out, tell me more about how you came to be involved.'

'All right.'

Stevie explained how he had tried to blow up an off-licence in Hornsey as a protest against Israeli settlements in the Occupied Territories – on the grounds that places that sold alcohol had to be anti-Muslim, and therefore Zionist. Raschid did not quite see the logic, but he did not bother to get Stevie to explain it; the very fact that Stevie could see a connection gave Raschid all the information he needed. Nobody who had interviewed Stevie after his arrest had been able to fathom it either. Stevie himself realised later that there were a few steps missing in his argument, but he stuck to his reasons proudly and unswervingly while the various psychiatrists and probation officers just scratched their heads.

Nobody got hurt in the bombing though Stevie did lose his hands. Inside, he read a lot, mainly deep and devoted religious study. At prayer he met the pornography dealers. They could see he was pretty fervent and they decided he might be useful as a less obvious contact for anyone coming from abroad. Stevie made a conscious effort to seem to have mellowed, which is how come he got maximum remission on his sentence. Since he's been out, he's settled down to some kind of *modus vivendi* with his dad. He doesn't have many friends, which is his way. The council have put Les in a ground floor flat because he's not good with stairs and Stevie tries to look after him.

It would have to be enough for now.

'We'll talk tomorrow.'

'OK. You hungry? Pizza all right?'

Raschid nodded.

'Here, how come you got a Brummie accent?'

'Because I'm from Birmingham,' replied Raschid, patiently.

Les's vast bulk lumbered in the doorway. 'Pizza? You're ordering pizza now? Get me one?'

'You're having salad. I told you.'

'Salad? What fucking good is a salad?'

'It's all you're going to get, OK? So that's a fucking end to it. I don't want an argument.' Stevie stared at Les with furious, beady eyes.

'But . . .'

Stevie exploded, frothing at the mouth, stamping and spitting.

'You're having salad because I say so because you're fucking killing yourself and it's doing my nut in trying to look after you and if you don't fucking shut up I'll wire your fucking jaw up!' Then, recovering his composure as if it was controlled by a switch, he said sweetly, 'Understand?' And smiled.

Stevie ordered the food and they sat down in front of the TV to wait.

Bridge on the River Kwai,' said Les. 'Just started,' and he ran the video.

They ate in silence, Les picking mournfully at his

salad and casting envious glances at the other two munching on their pizzas, until it became too much to bear. With a great deal of effort, Les got up on his feet and announced he was going to bed.

'All right, Dad. Look, Raschid's going to get his head down and I'm going cabbin' for a bit, yeah?'

'All right. You charging him rent?'

'No.'

'But he's using your room.'

'It's only a few days.'

'Where you going to sleep?'

'In here. He's a mate.'

'I'm going to bed then.'

'All right.'

Raschid got into the bath with an uneasy feeling. A tattooed white boy with metal hands was not the contact he had expected. Also, he was not keen on killing the comedian. His material was not blasphemous, its target was human not the Divine. On the other hand, Allah had granted Raschid the opportunity to start his new life; what if Allah were genuinely offended by the comedian's insults, and the killing of James was the debt Raschid had to pay before he could start again?

Raschid could hear Les out of bed again, walking about and, as he fell asleep, translated the slow thump of his tread into his dream like the rhythmic shelling of heavy artillery.

CHAPTER FOURTEEN

They've just finished a chicken vindaloo and a prawn pathia.

'You've never liked her, have you?'

'Who? Elizabeth? Of course I do.'

'You've never liked her and you're jealous of me marrying her because you fancy her. You've never forgiven us for getting together at that party when it was you who started chatting her up but me she went for. That's why you forgot we were cooking lunch.'

Henry turns to a passing waiter and asks for the bill. A second waiter, coming from the other direction, puts the bill down on the table with Henry's credit card and a slip. It's not supernatural, for Henry already asked for the bill ten minutes ago. He is very impressed. 'I told you the service was good here, didn't I?'

'You did.'

'Are you laughing at me?'

'No, I'm just smiling, that's all.' James leans

forward, and mimics the concerned manner of a psychiatrist he has seen on a TV show recently. 'Look, Henry, I know you're angry with me, and I hope you know I would never knowingly offend you . . . tell me what it was you wanted to talk about.'

He notices with great satisfaction the disarming effect this performance has on Henry, who looks at him with gratitude and surprise, then looks away to find the words, then back down at the table to deliver them.

'We've got a problem, James. Elizabeth and I, I mean.'

'What's up?' James smells juicy information and decides that playing concerned and caring is the best way to extract it.

'I can't make love to her any more.'

'Why not?'

'I don't want her to get pregnant.'

'That's not so difficult to avoid.'

'But I can't tell her why. It sounds so ridiculous.'

Henry goes on to tell James that his fear of the potential pain and suffering in the world have convinced him it's wrong to have children and subject them to the dangers of existence.

'The only good thing about it is that, if I go anywhere near her, I can't get a hard-on. So she thinks it's an impotence problem, but it's just the anxiety. I can't tell her the real reason, she'd laugh at me. Or maybe leave me for someone who does want kids.'

'I thought you did want kids.'

'I do, in a way. I mean, emotionally I do, it's just rationally I can't justify it. What am I going to do?'

'Well, I don't know.' Henry is speaking loud enough for the other tables to hear and they've all stopped talking, waiting for the next instalment. Protectively, James suggests they get some fresh air.

'I know! Let's go to Aldingtons and have a look round.'

'What? Walk up there, in the dark?' says Henry. It's almost a whimper.

'You've got to fight it, Henry. Come on, I'll take care of you.'

Stevie spends the evening ferrying people into the West End. He is blissfully excited. He knows Raschid's presence means something important is going to happen and he is going to be part of it. It's what he's been waiting for, ever since his botched bombing. Now there is a chance to be involved in something big.

Stevie is the runt of the litter – actually, that's not strictly true as he's an only child, but he's been the runt of every group he's ever been a part of. The one the others are always making fun of. Who's the kid on the bus whose shoe goes out of the window?

That's Stevie. The one with the Kick Me note on his back in the playground, the last one to be picked at football. Later on, he's the one who sticks most safety pins through his ears and cheeks – without the use of ice-cubes to numb the spot – to give himself some standing. Of course, he becomes the circus freak, doesn't he? Enjoys the attention, but what a price. Look at the scars, the raddled tissue where it all went septic. And the broken teeth – too many beer bottles opened on them.

Course, when he's tanked up, from time to time he'll go off on one. Like, normally, it's 'Stevie, stick this kebab skewer through your cheek' and it's stapling his face together like something out of Tom and Jerry. But every so often he'll turn and swear and it'll be *your* face getting kebabed if you aren't quick. He'll smash up anything and anyone. Like a man possessed. Only a scrawny kid but no one can handle him if he's in that kind of mood.

One day, sniffing lighter fluid round the back of the flats, someone's got a staple gun and they've brought a new girlfriend to see the fabled freak. This guy asks Stevie to whack a few staples in his arm. Stevie's not in the mood, the girl is pretty but Stevie knows she's never going to be interested in someone like him. He loses it in rage – and a little flash of foresight that his life is always going to be like this. Anyway, he squirts a jet of lighter fluid at this kid, flicks a lighter. Everyone scatters, there's a whoosh, the fluid goes up and burns both ways. Then Stevie slings the tin of lighter fluid just in time and there's a bang and a flash as the whole thing goes up and one of the slower runners gets a few metal splinters in his back.

That's it for Stevie. The equivalent of the light on the road to Damascus. Explosions. That's what he lives for from that moment on. Explosions are beautiful. He can still see the red and yellow and blue of the lighter fuel going up for days afterwards. Not all that surprising – they are virtually scorched on to his retina. And it's deeper than that. The noise, the way everyone runs for it. He can feel their fear. Before, there's always been an element of entertainment if he's gone off on one. Even if he's kicking shit out of whoever he's caught, the others are laughing, sometimes even the kid he's hurting. But nobody laughs when he sets the bomb off. They're just plain scared. For Stevie it's a divine revelation – terrible and fascinating. He has seen the face of God. Explosives equal respect.

Stevie starts paying attention at school.

As for Stevie becoming a Muslim, he's convinced he really is one. His understanding of Muslims is of angry protestors on TV burning the Stars and Stripes and the Union Jack; they hate the country Stevie lives in, and that's good enough for Stevie. The specifics don't concern him, he doesn't feel a need to dig very deep on the intellectual side. For him Muslim means fundamentalist, however ignorant this might be. So he too is a fundamentalist and has a reason and a cause to direct his bombs.

And, now Raschid's here, who knows in what exciting ways he might be called upon to serve the cause?

The supermarket car park is virtually empty now, and lit by sickly orange lamps shaped like giant mushrooms. James and Henry stagger in and are amazed to find the atrium flooded in cool blue light. A large crowd of young London trendies and those trying to pretend they are still young and trendy stand expectantly, penned back around the edges of the floor behind those tapes you get in banks to make people queue properly. Henry reflects that it is a sad comment on modern society that such devices are necessary in Britain. Duke Ellington's 'Take the A Train' is playing over the loudspeakers and, here and there, little groups are *Der*-der-der-dering along with the melody. Henry and James stand and wait to discover exactly what ritual they have stumbled upon.

The Duke Ellington fades out and there is a joyful cheer from the audience as the next track starts,

Annie Lennox's version of 'Keep Young and Beautiful'.

The six sets of automatic doors that separate the atrium from the supermarket proper are veiled by billowing clouds of dry ice, which suddenly change colour as they are hit by six spotlights, alternately pink and electric green. As Annie's vocals kick in, six lines of rollerbladers burst out of the garish clouds, one, two, three, four out of each door, all in different-coloured uniforms, fanning out into the central space at great speed, weaving in and out of each others' lines like a human kaleidoscope, the crowd whooping and singing along as the bladers spin, pirouette, skate backwards, sideways, do the splits, pas de deux, tango, all the while singing along and offering delicacies from huge trays which they somehow manage to keep horizontal.

The dry ice dissipates in almost perfect timing with the end of the song, and the dancers filter back into the shop to tumultuous applause. Security guards dismantle the barrier-tapes and Henry and James follow the surging throng into the shop.

Loretta, in the first group of roller-bladers back through the door, heads straight for the ladies. Loretta already has lit up and taken two quick drags on the joint and, as Yvette as joins her in the cubicle, she passes it over.

'Only four hours to go.'

'Fucking bullshit. I need this.'

'You and me both, baby.' Yvette hands back the joint. They've both had a shitty first shift, as if there's any other kind when you're working on a supermarket checkout. Loretta particularly dislikes Saturday afternoons. Somehow the volume of people turns all the customers into fugitive extras from *Night of the Living Dead*. And now she has to rollerblade until four in the morning with a smile on her face and put up with people who are sufficiently high on booze, pills and powder to think they are all infallibly and outstandingly witty.

So, when a young man with a glint in his eye correctly identifies the three salamis on her tray, she is keen to stop and chat, with only a brief acknowledgement of how bad things must be when this is the high point of her day.

'This Hungarian is very good,' James is saying, trying to keep his comments directed into the eyes of the roller-skating hostess, rather than at the crystal pendant that dangles in the hint of cleavage above the line of her lurex T-shirt. 'Just enough paprika.'

'Try the Milano.'

'Thanks. So, where are you from?'

'California.'

'Been in London long?'

'About a year. Just under.'

'Like it?'

'Yeah.' The guy is OK. A little drunk but he has a cool haircut and dresses pretty good. Diesel jeans, Nikes, North Face fleece. The other guy is cuter though – more soberly dressed – chinos, oxfords, overcoat but his hair is too long and rich for him to be a total square. But he's not saying anything.

James needs to keep her talking. It's obvious – the pendant – go New Age. 'You know, this supermarket doesn't have the greatest eco-friendly record in the world. I don't know if that bothers you.'

Loretta isn't sure how to respond. 'Well, when you need a job . . .'

'Sure, yeah. Doesn't waitressing pay better though?'

'I'm trying to fit some of that in too. But I have . . . there's other things to consider, that's all.'

'I like your pendant. Is it an opal?'

'Yes. From New Mexico.'

'Oh yeah. Beautiful place, Santa Fe.'

It picks along like this for a while with a stuttering momentum which quickly smoothes out and, before you know it, they're on to the Navajo and the Anasazi and the Pueblo and the art and jewellery of the South Western Native Americans and shamans and it's running really nicely, while Henry stays in the background and just grins benignly whenever Loretta invites him to join the conversation with nod or smile in his direction. Henry is genuinely impressed by James's knowledge, as Loretta is, but he can't help feeling, unlike Loretta apparently, that it's all coming out a little too smooth, a little too pat. James is too, pleased with himself. The conversation is about himself, somehow, not about any of the things he's talking about. And it dawns on Henry that that is what bugs him about his brother's stand-up act. He's never been able to put his finger on it before, but now he sees: it's clever, it's funny, it's brave, but ultimately, it's an act. Its main purpose is the furtherance of James, not the cause he seems to be espousing. He doesn't believe a word of it. And yet he goes round trying to expose politicians for doing precisely the same thing.

'What a fucking wanker,' thinks Henry. He's contemplating saying this when James cuts the conversation short.

'Look, I'm sorry. We're going to get you into trouble keeping you here the whole time.'

'OK, I guess I should get round some other people.'

'Maybe we could pick it up over a drink?'

'Sure, why not?'

James notes her number down and they say goodbye. Loretta moves down towards the back of the store, James and Henry towards the checkout.

James is very pleased with himself.

'Yes! A phone number, straight off the bat! Do you fancy another drink? We could go into town.'

'I ought to get home. I was hoping to see Elizabeth before she went to bed.'

'Come on, it'll be all right.' James puts an arm round Henry's shoulder, and shakes him cheerily. 'Anyway, I bet she's pleased, not to have had to talk to me for an evening.'

'That's true,' says Henry.

James is taken aback by this. He knows he isn't Elizabeth's favourite person, but the idea that she actually doesn't like his company is an affront to his professional skills.

'How do you mean?'

'Well, she wasn't looking forward to tonight. Like you say, she doesn't really like you.'

'Can't please everyone. Quick – there's a bus.'

They jog the final fifty yards to the bus stop and stand catching their breath. It's such a delight in London to catch a night bus without having to wait half an hour, a rare event – like getting all the way along Marylebone Road to the M40 on green lights, or finding a parking space within eight hundred yards of where you were going. The bus sails straight past.

'Might as well walk it.'

'OK.' Henry knows it's going to be a test of his fear, but it has to be done. That it shouldn't be a problem to walk half a mile down the Caledonian Road at night, but that it is going to be. That the more frightened he is, the more he's going to give out victim vibes and the more likely he is to bring the thing he fears down upon him. He feels pathetic. He's compelled to keep some kind of conversation going with James, simply because he feels that it implies he's relaxed, confident, able to take care of himself with any predatory youths, whom he imagines to be stalking them even now, even though there's no one else in sight. 'Oh fucking hell,' groans Henry.

'What's up?'

'I . . . I'm . . . nothing.'

'Come on, Henry mate, you'll be fine. No one's going to jump us. You just need the right body language in your walk. Lift your head up . . . that's it . . . drop the shoulders . . . slow down a little – look at me, look at me . . . that's it . . . and put this thought in you head . . . "I own these streets – I am the guv'nor . . . the guv'nor . . ." Yeah, that's it. Can you feel it? Henry, can you feel it?'

'Yeah, I can feel it,' says Henry. And hates his brother for making it so easy.

'Does Liz really not like me then?'

'Of course she does,' lies Henry. 'I was just pissed

off with you, that's all. She always looks forward to you coming over.'

'Really? Straight up?'

'Yes. Blimey, you're my brother, aren't you? She's married to me so clearly she's going to like you – we've got so much in common.' Henry is really hating himself now. To be able to come out with such bullshit so smoothly, just to avoid telling the truth. What a spineless git. And the idea that he and James are similar almost makes him throw up, literally, he realises. He despises James for appearing to buy what he's just said, despises himself for having said it, and then despises himself again when he realises that what he really dislikes about James is what he realised while he was watching James chat up the girl in the supermarket – that James is full of bullshit, and that he himself had just shown a capacity for exactly the same thing.

Elizabeth is up, welcoming and friendly.

'We were going to have a joint,' says James expecting her to back off with a whiff of disapproval.

'Excellent,' says Elizabeth. 'Just what I need.'

She doesn't want to get stoned of course, but she knows they don't want her there, which is a perfect reason for staying. She doesn't begrudge Henry an evening enjoying himself, of course she doesn't, but James's barbed offer of the joint is a challenge she is not prepared to back down from.

She sits saying little, just watching, a brooding presence, while the two men automatically choose topics of conversation which they hope will drive her off. They fail. Henry makes tea for all three of them, and offers whisky which James accepts and Elizabeth does not.

Henry hands the second joint back to James, pours two whiskies into square Finnish tumblers and puts one next to James's tea.

'I'm sorry I said all that stuff.'

'What stuff?'

'About you being a fraud and a charlatan. I didn't mean it.'

'That's OK.'

He takes another drag on the joint. His head spins.

'Actually, I did. You really piss me off, you know, pretending to be this ... avenging revolutionary angel, exposing injustice and righting wrongs like some fucking ... alternative comedy's answer to Batman when in ... in fact you don't give a shit about anything except yourself. It's just a pose. Like when you spent two years slagging off Comic Relief for being a "bourgeois palliative" because they'd only asked you to go to Blackpool and you wanted to have a week somewhere sunny where you could be filmed crying over lots of starving Africans.'

'That's not true. The reason I turned them down is because I was the perfect person to go to Central Africa to visit that clinic because I knew more about the politics than anyone else and they gave it to that twat off the soap opera because they said he was more well known than me.'

'And you turned them down flat when you couldn't get what *you* wanted.'

James knocks back his whisky in a single gulp. 'I'm not going to discuss this now.'

'No. Because you can't face the truth, can you, Caped Crusader?'

'No, because I've just heard the cab toot outside.'

James gets to his feet.

'Oh, by the way, Elizabeth, I don't know if it's my place to say this, but . . . Henry hasn't stopped having sex with you because he doesn't fancy you any more, Elizabeth. It's more complicated than that.'

Henry stares at James, stares at Elizabeth, who is looking at her lap. James smiles, says, 'Goodnight, good to see you,' and darts out to his cab before Henry can recover enough to punch his brother in the face.

Elizabeth stands up and walks briskly out of the room.

'Elizabeth . . .'

'We'll talk about it in the morning,' says Elizabeth, ascending the stairs with as much dignity as she can manage.

CHAPTER FIFTEEN

James gives directions to the driver and sits back, delighted that he has stirred things up so successfully.

'Serves them right,' he tells himself. 'Serves them right for . . . well, it just serves them right.'

James is pretty out of it but always likes to have a chat with minicab drivers, on the off-chance of getting something he can use for material. It's a long drive to Tooting and he doesn't want to get bogged down into a really involved conversation, so he waits until they are over Chelsea Bridge and coming into Clapham.

'Been busy tonight then?'

'Only just come on.'

The driver doesn't feel like talking, which is why when this ride tried to get in the front, he'd pretended the door would not unlock. Glancing at him now in the rear view mirror, for the fourth or fifth time, he's sure he recognises him. The geezer's hair is a different colour and he's got no goatee beard, but Stevie reckons he's a comic.

' 'Ave I seen you on the telly?'

James passes a hand through his hair, trying to appear modest. 'Might have, yeah.'

'What you do? Comedy, is it?'

'Yeah. Name's James. James Randall.'

'James Randall . . . yeah, thought so. Like your stuff.'

'Thanks, man,' says James, nodding from the waist, which he understands to be a streetwise way of expressing humility. He's expecting the usual sallies about how it must be the hardest job in the world, where does he get his ideas from? and the telling of a terrible, generally offensive joke, prefaced by the generous offer that James 'Can have it if he wants', but instead the driver never says another word until they get to Balham High Road. James notices the driver is wearing gloves.

'Left at these lights is it, mate?' says Stevie.

'Yeah, then second on the right. Number three.'

James gives him fifteen quid and tells him to keep the change, convinced yet another ordinary working person will be going round telling all his mates what a good bloke that James Randall is.

CHAPTER SIXTEEN

Caged birds sing. Raschid and the fair-haired girl lie naked on silken sheets on a broad divan limbs entwined her hair flowing to the tinkling of fountains and dapples of sunlight fall upon them through intricately carved screens while outside peacocks strut and call and heavy metal throbs gently from concealed speakers and Raschid's Harley Davidson ticks over quietly in the corner gleaming and proud. They smile at one another but he cannot see her face and then the fox or is it a small dog scuttles in across the mosaic floor, prostrates itself at their feet, the woman feeds the dog a tidbit from the silver platter. The animal rises on its hind legs, takes the morsel and then rolls over on its back and urinates in a golden arc high into the air. They laugh and as the liquid falls to earth it clatters and when they look it has turned into gold coins and Raschid turns towards her again knowing this time he will see her face . . .

. . . but of course Raschid woke up instead and saw the listless pale green walls of Stevie's bedroom with their heavy-metal posters.

The radio alarm said nine-thirty. He got out of

bed, took the towel and toilet bag from his canvas hold-all and found the bathroom. Soon the luxury of lying uninterrupted in steaming hot water soothed away the frustration of the unconsummated dream and he began to focus his attention instead on the material world, and what was to be done. There was a system of pulleys and ropes tied off above the bath whose purpose he could not discern – just one of many things about Stevie's place he needed to find out about. The thought of Stevie immediately brought with it the memory of the time Raschid had to transport a lorry-load of nitro-glycerine along a terrible mountain road. But at least he understood the volatile nature of nitro-glycerine.

And where was this recurrent dream coming from? He wanted to take it as a sign that he was right to leave the revolution, a Divine confirmation that there was a way to live his life in modest prosperity, with motorbikes and heavy metal, without betraying his faith. And what of the voluptuous female? Was she a symbol of a pure true love to come? Or an insidious temptation, clothed in beauty but rotten and corrupt within, a trap to lure him into sin, conjured up and whispered into his sleeping ear by Satan? Never mind. All would be revealed if he kept faith and waited for the signs of guidance that would come in their own time. For now, he lay back and savoured the water and the quiet.

NIGHT OF THE TOXIC OSTRICH

* * *

Henry and Elizabeth had a tense breakfast: a cafetière of the eco-conscious Colombian organic coffee with organic skimmed half-fat Welsh milk and poached organic West Country eggs on organic Italian bread lightly buttered with organic non-salted Breton butter and three Marlborough Lights (left behind by James, perhaps deliberately) on Henry's part and silent disapproval on Elizabeth's.

They ate silently and read the papers. Elizabeth concentrated on the restaurant reviews and the travel section, while Henry, having covered all the sports pages and as much of the actual news pages as he could manage without the anxiety overwhelming him, settled wholeheartedly into the longest article he could find in the review section, which happened to be about a newly-discovered relationship-threatening phenomenon called Emotional Bottling.

'What are you reading?' asked Elizabeth after a while.

Henry either did not hear or pretended not to.

'Henry?'

He looked up.

'What are you reading?'

'Oh, nothing. Just some pretentious psychobabble stating the obvious in puffed-up language. Amazes me how this stuff gets commissioned. Such complete garbage it's fascinating.'

He could tell from the way Elizabeth was tugging at her hair that she was intent on forcing him into serious conversation when, in the nick of time, he was given a stay of execution by the Archers' theme tune announcing the long-standing sacrosanct hour of silence which could only be broken with mock-serious pantomime-level remarks about the programme and the occasional offer of more coffee.

'About time too. Do you want to turn it up a touch?'

Raschid stood before the mirror and began to shave off his beard, as he had been ordered to do before he left Kabul. Beardlessness was a crime but they had given him special permission because it would make him less conspicuous amongst the heathen. Bit by bit his face appeared, and he thought it ironic that he was going undercover by revealing more of himself. Then he thought it ironic that he was thinking ironically, because that too was a suspect condition. Was he going undercover, or was he going over?

He went back to his bedroom, got changed into jeans and his 1991 Aston Villa away shirt and felt a great sense of liberation as he put on his old bomber jacket for the first time since he was last in England. He had never felt it was appropriate to wear any of his Aston Villa colours while enforcing religious law in Afghanistan in case people didn't take him seriously. There was also, of course, the small matter of risking imprisonment and death for flaunting the trappings of decadent infidels.

He found Stevie and Les in the kitchen.

'Right, Dad, I'm cooking you some soup, yeah? Fuck me you look like Imran Khan without your beard.'

'Eh?'

'Not you, Dad.'

'What use is soup to me?' said Les, forlorn.

'It's good for yer. It's got —' Stevie speared the box with the sharpened index claw of his right hand and brought it within reading distance. 'It's got ginger, garlic, miso, shit-ache mushrooms . . .'

'I need potatoes. Turkey. Christmas pudding.'

'No you don't, Dad, you need to cut out fats —'

'I'm trying to get fat, aren't I?' Les turned to Raschid for support. 'How am I going to get on TV as London's fattest man if I'm not fat?'

Raschid just stared at him, giving no hint of an opinion, hoping not to encourage Les. Unfortunately, this silence only made Les want to fill it, he was nervous of Raschid and wanted to be his friend.

'See, I wanna get on a TV programme next time they do one on fat people. "Eats so much because his wife left him." That'll show her, the bitch.'

Raschid looked at Les and estimated that he

weighed as much as all the schoolchildren in Kabul put together.

'All I did was kill a gerbil. I didn't even do it on purpose. And it was twenty-five years ago. I was thirty-eight stone seven before the scales broke. I'd be even more if this little bastard wasn't trying to starve me.'

'Dad, I'm trying to help you.'

'Well, you're making me miserable! Anyway, I'm not talking to you, I'm talking to your friend here. I've written off again – Vanessa, Trisha, Kilroy, Richard and Judy, all of them. I was going to send a picture but that booth up the post office is useless. Door's too narrow for a man to fit in it.'

'All you got to do now is heat it up in the microwave, yeah?'

'You could at least have got me a chocolate orange for afters.'

'Have you been to the toilet today?'

'That's my business.'

'Dad, it's not good for you . . .'

'I keep telling you, I've just got a slow metabolism.'

Stevie was clenching and unclenching his claws against the kitchen table. 'He ain't had a shit for weeks.'

Les slowly realised what Stevie was saying to Raschid and decided a defensive argument was appropriate.

'It's my arsehole, my guts, I'll do what I want with 'em.'

'All right then, Dad. Anyway, we've got to go out.'

'All right,' said Les. His tone was suddenly acquiescent and disinterested. Arguing so passionately for such a long stretch of time had clearly exhausted him. 'Here, thought you was on the minicabs again today.'

'Can't make it now, can I? But if the office phones, tell them I'm on my way, yeah?'

'All right.'

A long, tenor-toned fart speeds Raschid and Stevie through the door.

Instead of turning up the radio, Elizabeth switched it off. The silence hit Henry like a shovel in the face and he felt a stab of panic in his chest. This had to be serious. You didn't just snap off the Archers Omnibus like that unless... Oh God. She wanted to talk. Henry tried to pretend nothing unusual was happening and buried himself deeper into his article, praying for some miracle to deliver him from the inevitability of a Serious Conversation. Elizabeth was standing over him. Pretend it isn't happening, Henry told himself, and it still might go away.

'So what was it you could talk about with your brother last night that you can't discuss with me?'

Henry sat there, frozen. Where was the knock of

the Jehovah's Witness when you needed it?

'Are you having an affair or something?' She tried to make it sound no big deal, but her voice caught.

'Is that why we don't have sex any more?'

He looked up, put down the magazine and turned to her, took her hand.

'Of course not. Me have an affair? Christ, Elizabeth, I love you.'

There. He had been totally honest. Perhaps that was an end to it.

'What then? You told him.'

She was angry, and he realised she was entitled to be.

'It's just going to sound so stupid.' He glanced at the magazine which lay open in mid-article. He could read a strapline in bold print: Strategies For Freeing Your Emotional Constipation. But from this distance he couldn't read the advice itself and realised that, while reading, he had taken precisely nothing in. He was on his own.

'I don't care if it sounds stupid. Tell me.'

He paused.

'I just feel scared all the time. Of what can happen. All the terrible things that can – you know. We say, "It'll never happen to me," but it all does happen, so it has to happen to someone.'

'What?'

'Everything. Road accidents, madmen with knives,

bombs, fatal diseases, brain tumours, falling down the stairs, whatever.'

'You're going to get a brain tumour if you make love to me?'

'No!' Then he clutched at the straw he realised was floating past. 'Look, I told you it was going to sound stupid. If you're just going to take the piss out of me you can piss off because you'll just piss me off,' he said elegantly.

'I don't understand.'

'I'm scared all the time, OK? I don't know why, I know it's ridiculous but I've lost the ability to pretend everything's always going to be all right. And I'm scared of having sex with you because I'm scared of having kids because I just keep imagining how scared I'd be all the time that something dreadful was going to happen to them and it would just be too awful.'

'That's a risk that everybody has to take.'

'But don't you understand? I don't see it as a risk, I see it as an absolute certainty. Let's assume we have kids and they grow up. Chances are, they'll just end up despising us and turn into delinquent drug addicts who'll sell everything in the house to keep their habits going, or we send them to some expensive private school and they turn out as insufferable materialistic braying pigs who only care about their careers and treating their fellow men like dirt.'

'What on earth makes you think that?'

'Don't you read the papers? That's how they all turn out these days!'

Elizabeth tried to remain calm and reasonable. 'Why haven't you talked to me about this before?'

'I know how much you want to have kids. I didn't want to upset you.'

Elizabeth tried to keep her temper. She must remain sympathetic, she told herself, this was her husband. She could not help thinking, however, that this was not the man she married. The man she married was not a trembling puppet controlled by a paranoid fear of chance; the man she married was meant to be controlled by her. She'd always had the firmer, more assertive attitude, but she knew that Henry should be more confident than he was; and if he paid more attention to her, they would not now be having this ridiculous conversation. He was a corporate lawyer, for heaven's sake, and corporate lawyers didn't go round having thoughts like this. She knew. She was a corporate lawyer, too. He needed a good dose of commonsense, that was all.

'But if you're living your life assuming all the terrible things that could happen are going to happen, then that's the same as them happening anyway, even when they're not.'

Henry absorbed this. It was a good argument, but suddenly he had his answer. 'I know. But I can't help it,' he said, hopeless yet triumphant. She would now understand the depths of his distress, and help him.

'You're a pathetic wimp,' she said flatly.

To this, he realised, he had no answer.

'You could have told me first, you know. I am your wife, for God's sake. Instead you have to get pissed and blab it all out to James.'

'He's my brother.'

'Yes, he's your brother. And he loves you.'

Henry didn't hear the sarcasm.

'Yes.'

'He loves you for providing him with constant raw material for his comedy routines.'

'Don't be ridiculous. He wouldn't do that.'

Elizabeth looked at him and then decided it was time to do some ironing.

CHAPTER SEVENTEEN

In Tooting, James had got up feeling much sparkier than he was entitled to be, considering the caning he'd given his system the night before. He felt thoroughly up for a long session at the computer, turning Henry's confidences of the night before into a stand-up routine.

He pulled on some sweat pants that lay on a chair, found a sweater that passed the armpit sniff-test, made coffee, munched a banana, lit up and sat down at his desk. He envisaged a long tirade about how all the yuppy (could he still use that word. No, but come back later) Blairites were getting their payback for supporting the revisionist tendency by voting Labour in 97. All well and good, but where was the comic angle into it? Ah yes...

My own brother has just spent ten grand on a security system for his house. Ten grand. He's so obsessed with protecting what he has, that he's prepared to spend ten grand, ten thousand pounds – on home security. He applauds tax cuts (actually James wasn't sure if this was the case, but who cares) *and then spends more than he's saved on security systems that he wouldn't need if we lived in a fair society.* (Not funny, but if said with enough indignant outrage James knew he could get a round of applause on it.) *He goes round in a state of constant fear, fear of being mugged, fear of having his car scratched. Fear of being burgled, fear of trees falling on him. He thinks that it's enough to recycle his bottles and his newspapers – although he drives to the recycling centre in his Volvo – what else would he have but a Volvo? – polluting the city, burning up more energy than he's putting back, putting cyclists in mortal danger. He thinks that recycling and buying organic produce from Third World countries is a revolutionary act. Somehow, if Che Guevara was alive today, I think he'd be doing more for the struggle than refusing to buy coffee that's been grown with the help of fertilisers . . .*

He lit another cigarette and put a Lee Perry CD on the stereo.

James's mind wandered off the script and he found himself comparing Henry's house in trendy Islington with his own place in unfashionable Tooting, where he had studiously chosen to stay for the last eight years. He felt it leant credibility to his status as an ascetic iconoclast and very few people realised he had in fact bought the other two flats in his house. His long-term plan was to convert the whole place back into one dwelling, but that would have to wait until he had the funds available to do it exactly the way he planned. In the meantime, the two flats remained empty. One for eight months now, the other for over a year. He had considered letting them out but did not want to become a member of the capitalist-rentier class; he also preferred the guarantee of silence above and below him. However, he now bought up to six or seven copies of the *Big Issue* a week to redress the balance. And of course, the more copies of the *Big Issue* you bought, the more likely you were to be recognised buying it, and the wider your reputation would spread as a caring charitable person. People would say to their friends – 'I saw that comedian James Randall buying the *Big Issue* the other day – he's just as good a bloke in private as he is in public.' As a result, he felt it legitimate to offset this against tax, under Presentation (the same category under which, as an Equity member, he could haircuts, manicures, and pedicures).

It didn't occur to him to write any of this into the new routine.

He was losing concentration, starting to think about sex with Loretta and then, unavoidably, about sex with Stride Boswell. He considered the positives for doing it with Boswell, making lists. There were many good reasons.

It would make him identify more intensely with the common predicament and suffering of women in this ... phallocratic society. Note – was that a new word?

He reflected on some of the psychological and anthropological stuff he'd been reading lately. Suffering on the way to new levels of power was a constant in the experience of the priest or shaman – and had he not been described in various reviews and columns as precisely that – 'a shaman for the information technology age'? Well then, it was a necessary ordeal on the road to enlightenment.

Plus, it would get him a gig in space – the biggest stand-up gig in history – and set him on the route to global wealth and fame.

James finished a draft that he felt was ragged but promising and, on the updraft of confidence this gave him, decided it would be a good time to ring Loretta.

Loretta was doing yoga and watching TV when Yvette came into the living room with some toast and a sceptical expression and slumped into an armchair.

'I thought maybe we could go to the Island Queen

for lunch,' said Yvettte, flicking crumbs from the lap of her silk tiger-print dressing-gown.

'I can't,' said Loretta putting her forehead gracefully on to her outstretched knees. 'I'm meeting Stevie at lunchtime.'

Yvette flicked her eyes at the ceiling.

'Stevie. What is it with you and that guy? You're not going to fuck him, are you? He's disgusting.'

'His dad's sick. He wants some advice.'

'Yeah? So what's it to you?'

'I feel sorry for him. Maybe I can help.'

'A mercy fuck? With that arsehole? Jesus.'

Loretta sat up. 'Why does it always come down to sex with you? I'm not going to fuck him, OK, I'm just going to listen to him about his dad, is all.'

'Sure. That's what you think. He's crazy about you. I bet he don't even have a dad. He just knows how to get your company.'

'I trust him.'

'Trust him? Fuck. Yeah, I would trust him. I would trust him to fucking kill me in a dark street. He has got metal hands or didn't you notice?'

Loretta went back into the stretch.

'Anyway, it's not that I always think about sex. Actually, maybe it's good that you're seeing Stevie today.' She glanced at the ashtray by her chair. 'Want some of this joint? Quite a big roach here.'

Loretta shook her head.

'What do you mean?'

'I've been thinking about those birds. Stevie could help us...' Loretta unfolded herself from the ardhamatsyendrasana spine-twisting pose and sat up on the sofa.

'You serious about letting them out then?'

'Aren't you?'

'Well...'

'Christ sake Loretta — you saw the conditions they're in. It's fucking outrageous.'

'Yeah, but...'

'But what? It's illegal? You're such a typical American liberal you know — you bleat about everything and you're too scared to do nothing.'

Fair point, kind of, thought Loretta. *The only time you ever put yourself on a limb was before the courier job — and that was totally for you.*

'OK, you're right,' she said, assertively. 'Let's do it.'

'You serious?'

'Yes, but no violence.'

Yvette looked at her, uncomprehending.

'There doesn't need to be any violence. That's my only condition.'

NIGHT OF THE TOXIC OSTRICH

Yvette exhaled the last of the roach. 'OK. No violence.'

CHAPTER EIGHTEEN

'Thing about my dad is,' said Stevie once they'd got outside, in a tone that implied he was going to let Raschid into a secret, 'he's overweight.'

'I see,' said Raschid, trying to sound surprised.

'Yeah, I keep trying to make him eat more sensibly and that, but he won't have it. He's totally into this Christmas number. I wish I could get him to convert, then Christmas wouldn't mean the same to him. Plus he could do with a few Ramadans inside him, innit? But like I say he won't have that neither. So anyway, Loretta, she's into all this like Chinese medicine stuff and, well, she's from California and you know what they're like with fucking health food and all that so she's going to help me out with him. Dunno why I bother though, the fat stupid twat.'

They walked down the street, Raschid slightly ahead. He stopped by a dented Nissan Bluebird whose front bumper was attached to the body at a jaunty angle by a length of electrical flex.

'How did you know this was my car?' said Stevie.

'You said you were a minicab driver.'

'Oh. Right.'

The door opened with a fatigued squeak. Stevie leant in and flicked the passenger door open.

'I'm impressed with those hands of yours,' said Raschid as he watched Stevie click on his seat belt.

'Yeah. I was very lucky to get these actually.' Stevie held them up for Raschid to get a better look. 'They're just like me own really. Light, stainless steel, so they don't rust. I got this little attachment here' – he pointed to an arrangement of grooves in the palm of the left hand – 'which allows me to unscrew the tip of this finger' – he tapped the index finger of his right, then placed it in the palm of his left, and unscrewed it, 'and then I got these attachments I can put in – screwdrivers, blades, whatever. This geezer inside made them for me. I used to give him all my tobacco and that. He won a prize for these. I still got the National Health ones for special occasions. They're skin-coloured. Don't stand out so much.'

The car started at the third or fourth attempt and, with a squealing clutch, Stevie eased them out into the flow of traffic.

CHAPTER NINETEEN

The high-pitched shriek of the clutch dwindling into the distance caused Les to break into a smile. More accurately, deep beneath the quilted festoons of flab, what were left of his facial muscles caused the surface to twitch a little, some seven or eight minutes after the message had been sent out from Les's stagnant nervous system. By this time he had moved from the window and entered Raschid's bedroom.

As usual Stevie had removed all food and money from the flat, but Les was counting on the possibility that Raschid might not have been so conscientious. There must be something amongst Raschid's possessions that Les could convert into food. As he searched through Raschid's Spartan collection of clothes, rifling the pockets of the one spare set of trousers, Les became desperate. Nothing. In Raschid's toilet bag he found a standard sized tube of toothpaste, and a smaller one, provided by the airline, which he squeezed lugubriously into his mouth.

There was nothing else. Then as he rummaged at the bottom of Raschid's bag, squeezing his pudgy fingers beneath the flap which strengthened the base, he detected a hard surface. There was too much bulging fat beneath his skin for him to work out exactly what it was by touch alone, but in a state of great anticipation he pulled the object from its hiding place, hoping against hope it might be a huge bar of chocolate. It was a video cassette.

Les tried to be stoical, and went through to the living room to play it. By the time he reached the sofa, he felt he had done enough for the moment and decided to reward himself for his strenuous workout with a little rest, and flopped down on to the cushions. By the time the rest of his body had settled down around him, he was fast asleep.

Stevie did not speak at all as they drove, except to swear at other cars, and Raschid was happy to avoid the interrogation he had expected. He noticed Stevie's swearing increasing in invention and intensity as they went along, and sensed Stevie was nervous about something – which indeed he was. He'd bought two tickets for a heavy-metal extravaganza at the Astoria that evening and was hoping to take Loretta. But for the past six weeks he had failed to find the courage to ask her. To his frustration, the only things he had dared talk to her about were wildlife videos and the state of his father's bowels. He knew that this meeting in the pub was his last chance.

The Prince of Wales Feathers was an old Victorian gin palace, huge, sturdy, sad. Almost all the other buildings of its generation were long gone, replaced by a variety of sixties mid- and high-rise, and thirties tenements.

There were a few old blokes leaning at the bar, a couple of tables of twenty-somethings, and a thin, balding man in a suit with a dog who stared straight ahead and reacted to nothing. The dog, a terrier, sat by him on the bench and also stared straight ahead. The dog and the man gave you the feeling they'd just had a big row and weren't speaking.

Occasionally the man would sip from his glass or pour more brown ale into it without looking, the only movement in his whole body the right arm between elbow and fingers. It was perfection really; everything unnecessary pruned away, just the beer and what was needed to drink it. Nothing wasted.

The men at the bar turned towards the door each time it opened. Stevie ignored them, bought a pint of lager for himself and a Coke for Raschid.

Raschid knew it was only a matter of time before Stevie would ask what Raschid's mission was. Raschid was unsure if he wanted to tell him or not. He could feel in his bones that Stevie was unreliable, especially as he'd just bought himself a pint of lager.

From what Stevie had told him, Stevie's passion for Islam was fundamentally a reaction against the world he lived in, rather than a positive belief. Certainly the sense that Western decadence was threatening the righteous contributed to a zealous rage and siege mentality amongst many in the Muslim world, but – and Raschid was interested to notice he was phrasing his next thought in a peculiarly English understatement – there was a little more to it than that. Ironically, Stevie, despite his devotion, was no different to the majority of the ignorant Western World, in that he, like them, believed that all Muslims were mad fanatical fundamentalists. Primarily, Stevie was angry and alienated and, even if he didn't understand this himself, had latched on to Islam as a device for venting his own personal problems.

Furthermore, Raschid was not entirely convinced he ought to seek out this comedian, James Randall, and kill him. Hadn't he laughed – albeit inwardly – at the material and the reaction it had caused? On the other hand, if his own future lay outside Afghanistan – and he certainly did not want to return there – perhaps carrying out his mission was the price he had to pay before he could start a new life? There was less likelihood of himself becoming the hunted if he did so, and perhaps it was the Divine Will. What if his abhorrence for his masters in Kabul was a short-sighted, human frailty? If so, failing to kill the comedian would bring Divine as well as human wrath down upon his head.

Raschid was confused, but he knew he wanted to keep his options open, and that as soon as he confided in Stevie there would be no going back. In his insanity, Stevie would seize upon the mission with blood-thirsty glee. On the other hand, Raschid did not know for sure how well-connected Stevie was. Were there others watching them? Others waiting to see if Raschid was trustworthy and ready to dispatch him if he showed any hint of weakness?

And where was his dream coming from?

As if in reply to this last question, his dream walked in through the pub door.

She was bathed in the autumn sunlight streaking in through the tinted glass of the pub windows. She had long golden hair and her face was obscured, like it always was in the dream, though now it was because of a grey cloud of tobacco smoke which hung thick in the air, illuminated by the sunlight. And then Stevie, who was about to ask Raschid the difficult question, spoke to her.

'Loretta!'

She responded with a wave, emerging from the tobacco cloud smiling like an angel. Raschid was amazed.

'Hi, Stevie.'

'This is my mate, Raschid.'

She had pulled up a stool and was sitting down opposite him at the table, extending a hand.

'Hi.'

'Hello.' He shook the hand, looked her in the eye and felt breathless. Not only that, but noticed a look of amazement in her face in turn.

Oh my God, it's him, went a voice in Loretta's head.

'Wanna drink, Loretta?'

She did not seem to hear him immediately.

'Oh, sure, er, a beer.'

They were left alone while Stevie went back to the bar. Neither of them knew what to say. Then there was a sudden outburst of crude laughter from the next table. The man with the dog had leapt to his feet, appalled, while his dog lay on its back in the bench, legs splayed, pissing into the air. Loretta would later describe it as the most romantic moment of her life up to that point. For when Raschid and Loretta looked at each other, they felt a charge so strong between them you could have lit a fag off the sparks. They didn't have to say anything. They just knew.

'Half of Stella,' said Stevie, breaking the spell.

Stevie didn't like the way they had been looking at each other.

Loretta took a big swig and tried to clear her head. Surely she was hallucinating, imagining things. *Get a grip, girl*.

Stevie got straight down to business.

'Right well, thing is, my dad's getting really fat, you know, and also he ain't... he ain't...' A beam of light dappled on to Loretta's lovely face. She was listening patiently and entirely to Stevie, emanating serenity and concern. He wanted to phrase it as delicately as possible. 'It's like I was saying, he ain't had a shit for weeks. He's in pain.'

To his relief, Loretta seemed unshocked. Raschid, on the other hand, swooned at the mental image of Les, straining on the lavatory like a huge lump of modelling clay with a little head stuck on it.

'Why won't he go to a doctor?'

'Pride. He don't like going out much.'

'Well, if he's as bad as you say, he really ought to.'

'He won't.'

'OK... well, you know I would recommend an enema.'

'Enema? Enema? He won't even eat All-Bran without a fight.'

'If he won't go to a doctor, an enema would certainly unblock him. They're great. There's a very spiritual element to them, somehow, if that doesn't sound weird. Like a rebirth sometimes – it might change him. He might get into it. I've brought this instruction leaflet. It's real easy.'

'Thanks. Hope I can do you a favour some time.'

'Well, maybe.'

'Actually, Loretta, there was something else . . . I was wondering . . .'

He wanted to say, 'I was wondering if you wanted to come to a gig with me tonight,' but the words wouldn't come. He was too terrified of the inevitable rejection. He kept telling himself it was better to try, that if you don't ask you don't get and yet these commonsense saws were not helping.

'I was wondering . . .'

At that moment Loretta's mobile rang.

'Excuse me just a second.' She answered the phone.

'James? Oh hi!'

Loretta was hoping, willing James to ask her out. She needed distance between her and this guy opposite straight out of her dream, courtesy of Cochise the dolphin . . . 'Tonight? That sounds great. OK. Say, can I call you back in a little while?'

She flicked the phone shut and returned to Stevie with her big smile.

'So . . . ?'

'Don't matter,' said Stevie. 'Well, we'd best be off.' He threw three-quarters of a pint back in one movement and rapped his glass back down on the table as he shot to his feet. 'Wanna tell me dad about this as soon as possible, innit? Thanks, Loretta.' Raschid stood up with Stevie, not trying to hide his disappointment from Loretta that they were leaving so soon.

'OK, Stevie, see you at work.' She smiled at Raschid. 'Nice to meet you, Raschid.'

'You too.'

CHAPTER TWENTY

Stevie walked out of the pub at an electric pace, and tried to kick a lazy pigeon which hopped minimally out of the way with a couple of flaps of its greasy wings, whereupon Stevie landed a huge rasping gob of phlegm on its head. The pigeon didn't seem terribly bothered, so Stevie did it again.

He unlocked the car and wrenched the door open so vigorously one of the hinges snapped.

'Fuck.' He jumped in, jabbing his claws into the plastic door lining to get a tight enough grip to pull the door shut. The lining tore, and Raschid, still on the pavement calmly lifted the door level and closed it. Stevie glared at him, feeling that in some way Raschid was mocking him, and grudgingly leant over to open the passenger door.

'So tell me about what you're here for.'

'The others haven't told you?' replied Raschid calmly.

'What others?'

'There's meant to be another group here.'

'Not as far as I know.'

'Oh,' said Raschid, trying to mask his relief with a tone of disappointment.

'Just you, mate. You and me.'

'Yeah.'

'So, what is it?'

Raschid felt he had to throw a bone.

'It's . . . pretty serious. That's all I can say.'

'That's all you can say?' Stevie had been knocked back by Loretta. He wasn't having more of the same from his comrade-in-arms within five minutes.

'If they've sent you all the way from Afghanistan I reckon there must be something pretty fucking serious in it, innit?'

Raschid said nothing. Stevie angrily picked his nose and swore as the car hit a bump and his metallic finger speared into his septum. He accelerated to overtake a Volvo on the inside that was turning left a hundred yards ahead, scraping past with a massive blast on his horn and a savage look at the terrified middle-class woman at the wheel. 'There's some anti-freeze in the glove-box. Get it out and give us a squirt up the nose will yer? Stops the bleeding. Ta.'

Watching Stevie steer and change gear with his metal claws made Raschid a little nervous.

'Don't worry, mate, I got the knack of it now. You must be starving. Fancy a kebab?'

There were two or three spaces just short of the take-away but Stevie ignored them, drove fifty yards along the road on the wrong side and double-parked directly outside the door, on a zebra crossing. Ten minutes later they were both back in the car with a doner kebab and salad.

Stevie jabbed into his pitta bread, coming up with a piece of lamb on each of his four fingers, and started the engine.

It took several minutes to get moving as the traffic flow was snarled in both directions. ''Cos of all these wankers double-parked,' Stevie explained. As they drove along Stevie bobbed down to snatch the meaty chunks off his spears one by one, chewing ruminatively, until finally he turned to Raschid:

'You're here to kill someone. Gotta be.'

'What makes you say that?'

'One, 'cos you've come all this way and, two, because I feel like I wanna fucking kill someone and Allah owes me a fucking favour after the way Loretta just blew me out.'

'I will tell you everything when the time is right. Those were my orders.' Raschid glared at Stevie with cold eyes and Stevie knew to shut up.

Les awoke and felt something itching his stomach. He fumbled around in the folds of his guts and pulled out the videotape. After a moment he remembered where it came from, rolled off the sofa on to the floor, turned on to his hands and knees, crawled to the machine and ran the tape. It was a comedy show. Though there were no Christmas trees on the set, Les returned to the sofa to watch it anyway.

James Randall was just being introduced as Raschid and Stevie came through the door and Raschid could not conceal a brief reaction which Stevie's ratty eyes caught. Stevie paid close attention to the tape.

'What's this, Dad?'

'It's your mate's.' Les turned to look up at Raschid. 'Hope you don't mind, mate. Only, a mouse got into your bag and I found it when I was chasing it out. It ate your toothpaste, little bastard. I love a bit of comedy, see. What's life without a laugh?'

'Shut up, Dad, I'm watching this.'

James was in full flow about Afghanistan.

'One of them fucking alternatives,' Les grumbled, and was soon fast asleep again. The set reached James's fearless challenge and Stevie killed the tape, began giggling uncontrollably. Then, with a glance at his dad, he jigged into the kitchen, beckoned for Raschid to follow. He was almost hyperventilating as he looked at Raschid with an ecstatic grin on his face. He was smiling so widely his eyebrows stuck out like little horns, poked up by the tautness of his skin.

'James Randall! James fucking Randall! Surely Allah is merciful! James Randall!'.

'You know him?' Raschid felt Stevie's laughter did not herald anything amusing.

'You're fucking joking! James Randall? Do I know him?' Stevie brayed and whooped. 'Better than that, mate – I only gave him a lift home last night. I only know where he lives. It's Divine Providence if you ask me. We could do it tonight.'

'Tonight?'

'Yeah. We've got an alibi.' He produced the tickets. 'Crackin' gig – in the West End. Three of the best heavy metal bands in Swindon. My treat.'

'Excellent.' What else could Raschid say? He had to keep his cover. Besides, how could it be that his victim was falling into his lap like this? Perhaps Allah was indeed demanding a blood debt in return for Raschid's freedom . . .

Raschid could not really mount a plausible argument for delay, and decided that if Divine Providence really was guiding his life at the moment, then James would not be at home this evening. Or maybe he could contrive to leave Stevie outside?

'Great!! What's he done, by the way?'

Raschid persuaded Stevie to leave the house and continue the discussion outside. It was unlikely Les would wake up and eavesdrop on them undetected, but it was not worth the risk. Raschid also thought a walk might calm the buzzing, jumping, quivering Stevie down a little.

'OK, OK. How about a bomb – I could do one up easy...'

They forked apart to allow a woman pushing a push chair to pass by. The woman was wearing a pair of leggings and a lime-green anorak which Raschid could only assume had been given to her as some cruel practical joke which she was rising above by wearing.

'... or we could take some knives out of the kitchen... Oh, poor little thing.' Stevie knelt down and stroked a timid-looking dog that was tied up outside a training-shoe discount shop. 'Or maybe pool cues...' He saw a look on Raschid's face which he took to be professional disdain. 'Or just my shooter.'

'You have a gun?'

'Course I got a gun. This is London, twenty-first century, innit?'

Raschid was appalled at Stevie's casual enthusiasm. Raschid had killed, but for a reason. He supposed he could do so again, if he had to. But Stevie wanted to do it for its own sake and that scared him. Raschid had seen the same callous attitude in snipers, but they didn't get so animated about it.

'You like the idea of the shooter then?'

'Maybe. Although I think we could do it more quietly.'

'Fancy another drink? Football's on in twenty minutes. Boozer just round the corner.'

'Sure.'

When they entered the flat a couple of hours later, after watching Aston Villa draw with Coventry, muffled cries could be heard from the bathroom. Stevie swore.

'Give us a hand will you, mate?'

Raschid followed Stevie into the bathroom, where Les lay pink and naked, in constant movement, like a shimmering blancmange, stuck fast in the tub.

'I can't get out.'

Stevie was already untying the canvas harnesses and lowering them down, passing them under Les's head, and arms. 'Yeah, all right, don't worry.'

Raschid and Stevie pulled on the ropes and eventually Les was almost upright. Stevie signalled to Raschid to stop pulling, and tied the rope off on a cleat. 'What you stopping now for?' moaned the helpless Les.

'Cos I want you to listen to me.'

'What?'

'What do you mean what? You're in big trouble, Dad. You're fatter than ever—'

'I'm trying to get on TV.'

'You'll be dead first. You're gonna kill yourself — you understand me? Right, now I think it would be a good idea for you to think about having an enema...'

'An enema?'

'Yeah, it's when—'

'I know what an enema is, thank you very much! You think I'm going to stick a tube up my arse, you can fuck off! Now let me up.'

'Not until you hear me out. My mate right, Loretta right, she says they're really good for yer. People in California have them all the time.'

'Yeah, I bet they fucking do. They're all fucking mad over there. They're sticking things up their arses the whole time over there, aren't they? All kinds of things. Piece of rubber tube ain't going to make any difference to them Californians, is it? Disgusting.'

'It's good for you.'

'Oh yeah? You going to have one then?'

'I might,' said Stevie, but the pause before he spoke gave him away and Les jeered him.

'Look, Dad, my insides aren't fucked up like yours are! Now, you listen or I'll leave you here all night. There's various health benefits to having an enema, including—'

Les was getting cold. 'All right, I'll think about it.'

'You promise?'

'Yeah. Let me up.'

They hauled Les up the remaining forty-five degrees and left him alone to get dried and dressed.

Ideally Raschid would have liked to keep putting off the mission until he could get enough money to disappear, or engineer a way of getting down to James's flat on his own so he could quietly explain the situation and get some money out of him in exchange. There was a risk involved, of course. James might not take him seriously, in which case Raschid would have to convince him he wasn't joking. And, if he left James alive in those circumstances, he might find himself on the wrong end of a manhunt.

The longer he left it, the more chance, he feared, that Stevie would become suspicious of his credentials. Word might even get back to his superiors. He wasn't sure who was next in the chain between Stevie and headquarters, but he knew they must be somewhere near and that possibly Stevie was reporting to them. The longer Raschid left it, the more danger he was in. It was possible that Stevie would take it on himself to carry out the mission. The Providence that had let Stevie know where their quarry lived was forcing Raschid to decide what he must do – the quicker the better. He could deal with Stevie, if he had to. In which case, doing it in front of James would be one way of convincing James that Raschid was genuine.

He prayed that, when they went round, James would be out. Then they could leave a warning and James would get police protection. Raschid would lay low for a while, but eventually he could disappear or they would send someone else, in which case James would have to hope Special Branch weren't fed up protecting people whose words had offended the sterner factions of his faith and take his chance. It wasn't ideal but it was better than James could otherwise expect. Raschid thought further. The more time he took, the better the chance that Stevie would improvise some scheme of his own – like a bomb. Just great, thought Raschid, I'm billeted with someone crazier than the madmen back home. Raschid concluded it was some kind of test that had been set for him from on high. That if he looked inside himself then he would overcome the obstacles and gain reward. All he had to do was keep calm. Keep faith and He will provide.

The other thing that worried Raschid was that Stevie didn't appear concerned about getting caught. Raschid had not come three and a half thousand miles to go to prison.

'We'll do it tonight,' said Raschid.

'Tonight! Excellent! Before or after the gig?'

'Before.'

Suddenly Stevie grabbed his arm, pulled him to the window. 'Keep perfectly still,' he whispered. 'In the tree, there, a goldfinch. See?'

'Yes,' whispered Raschid, puzzled.

'Very rare to see one in London. Ain't it beautiful?'

CHAPTER TWENTY-ONE

James had suggested Loretta meet him at the Queen's Arms, a pub in Crouch End he knew well because it had a Comedy Club in the basement. Twenty minutes after his opening question, which had been 'How are you?' she was still answering it; wittering, avoiding thinking about what was really going on in her head, for she was confused. She did not want to tell James that she believed she had met – literally – the man of her dreams. This was not only because she knew it would not be kind, for she could tell James was attracted to her. It was also because it was so weird she was not sure she had the courage to believe it herself. Even if it were true, she did not feel entirely comfortable with the idea that she was maybe close to getting what she wanted.

Therapist after therapist had detected in Loretta a self-destructive tendency to feel guilty about being content and an urge to sabotage her chances of happiness. So, on the one hand, she was split between deciding she was imagining the charge that seemed to flow between her and Raschid and, on the other, believing he really was The One and giving herself the confidence to embrace it.

She had resolved to treat this evening as a test – would Raschid still be figuring so vividly in her thoughts by the time she got home? Since it wouldn't be right to tell James he was just the control in an experiment, she was pouring out a constant verbal smokescreen.

She had begun by telling him how she felt when she got up, how she had shared a mid-afternoon joint with her flatmate and how this had not really been a lapse in her no-drugs regime because it was Italian and organic, which led into a colourful digression into what drugs she had used in the past, and why, and what strategies she had used to stop using them, and how yoga was changing her life especially when she did it at her friend's place in the High Desert in New Mexico, how it was OK doing it in the low desert at night but you didn't get quite the same vibe and how she didn't drink alcohol but red wine was good for the heart.

'I'm talking too much,' declared Loretta. 'What about you?'

I agree, you're talking too much, thought James. 'I like listening to you,' he said, smiling.

'You sure?'

'Sure. Why don't we go downstairs and watch the gig?'

'Oh, OK.'

People were queuing all the way down the stairs, but James took Loretta's hand and they squeezed past down the two short flights. A couple of people turned round, ready to object but then seemed to recognise James or whisper to their friends who then nodded in apparent acceptance. Loretta was amazed to be participating in the unimaginable experience of sanctioned queue-jumping, in England! Whatever else happened this evening, it was already one she would never forget. The walls of the stairway were covered in small home-produced posters advertising old gigs at the venue, evidently stretching back several years. James casually pointed to his name on a couple of them and whispered, 'That's me', trying to conceal the bragging by saying it in a comic little boy's voice.

'I didn't know you were a comic,' said Loretta. James turned back to her with a look that was intended to be sweet and modest but somehow came over as smug.

'There's a lot you don't know about me,' he said. A girl sat at a small table by the doorway, taking the money. James greeted her effusively and Loretta could tell that the girl was not equally delighted to see him. James did not introduce Loretta.

On the right of the door was a little window, and behind it a small room containing tape decks and other sound equipment. The window opened and a cheery-looking man, probably in his forties, with a boyish face, reached out and tapped James on the shoulder, smiling.

'Mr Peters!' said James ebulliently. 'How's it going, man?'

'Nice to see you. Wanna do five minutes?'

'Just watching tonight. Later, yeah?'

Loretta didn't like the way James was still holding her hand and she pulled free, asking him what he would like to drink. They crossed the low-ceilinged room to the bar, and James encouraged her to continue her life story.

There were tales of drugs and bands and shrinks and yoga and retreats and little phrases plucked willy-nilly from any number of esoteric books of wisdom and the Western psychological tradition and, beneath it all, the minimal outline of a badly failed relationship. Disconcertingly, James kept waving and nodding to various people behind her as they headed into the sound room or placed microphones on the stage area, which was not raised at all, just an oblong section of the floor covered by rubber matting. If it had been raised at all, only midgets could have performed without hitting the ceiling.

'I believe you can divide the whole world into four

groups, depending on which side of *Blonde on Blonde* they like best. Does that make sense to you?'

James could not resist a little teasing.

'Which side of what?'

Loretta looked like a startled meerkat. '*Blonde on Blonde*. Bob Dylan?'

'What about the group that have never heard of Bob Dylan?'

Loretta thought about this, and had to finally accept it was a possibility, even though it went against everything she had ever believed. 'I never thought of that,' she said.

James could listen to anyone once he had decided he could use them as a character in a routine. Eventually though, he became bored and started talking about himself, his career, his motives, his sense of merely being a conduit for the talent that somehow lay within him.

Loretta found it interesting at first, but after a while it wore her down. She had to find some way of breaking the flow.

'What star sign are you?' she asked. This, she had found, was normally enough to deter most English suitors.

'Capricorn,' he said. He could put up with her being flaky, he'd put up with anything, just to get her clothes off. He then went into one of his routines on astrology, breaking it up and disguising it so it came out like he was making it up off the top of his head.

'I don't believe this, he's doing his act at me,' thought Loretta.

CHAPTER TWENTY-TWO

Raschid and Stevie crept out of the house leaving Les asleep on the sofa, which creaked meekly in rhythm to his snoring. He had a red paper hat from a cracker on his head.

They got in the car and squealed off down the street. Raschid could only hope that James would not be at home. He had taken his passport and all his money in case he needed to escape immediately.

At Raschid's suggestion they parked a few streets away from James's. Raschid explained to Stevie why this was. 'The car makes so much noise there's too much risk someone might notice us.' It said a lot for the organisation and intelligence-gathering skills of his masters that they were prepared to use a lunatic like Stevie as a safe house, he thought. Then he remembered they had originally been trained by the CIA.

Raschid had convinced Stevie that the best way to do the job was with bare hands and a rope, for silence. If James was in and Stevie needed to be overpowered, it would be better if he were unarmed. Dim light glowed behind the shutters but the front door had no outer lighting, which was a relief to both of them. They stepped quietly up the path. Stevie unscrewed the index finger of his right claw and slotted a lock-pick in its place, winking as he did so. Within a couple of minutes they were in. Together, they checked every room. The flat was empty.

'What we gonna do then? Wait?'

'We don't know when he'll be back.'

'Don't matter. There's plenty of food in the fridge. Shall I put the kettle on?'

'No! And anyway, what if he doesn't come back on his own?'

'We can take 'em.'

'He's the one we want. I'm not someone who kills innocent people.'

Stevie looked momentarily disappointed. 'S'pose you're right,' he shrugged.

'And anyway, if we stay here all night, we'll miss the gig.'

'Good point. So we come back another time then?'

'Yes.'

'I'll just have a piss.'

'Can't you wait?'

'Be OK, mate. Chill out.'

The room was filling up, so James suggested they

bag a place in front of the sound box dressing-room, leaning against some wooden box units about chest high.

'Hi, guys,' said James to a group of men chatting to the sound man. They all acknowledged the greeting, and one of them called out.

'What you doing down here then? Come to get some new material?'

The others laughed, but James clearly didn't find it amusing.

'I'm going to be going quite fast this evening, Jim – hope you can get it all down.'

The group chuckled again.

'Are they accusing you of stealing material?' Loretta asked.

'Yeah, it's just a running joke.'

He didn't seemed to find it very funny.

The man who had been setting up the microphones approached them, hand extended, beaming, then introduced himself to Loretta.

'Thomas Hughes. How do you do?'

His accent sounded upper class to Loretta, and she liked the firmness of his handshake. Though he was in good shape he had greying hair, which indicated he was older than he looked. His posture implied confidence and his eyes a generous nature. Loretta couldn't decide if he was handsome or not. If James Bond came back as a gargoyle, she thought, this would be it. She found him very attractive.

'Loretta Borgesson, hi.'

James looked uncomfortable. He knew Tom Hughes specialised in young attractive women, and his success rate was so incredible that James hated him deeply. He wasn't even famous, and he would beat James to the pull every time – in the days before James was gay.

Hughes was clearly interested in Loretta. James tried to intercept him.

'So how's it going, Tom?'

'Disastrously dear boy, terrible. My life is in ruins as usual.' He was laughing as he spoke. 'Crippled by alimony and school fees as ever, bent and broken by the demands of rapacious young women who treat me as a cross between a cash point and a sexual plaything. Bleak! Bleak! Nothing works; there is nothing but despair and constant anxiety. You're so lucky to have thrown off the tyranny of female allure! Hahaha! Well, better get the show running. Lovely to meet you Loretta.'

Next minute this peculiar man was on the stage, explaining to the audience, almost in the tone a kindergarten teacher would use with her charges, that they were in the club to enjoy themselves and to do this they would need to abandon their inhibitions.

'Don't worry about feeling stupid, that's the key. I'll show you what I mean.' He proceeded to impersonate a gorilla and a bulldog, play two recorders through his nose and, guitar in hand, persuaded the whole audience to sing 'The Teddy Bears' Picnic' not once but twice. Then he brought on the first act to huge and uninhibited applause. Loretta was staggered that anyone could get English people to behave like this.

James laughed only occasionally at the acts, very loudly and generally at points when the rest of the audience was merely chuckling. This, Loretta realised, was to ensure they looked round and recognised him.

At the interval, James continued to keep Loretta to himself, at one point even turning his back on Tom Hughes whom he had seen advancing out of the corner of his eye, leaning in towards Loretta as if they were engaged in a deeply private conversation. He was actually name-dropping his way through some of the top-profile charity gigs he had done over the years. Loretta had had enough. She had spent two or three years in her teens playing Lolita-slut-groupie around Los Angeles, consorting with far bigger showbiz names and egos than even James Randall would ever have. He was talking about a Greenpeace benefit where he'd met Sting, when Loretta decided to cut him off.

'Have you ever done any direct action?'

'Sure, I go on marches, demos ... I did this

fantastic gig in Trafalgar Sqaure once – a hundred thousand people – for the health workers . . . there was me and Mark Thomas on stage right, and—'

'No, I mean, direct action. Illegal stuff.'

'Oh sure. Not for a while but you know, hunt sabbing, laboratories. I've been there,' he lied.

'Well, if you're interested, some people I know are planning this raid.'

James decided to bullshit along.

'Yeah?'

Loretta explained the ostrich situation, without being specific. 'I can fill you in on some more details if you'd like. I think they could use any available manpower.'

'OK, sounds great.'

'Great. Well, call me.'

'What, you're going?'

'I'm sorry, I have to get an early night, I had a long shift yesterday. I'm exhausted. Is there some place near I can get a cab?'

James wanted to tell her to go and fucking find her own cab. But he restrained his anger and decided that playing the gentleman would still leave him with an outside chance.

'You'll get one on the street, I'll come out with you.'

'No, that's OK.'

'Really, please, I insist.'

NIGHT OF THE TOXIC OSTRICH

* * *

They saw a cab almost immediately. As it pulled up, James tried to kiss her, but she just pecked him on the cheek and opened the door of the taxi. 'Fuck,' said James to himself. That was stupid.

'Look,' said Loretta and paused. Looked down. Oh fucking hell, thinks James, it's going to be an 'I-really-like-you-but-I-don't-think-we-should' – after all that hard work! After all this time, for God's sake . . .

'I really like you, and this has been a great evening, but I have to tell you I met someone really special recently and, well, I wasn't sure, but now I am, and well . . .'

'I understand,' said James, working hard to keep his smile going. 'Look, I'll call you about the thing.'

'Great.'

He unnecessarily helped her climb into the cab, and closed the door.

James returned to the club and ordered the first of several large vodkas and ice.

Stevie reappeared from the toilet looking even paler than usual. His pimples stood out like spatters of tomato ketchup on a snow-covered plain. He was shaking. In his left hand he held a framed picture of a football team. He held it out for Raschid to see.

'Fucking twat's an Arsenal supporter!' Stevie

could barely get the words out. Saliva sprayed out as he spoke. He stabbed at the photograph with his right claw, clearly forgetting he had replaced his index finger with the lock pick, which bent. This only made Stevie more enraged. He raised the photo above his head and, with a furious grunt, hurled it on to the floor, jumped on it with both Doc Marten's, picked it up, shards of glass flying as he smashed it down repeatedly on to the coffee table. He then skimmed it at a standing lamp, which tottered and flickered. Stevie jumped through the top of the coffee table, grunting all the while in time with his kicks.

Raschid, who had been caught by surprise, grabbed Stevie by the shoulders.

'Hey, come on, Stevie! Calm down! The neighbours might hear!'

Stevie shook himself free, screeched like a cornered rat and pushed Raschid backwards with such force that he was slammed into the far wall and winded. Stevie kicked away the shattered table, grabbed the standard lamp and bayonetted the television. He then slung it broadside on at Raschid and scuttled at cartoon speed into the kitchen, slamming the door behind him. Raschid sprinted after him and was met by a barrage of kitchen implements and crockery. He was momentarily stunned by what looked like a food mixer (in fact, a top-of-the-range pasta machine – a present from Sid).

Stevie shot past him again, tearing pictures off the wall as he ran into the bedroom, which Raschid entered to the sound of ripping material – Stevie was slashing at the bedding with his claws. Raschid advanced towards him, arms wide, speaking soothingly:

'Stevie, cool it! Think of the neighbours, OK?'

Stevie nodded in agreement then, when Raschid was a pace in front of him, lobbed the shredded duvet over his head and threw him to one side. Raschid cursed and ran after him but by the time he reached the bathroom, Stevie had locked the door. Raschid heard taps running and a crunching sound, followed by a crash. He got his shoulder through the door just as Stevie hurled the handbasin into the cast-iron bath, where it cracked into pieces. Water was spurting from the severed, mangled pipes.

'Stevie!'

Raschid moving swiftly, caught him on the jaw with a straight left, then hooked him with a right to the temple. Stevie wobbled and Raschid seized him by the elbows and wrestled him back into the living room. Stevie's distorted features resembled a life model from Picasso's cubist period, as he continued to moan and grunt. After a minute or so, his face clicked back to its usual furtive mask and Raschid felt him relax. Stevie looked at his feet as if noticing them for the first time, then at Raschid. He shook himself like a cat pretending it hadn't just missed its footing and fallen off a table, and turned back to Raschid.

'I hate Arsenal,' he explained.

CHAPTER TWENTY-THREE

James got out of the cab feeling pissed and wishing he was more so. To get so near to charming the pants off that gorgeous American airhead only to blow it by overdoing the platitudinous New Age bullshit psychobabble... 'A duck-billed platitudinous,' he said out loud while paying the driver.

'What mate?'

'Nothing. Good night.'

To get so close... he'd judged her so well, knew what she'd respond to, and then – *I blew it because I was too good*, he said to himself, zigzagging up the path. *Fucking dustbin. Keys.* In through the door like a javelin thrower trying to keep this side of the line, on with the light and – *Oh fuck what's happened? Fuck, they might still be in there... leave the door open... shout that you're here but you're not going to try and stop them, then run round the corner and phone the... police... shit.* 'If you're still in there, I am not going to try and stop you from leaving'... *too wimpy*... 'you fucking bastards... I'm sorry, that was confrontational, but you must accept I've a right to be angry . . .'

A curtain across the street twitched in a bedroom opposite. Cat Woman (so-called because she kept cats) turned to her paramour — a wheelchair-bound ex-body builder whom she had abducted from outside a supermarket six months before and kept as her toy boy under lock and key — and said:

'He's talking to his front door now. Having a row with his front door. Can you bleedin' credit it? All that money on the licence and there's a poof off the telly out of his head on Gawd knows what except he's bought it wiv my bleedin' money.'

'Actually I think he's on Channel Four,' said the captive Adonis.

'What's that got to do with it? I'm ringing the papers. I really am this time. Fancy that — talking to his bleedin' front door.'

'Will you let me go now please?' added Adonis, plaintively.

'Shut up and loosen your sweat-pants.'

James was searching for the stop-cock, frantic and cursing, when his phone rang.

'You fucking Arsenal scumbag! Thought you could slag off the Taliban and get away with it, did yer?'

'Who is this?'

'Your worst fucking nightmare, that's who this

fucking is. You're fucking dead, mate! We'll be back – that's all you need to know!' Then the voice began to sing. '*My old man/Said be an Arsenal fan, I said fuck off I'll follow the Spurs! You're a dead man/Off the Taliban/ fuck off bollocks you're a cunt!* Jihad!'

And then cut off.

Sitting next to Stevie in the car as he performed this on his mobile phone, Raschid was staggered, although impressed that Stevie could improvise song lyrics, however crude, so instantly.

'Just made that up,' said Stevie.

Raschid also wondered when and how exactly Stevie had managed to memorise James's phone number in the middle of his raging fury.

'S'all right, Raschid, I wiv'eld me number, innit?'

Maybe it was to James's credit that he did not collapse into a heap, fearful and penitent, when the full consequences of his actions were revealed and it seemed as if the Taliban had actually taken up his televised challenge to them to kill him. Perhaps he felt it was simply the kind of risk he had to accept in his chosen vocation. But actually, his initial reaction was a thrill that he might appear to be someone who was prepared to die for what he believed in. It would make a wonderful passage in his autobiography. Besides, he did not believe that any death threat could actually succeed – he was too big, too chosen, too cool. Surely, if he was meant to die, he'd have been in when they'd come round.

He was certainly not going to tell the police about it. He didn't need the organs of state oppression to help him – apart, of course, from giving him a crime number for the burglary, for insurance purposes. Plus, if he was honest, the voice on the phone had sounded so hysterical and untogether that he doubted its owner could carry out its threats.

However, he needed somewhere to stay. He thought of various of his comedian colleagues, but then it occurred to him that Henry and Elizabeth were going away. Their house was much more comfortable than most of his friends', and also it was nearer to Loretta . . .

If the detective who arrived an hour and a half later had been an actor, he would only have ever been cast as a detective. His face had a look of stoical patience, born of long and depressing experience of seeing people at their most dangerous, bereft and stupid, mixed with a contempt for anyone who saw the world differently to him. He looked like he would enjoy being provoked from time to time into using his fists.

The detective was going through the formalites, and James sensed he had recognised his face immediately, and was using most of his brain to place it.

'And your name?'

'James Randall.'

'James Randall,' the policeman repeated slowly. 'Of course, you're on the telly.' Although the policeman smiled as he said this there was something in his voice that made James fear he had been provoked past the point of restraint. Suddenly the publicity benefits of the exercise seemed pointless. He tried to stay cool.

'From time to time, yeah.'

'You're a comedian aren't you?'

It was a tone of excitement, a hint of deference even.

'Yeah,' he said. Delighted and slightly less nervous.

'The gay comedian,' deadpanned the policeman. 'So what's missing?'

'Nothing actually . . . I mean, the whole place is trashed, but as far as I can see there's nothing missing.' James thought this was probably unusual, and the detective's reaction, a sudden turn of the head implied he did too. James awaited his impending expert opinion.

'The gay comedian who did that piece about homophobia in the Met?'

'Yeah.'

'Did that stunt with the drag queen . . . ?' The detective was beaming at him now, but it was impossible to say what his look meant. James could only smile back.

'Yeah.'

'Upset a lot of people in the Met that did.'

'Right.'

'Found it very funny myself.'

The detective held his smile a second longer than felt natural before emitting a gruff cackle. It was hard to say if he was laughing at his memory of the programme or at the awkward position James now felt himself in.

'Well, we'll be in touch. Do you have a contact number and somewhere to stay? Not even a straight bloke could live in conditions like this, eh?' It was impossible to tell how the joke was meant. But James knew how it would sound when he related the stage version of the incident.

'No. I'll be staying at my brother's.'

James called Henry on his mobile.

'Elizabeth?'

'Yes.'

'It's James.'

'Oh. Hello.'

'Look, I'm sorry to call so late but it's been really worrying me what I said last night.'

Silence.

'And I want to apologise. It was not my place to say it.'

Silence.

'It's just that, well, it's important to me, you and Henry, and when he said you were, that things weren't actually a hundred per cent, I wanted to try and help. And I knew he was finding it difficult so I thought I'd try and loosen up the log-jam as it were.'

Silence. Come on, thought James, I'm giving it everything here, she's got to crack.

'And I realise I'd had a few drinks and it might have come out as malicious, which was the furthest thing from my mind. It's been eating me up all day. I had to get it off my chest.'

'Thank you.'

'I'm sorry.'

At her end, Elizabeth was sure the call was leading up to something else. She was not about to give James the benefit of a warmly accepted apology. Neither was she going to be forced to abandon her habitual decorum just because she didn't like him. She was, perhaps, also interested to find out just how much cheek he really had.

'There's nothing else then, James?'

'No, well actually, yes, there is, coincidentally . . . well, I've been burgled and they've trashed the place . . . no, I'm fine. It's just that, I've nowhere to stay and I was wondering . . . thanks.'

Elizabeth put the phone down and congratulated herself on having been so perfectly generous. She had felt the grovel in James's voice and knew he felt even smaller for not having heard the slightest hint of indignation in Elizabeth's tone. She woke Henry and began preparing the spare room.

James sat back in the cab and decided his luck was changing for the better when he realised he had escaped a talkative driver. So, he was the target of a death threat. That was pretty cool. In fact, it was totally on the edge. Next time Henry accused him of exploiting his position for narcissistic ends, he could put him down, bam, just like that – 'I put my life on the line for my art.' Except, of course, he couldn't because if he mentioned to Henry that he was the target of a death threat, Henry might be less keen on James staying in his house. He asked himself if it was fair of him to put Henry and Elizabeth at risk like this . . . what if they killed Henry by mistake?

James drifted off into a reverie, picturing himself on television – tearful, distraught, guilt-ridden, mourning his brother's death. James Randall as he had never been seen before – vulnerable, bearing his pain with dignity but not afraid to show his emotions. An icon, a role model for post-post-feminist man in the new millennium. Strong, courageous, and yet emotionally literate. He would instigate a memorial concert in his brother's name, a star-studded affair where the cream of radical British performing arts would testify their defiance of tyranny. It almost brought a tear to his eye as he imagined calling Elizabeth up on stage to receive the inaugural cheque for the Henry Randall Foundation for Freedom of Expression.

Or, perhaps, they would kill James himself. He'd have an award named after him. He'd be a martyr. Immortal, he would outlive his rivals and eclipse them – become an icon, like Che. He made a mental note to get some new publicity photographs. Maybe let his beard grow first . . .

But what if it was for real? *Someone is trying to kill you. Doesn't that worry you?* Not really, I don't think they're serious. *Isn't that just another way of trying to deny this is happening? Someone broke into your fucking house and wrecked it – doesn't that upset you?* Nothing upsets me. I am impervious to emotional pain. Anyway, I'm too successful to die young.

Of course he wasn't putting people at risk, there *was* no risk. And more important than that, he wanted to get laid. If he invited Loretta round for dinner at Henry's place, he might still be in with a chance.

Elizabeth and Henry were waiting up for James when he arrived and, over tea and whisky, he told them the edited version of what had happened and they said he could stay as long as he liked. James felt the evening had turned out well. Elizabeth always had a freezer full of excellent home-made food. He knew how to use a microwave. It would make a change from kebabs.

CHAPTER TWENTY-FOUR

Raschid did not speak to Stevie on the drive home.

He was too angry. He decided to remain silent, let Stevie calm down without risking provoking him in any way. When they parked, Stevie offered a sheepish apology to which Raschid simply replied that they would talk about it in the morning.

Les was asleep in front of *The Great Escape*, with a paper hat cloyed to his brow with sweat, and the remains of a turkey pizza clamped in the folds of his relentless stomach. His snoring reminded Raschid of a T-52 tank with transmission problems trying to change gear.

'Do you want a cup of tea or something?' said Stevie softly.

'No thanks. Good night.'

The next day, Henry and Elizabeth were up and ready for an early start. (Henry preferred to do any motorway driving when there was likely to be little traffic around, even if it meant reaching his destination well before anyone there was awake.) Elizabeth had been unhappy when James hinted he would like to stay for a few days, but Henry had been delighted. The idea that someone would be house-sitting took a weight off his mind. Despite the timer switches on the lights, the window locks and the Chubbs and the Ingersolls and the state-of-the-art alarm system, he felt there was no substitute for someone going in and out the front door. That it would be his brother going in and out the front door did not, for some reason, worry him. Elizabeth had tried to signal her objections but Henry, stung by her accusations of his ineffectual nature from the day before, was determined to be assertive and she relented. She could see the logic of Henry's position, but just felt uneasy that the house-sitter was James.

At five-thirty, Henry hammered on James's door and insisted he get up so he could show him round the security system and make him familiar with the massive array of keys and locks. James followed Henry round, grunting and nodding vigorously – or as vigorously as James could do anything at that time of day – to indicate he had understood. Henry then handed James several sheets of paper. 'I've written it all down just in case.'

'So what did you get me out of bed for?'

'There's no need to be like that, James. This is my

house. And I'd have thought you'd be sensitive to the need for good home security at the moment.' James recognised Henry's stubborn and petulant tone. 'You can always stay somewhere else if you'd rather.'

'OK, OK. Just a bit early for me.'

Elizabeth reminded James politely not to smoke in the house. James reminded Henry to be sure to give his love to their mother, and assured them he would ring in the week to tell them which train he would be on next Saturday.

Despite various hints, in the shape of grimaces and exhalations of breath, James did not help Elizabeth carry any of their luggage to the car, and closed the front door behind them without bothering to say goodbye. Then went back to bed.

'I feel a lot safer having someone in the house,' said Henry as they drove off. Elizabeth said nothing.

At noon, James got up again and went about his regular morning exercises – coffee and three cigarettes. He then picked up the phone to tell Sid about last night.

'Sid, it's James.'

'Hi, darling.'

'Look, I'm staying at my brother's for a while.'

'Brother?'

'You were in his house on Saturday.'

'Oh, of course . . . actually, I wanted to talk to you about that . . .'

'Well, first things first, yeah? I'm staying at my brother's 'cos my place got trashed last night.'

'Who were you with?' leered Sid, smelling gossip.

'No one. My flat got trashed by some people who said they were going to kill me. They rang and told me.'

'Are you serious?'

'Course I'm fucking serious. They said they were from the Taliban . . .'

The thought shot through Sid's mind that James didn't really have enough product – just the one video – to fully exploit a posthumous sales opportunity, but she didn't say so.

'Sid?'

'Sorry, I was just thinking . . . Taliban. . . . Must have been that piece you did from the Astoria last autumn then . . . very funny, inviting them over to London for a good seeing to . . . which reminds me—'

'What?'

'Nothing. Do you think it's for real?'

'I dunno.'

'What do the police think? Or didn't you call them?'

'Course I called them. I needed a crime number for the insurance. Didn't tell them about the death threat though. It's bullshit.'

'You don't think you were followed to your brother's or anything?'

'No.'

'Good oh. Stride Boswell's in town from Wednesday and it might make him nervous having dinner with you if he knew a hit-man was lurking round the corner. And we want him relaxed.'

'Dinner? You've spoken to him?'

'Yes. He's dying to meet you.'

'Yeah? Where do you think we should go?'

'Well . . . It occurs to me we might take advantage of your brother's lovely house. It's the perfect venue for an intimate dinner.'

'You want me to cook for him?'

'We could hire caterers.'

'I don't know if I want to . . . see this guy.'

'Of course you do. He's going to give you a slot on the highest-profile gig in showbusiness history.'

'But . . .'

'But what?'

'You know . . . you said . . . he . . . likes me . . .'

'This is your career we're talking about here, James darling. It's not as if it's just a cheap tawdry physical encounter. It's a strategic move.'

'So you're telling me that this guy has said to you

that he will definitely give me a slot on this gig if I . . .'

'Of course not. Not in so many words.'

'Or did you suggest it to him?'

'Well, I might have. But not in so many words. It's your best interests I'm thinking of, for heaven's sake. Are you still there?'

'Yeah.'

'Right, well, let's say Saturday night. You'd better give me the address.'

James paused. Was he really going to give her the address? He could always cancel later, of course, but he knew if he gave her the address it was somehow whittling away at his objections. Did he really want success that badly? Was there no part of himself that was not subjugated to his desire for fame and attention? Did he have no self-respect? Because if he gave out that address, that's what he was saying.

'James? Hello? What? Yes, of course I've got a pen . . . and that's N1, yes? Lovely. See you Saturday.'

He could ring up tomorrow and cancel, James decided, and dialled Loretta's number. Might as well have another try. Exploitative sex was much more attractive if you weren't on the receiving end, he thought. Also, it took his mind off the possibility that someone was trying to kill him. Then he thought again. There couldn't possibly be someone really trying to kill him. It would interfere with his career so badly. It couldn't happen. No answer.

He rolled a joint, then phoned a couple of friends he hadn't spoken to in ages because they were in New York and it was too expensive to call from home. As a result, by four-thirty he still hadn't got round to doing anything about getting the flat repaired. He rang Sid again and explained he was traumatically damaged from the experience, and wondered if she could get someone from the office to arrange it all tomorrow. He suggested they send a bike in the morning to pick up his keys. He rolled another joint and, realising it was now six o'clock, began phoning friends he hadn't spoken to in ages because they were in Los Angeles.

After an hour or so James had discharged these long-standing obligations to exchange gossip with people on the other side of the globe and decided to reward himself with another joint. As he lay on the sofa he began to think about Saturday. Was he really going to go through with it? Would it hurt? Surely this was going too far? But look what he would get in return. A slot on the first gig in space. That was a guaranteed profile-raiser, plus a place in the record books. And then Sid had mentioned the possibility of a couple of movie roles. It would be the perfect next step. Get away from the small screen into the serious stuff. When he weighed it up like that . . .

and yet, he didn't feel comfortable. For God's sake, how many Hollywood actresses have done the casting couch? If it gave him his big break then of course it would be worth it – a small price to pay for immortality. *Must get some heavy duty condoms in. And some lubricant. Lots.*

He went back to his earlier thoughts about identifying with women. It would enable him to understand a woman's experience of this patriarchal oppressive society much more vibrantly. Yes, that was it! He would not be prostituting himself, but committing a revolutionary act of abasement to put himself in touch with the condition of an oppressed group. Two oppressed minorities, in fact. God he was brave, when he thought about it. He sat up and decided to reward himself with another joint.

As usual, in moments of stillness with nothing to do, James's thoughts moved to his groin. He decided to try Loretta again. He knew their date had not gone well, but he calculated there was still a chance of regaining lost ground and impressing her.

'Loretta, hi. It's James here. Look, I'm sorry about last night. To tell you the truth, I'd done a couple of lines and I'd forgotten how it always makes me act like a complete bullshitter.'

'I didn't think you were bullshitting,' replied Loretta. She wanted to add, 'It's clear you're like that the whole time,' but restrained herself.

'Well, you're very kind. Anyway, the reason I'm phoning is because I'd like to help you out on this raid. I think it's important, and I want to, you know, do my bit, to make a difference.'

He congratulated himself on finding this American phrase to finish on, and waited.

What the hell, thought Loretta, *we can do with all available bodies*. She gave him the details of the rendezvous.

CHAPTER TWENTY-FIVE

Henry and Elizabeth had a clear run up the motorway and reached his mother's in record time. Henry was delighted. Elizabeth wasn't. Sitting in a three or four hour tailback was infinitely preferable to being in Henry's mother's house for the equivalent period of time. Before each visit Elizabeth would try to wipe away the memories of the previous ones but, somehow, whenever they turned into that familiar road and saw the house at the foot of the hill, a miasmic sludge would seep into the car. As always, the soundtrack from *Psycho* would play in her head though she could never recall it at any other time.

She saw a net curtain twitch in the living-room window. They pulled into the drive and Henry hopped out on to the gravel brightly, saying, as he always did: 'Pretty good run, eh?'

Elizabeth smiled bravely and stayed in the car, fiddling with her handbag and rearranging things in the glove box, grasping on to the last seconds of freedom and calm she would experience for a week.

Formerly a vicarage, the house was seventeenth century, square and large, with thick white plastered walls that repelled virtually all sounds of outside life that might infringe upon the interior. Climbing roses adorned the frontage on both sides of the wide black door. It stood a little distance from the rest of the village, at the foot of a wooded hill, on the other side of which began the Welsh mountains. There was rich and abundant birdlife all around, though curiously Elizabeth always had the impression that little of it ventured into the walled garden of the Old Parsonage itself.

Mrs Randall was originally from Lincolnshire and Elizabeth knew that she had chosen deliberately to live in isolation, on the other side of the country from anyone who might know anything about her. If it didn't exactly make her happy – what did? – it must have been a relief for her former neighbours when she had headed into the sunset for good.

Henry had already tapped on the door in his usual jaunty manner and had turned to survey the front garden. He winked at Elizabeth as she summoned the strength to join him. She couldn't help admiring his goodwill and optimism, which somehow had not curdled throughout the years. He genuinely thought his mother was going to greet him warmly this time, genuinely anticipated a happy family experience. He was capable of believing there was some good in the old witch and, for this generosity of spirit, Elizabeth loved him, even though he drove her mad. She had decided he deserved all the support she could give him and she skipped up to join him on the step.

At last the door opened slightly and Mrs Randall's spectral form scowled out.

'Hi, Mum!' Henry bounced forwards like a labrador and embraced his mother, who received his kiss stonily, absorbing his energy like a black hole. Elizabeth took her turn, forcing out a huge warm smile, 'Hello, Mrs Randall! Lovely to see you again!'

'I was in the bath,' Mrs Randall lied.

'Oh, sorry,' said Henry.

His mother stared at him, as if waiting for him to confess he had deliberately timed their arrival to cause her maximum inconvenience. Behind Elizabeth's gritted teeth an angry crowd of abuse was jostling to get out. 'No, you weren't, you lying old bag. You were downstairs – I saw you twitching the curtains. And this house is much too delightful to have net curtains in it anyway. Or you for that matter.' But instead she set her smile even wider and observed how wonderful the roses were this year. With a sniff Mrs Randall conceded that indeed they were. Elizabeth suspected Mrs Randall considered the dazzling array of creamy white and blood-red blooms were the price she had to pay for having the house bedecked with thorns. Elizabeth proffered the flowers they had bought in town.

Mrs Randall looked at the opulent display of lilies and for a moment her grim face twitched into a hint of a smile before regaining its customary sub-zero demeanour. As her mother-in-law's hand closed around the bouquet, Elizabeth fully expected to see it wilt and snap, as if cut down by a late frost.

'I won't take the cellophane off. My hay fever's bad enough as it is. You'd better come in.' She turned and led them into the living room. A skilled mime artist would have killed for her ability to express resentment so purely in a simple walk.

'I hope you've had breakfast. I can't carry much shopping these days.'

'Not to worry, Mum! We've brought lots of stuff. I'll run you down the supermarket later if you like and we can stock you up for a month.'

'If I last that long.' She put the flowers down on a sideboard, histrionically, as if she were placing them on her own coffin.

Elizabeth knew what was next in the ritual. It was always the same. Three, two, one . . . yes – there she goes, dusting the array of photographs on the mantelpiece. Elizabeth always found it disturbing that most of them were of Mrs Randall and James, and that in them Mrs Randall seemed a completely different person. Smiling, lively. Human even. Henry never discussed the fact that he only featured in one or two, and in the most recent was about eight years old.

'James not with you?' As if it was Henry's fault.

'No, sorry. He's going to come up on Saturday though.'

Mrs Randall looked at the flowers as if they had suddenly turned into a bag of rotting fish and handed them back to Elizabeth.

'Would you mind taking these through to the kitchen, please?'

'Of course.' Then she jumped in to pre-empt the inevitable request. 'Why don't I make a pot of tea while I'm in there?' A small victory.

'Don't overfill the kettle.'

'Right-o.'

And they were here for a week.

CHAPTER TWENTY-SIX

Next morning, Raschid rose and found Les in exactly the same position on the sofa, if anything snoring in a more metallic and disparate way.

Softly, Stevie spoke behind him. 'I usually leave him just to wake up in his own time. Want some tea?'

'Yes. Perhaps we should go to a café. We need to talk about things.' He held a piercing thousand-yard stare on Stevie who looked away first.

'Just get me jacket, yeah?'

A woman in her fifties with a beehive hairdo like rusted steel-wool was ordering breakfast, giving specific instructions as to how she wanted her toast, speaking in such a quiet voice that the Greek girl taking her order was having to lean right over the counter to hear. You could tell from the look on the girl's face that the woman's toast was going to be whatever colour it came out of the toaster. MTV was playing on the television in one corner, while the set at the other end of the same wall was tuned, with the sound down, to the newest cable station, the War Channel. It showed cockpit video footage of the latest hi-tech interventions around the world, cutting to military uniforms in press briefings trying to maintain confident body language, cutting to colour footage of massacres, cutting to bands of guerrillas in turbans and kaffiyehs and baseball caps traversing snowy mountains and steamy jungles and parched savannah, cutting to adverts for Benetton and training shoes and weather-proof woodseal and video games, cutting back to guided missiles destroying a bridge from the pilot's point of view.

Filling the wall space between the two televisions was a watercolour of an alpine chalet, an oil painting of a Greek fishing village and, in the centre, a portrait of Princess Diana.

The woman with the specific toast requirements sat down at one of the red formica tables and took a half-smoked cigarette from behind her ear, then got up to take a light from the waiter, who was smoking at the side of the counter.

'This is on me, Raschid, yeah?' said Stevie.

He ordered two full vegetarian breakfasts and they sat down in the corner furthest from the televisions.

'I try and get my dad to come down here sometimes, you know, get him to eat something different once in a while but he don't fit in the seats no more.'

'He doesn't seem too well.'

'Yeah. He don't take no notice of what I tell him though. But you gotta keep trying, innit?'

The waiter brought their food. When he'd gone, Stevie leant towards Raschid.

'Look, I know I was out of order last night, know what I mean?' said Stevie, in between chewing a slice of toast which he had impaled on his claw and rotated and munched on until it looked like a large bread cogwheel. He had attracted an audience, an old Greek man and two black women. Stevie glared at them: 'What's the matter? Never seen someone eat a bit of toast before?' They looked away and Stevie huddled closer over the table.

'Yes, you were out of order,' said Raschid finally. 'The police will have been alerted. We must do nothing for a few weeks. Let everything calm down again first. He will probably not be living at that address now. It may take us a long time to find him again.'

'It's just, you know, him slagging off the Taliban *and* being an Arsenal supporter – it's like he's really taking the piss, know what I mean?'

Raschid was disturbed to see that Stevie genuinely believed this was a rational argument. He also knew that because he had nowhere else to stay, he would have to opt for diplomacy.

'Stevie, you must not allow your personal feelings

to interfere in an assignment such as this. You see where it leads.'

'Yeah, yeah. But you gotta admit, we had to go for it. I mean, what were the chances of me picking the geezer up like that? Can you pass the ketchup? Thanks. It was like, divine intervention telling us what to do.'

'And what is it telling us now?'

The woman with the steel-wool hair was pointing to a specific patch of colour on her toast, explaining she wanted two more slices that were all that shade of light brown. Stevie turned back to Raschid.

'Yeah, yeah, I know what you're saying . . . But on the other 'and, if we did find out where he is, they'd never be expecting us to try again straight away, would they? We'd have the element of surprise.'

'We cannot take the risk.'

'Hang on, mate, we're Islamic fundamentalists, innit? I mean, surely the whole point of being a fundamentalist is that you do things on impulse? That's partly why I joined, frankly.'

'OK. Listen to me. I have spent ten years as a Holy Warrior fighting a vicious guerrilla war. You once left a small bomb outside an off-licence in North London. Who has the greater experience of Jihad?'

Stevie was stung and Raschid saw it in his eyes. But it had needed to be said.

'All right, point taken. I just think it's playing into the enemy's hands if we behave according to their methods of rational analysis and sensible planning.'

'Listen, Stevie, if we don't take this seriously and plan things right, we'll get caught. And if we get caught, how are you going to look after your father? I mean, you told me yourself, you're working two jobs to save up and take him on a surprise holiday at Christmas. What if you're not here then? What will he do?'

Stevie hadn't really thought of this. It worried him.

'Like you say, Raschid, you're the boss.'

'Good.'

'There's something else, mate . . .'

With a slight lift of the head, Raschid invited him to continue.

'It's like, how long are you planning to be staying here? I mean, obviously I don't mind how long it is, but, you know, our flat and me dad and everything . . . he likes his privacy and, well, I'm committed to the cause but I've got to respect his privacy and that and, you know, he's a bit of a nosey git as well so, like, if he starts sniffing round and finds out where you're from plus there's the question of money . . .'

'Believe me, I don't want to be here any longer than I have to be. Perhaps in a few days I could find somewhere else to lodge. The most important thing is for you to understand that we are suspending all operations indefinitely. Is that understood?'

Stevie nodded his assent and wondered if Raschid was talking sense or had gone soft.

As they left, MTV and the War Channel were both showing the same advert for the National Lottery, and Toast Woman and the waitress had both broken off their latest exchange to watch it.

CHAPTER TWENTY-SEVEN

They stopped off on the way home at a health-food shop. One look at Stevie, with his faceful of tattoos and body jewellery, and the assistant was virtually in the process of handing over the contents of the till.

'I want some peppermint tea and something for someone whose guts are bad.' There was a touching concern in Stevie's voice which immediately turned the assistant's mood from fear to sympathy. She drew more details out of him as if talking to a frightened little boy which, somehow, he had now become.

'They're like, well, clogged.'

The assistant suggested dried apricots, which Stevie took. At the door, he turned and muttered a timid thank-you. The assistant smiled with kindness.

Raschid dropped into a newsagent's and bought a *Guardian*. It thrilled him to think how much trouble he would be in at home if he were caught with an English newspaper. At home? What home?

Afghanistan wasn't home any more. He didn't have one any more. Yet. He bought a *Daily Star* as well, just for the outrage of naked female flesh.

Back at the flat, Les was sitting at the table, across two chairs, drinking a mug of tea.

'Here y'are, Dad, I got you some more peppermint tea.'

'Peppermint fucking tea.'

'And some apricots. Be good for yer. Woman in the health-food shop said.'

'Health-food shop? Made of money are we? Fuckin' 'ell.'

Raschid cleared some paper chains and tinsel from an armchair and lost himself in the *Guardian*.

'I'll make you one, shall I?'

'I got a cup of tea.'

'Yeah, but this might help your guts.'

'The cab office rung up. Wanted to know what time you was coming in today.'

'Oh yeah. Right.'

'He said you gotta come in today or don't bother coming in at all.'

'He's bluffing.'

'He said you've missed four shifts in a week. He said that's taking the piss even by their standards.'

Stevie considered this, and conceded the argument with a frown. 'Yeah. Raschid mate, I'm going to have to do some cabbing this afternoon.'

'That's OK.'

'And a bird phoned.'

'What bird.'

'A Yank bird. I said you weren't in.'

'She leave a message?'

'I told her to call back when you was in.'

'Great.'

'Right, I'm going to have a lie-down. I'm worn out taking all these phone calls. By the way – have you hid my mince pies?'

'You shouldn't be eating mince pies.'

'Don't tell me what I should and shouldn't be doing in my own house.'

Stevie wasn't listening, he was already halfway through dialling.

Les picked up on the urgency in the way Stevie was punching the numbers.

'Aah, look at that!' said Les in a mocking sing-song. 'He fancies the Yank bird! Ain't that sweet! He looks like a scarecrow with half a ton of scrap metal in his head and he thinks some bird is going to fancy him!'

'Shut up, Dad.'

'Blind is she? Must be blind or bleeding desperate if she's phoning that up.'

Stevie switched the phone off.

'Just shut it, all right?'

'How much does she charge then?'

Raschid moved quickly to intercept Stevie as he hurled himself, claws first, at his dad.

'Calm down, Stevie. He's only joking.'

'Yeah, I'm only having a laugh. Like that bird probably is if she's phoning you up.'

Stevie struggled to get free, but Raschid was too strong.

'You fancy the Yank bird! You fancy the Yank bird! Want to kiss her, do you? Want to kiss her? If you was ever going to kiss a bird in your life, son, it would have happened by now. How you gonna kiss her with all that shrapnel in your face? You'd rip her to shreds.'

'Les, be quiet,' said Raschid. 'Or I'll let him go.'

'Just fuck off, you fat twat,' spat Stevie.

'Fuck off yourself.'

Raschid gently released his grip on Stevie's arms and handed him the phone. With great self-control, Stevie limited his retaliation to a sorry shake of the head and dialled again.

'Loretta? All right?'

Les turned in the doorway – a more challenging manoeuvre than for the average person – and, of course, he was only prepared to make that kind of effort if he could get in a good dig at Stevie's expense.

' 'Ere, is she the one who told me to shove that tube up my arse?'

'Hello, Loretta? It's Stevie. No, I'm working the cabs today—'

'Tell her to shove it up her own arse.' Les's voice dwindled. He had lost interest in provoking Stevie after the sight of the topless blonde on the front of Raschid's *Daily Star*. He picked it up and waddled off for his nap. 'Tell her I'll decide when I have a shit in my own good time,' he mumbled without conviction. 'Keeping it in or letting it out is my business. Freeborn Englishman, that's what I am.'

Raschid watched as Les forced himself through the doorway and wondered if he had been transported to hell by evil djinns. But he couldn't be in hell, or he would never have met Loretta.

Stevie asked Loretta to hang on and turned to Raschid.

'I was wondering if you could do me favour. Loretta's got the enema tube for me dad. She wants to talk me through how it works and that but I got to go cabbing, else they'll fire me. I'm two days late, like. So I was wondering if you'd cover for me. You've seen me dad – he's in a right state . . .'

Raschid tried not to look too excited by concentrating on the thought of the enema lecture rather than on who would be delivering it.

'OK, sure.'

But Stevie had noticed, and he scowled.

CHAPTER TWENTY-EIGHT

Stevie was tense and brooding as they rattled along Holloway Road, using his horn and swearing at other motorists even more than usual. Forced to halt at a red light for once – the car in front had stopped – Stevie spoke for the first time. 'Me and Loretta, right – we're together, yeah?' It was such a preposterous idea, Stevie himself could not even utter the lie with any conviction. If he'd claimed he used to be the lead singer in the Supremes it would have sounded more plausible. But Raschid nodded politely. It was not worth upsetting his psychotic host in any way. Stevie overtook two cars and a bus, immediately cut in tight in front of them and braked sharply, causing a tirade of angry horns. They were on a pelican crossing opposite the Camden Town Sainsbury's.

'Tube zoverair,' he growled, indicating the station with a sharp jerk of the head. Raschid had barely time to close the door before the car was moving again.

He couldn't see Loretta, so he moved in a slow circuit through the ticket hall, out the other side and back to the pavement where he'd started. Here Raschid lingered a little while, leaning on the railings, then moved off casually as he saw in his peripheral vision a thin red-faced man detach himself from a group of alkies and totter towards him. Raschid settled against the railings outside the other exit to wait for Loretta.

She was ten minutes late but greeted him with such a warm smile that Raschid felt he had momentarily been transported a million miles closer to the sun. If Stevie had seen it he would probably have stabbed them both.

'Hi. Stevie couldn't make it?'

'No. He has to go minicabbing.'

'Oh. OK. So, just the two of us.'

'Yes.' Raschid tried to hit a neutral tone.

'OK ... well ... wanna eat something?'

'Yeah, great.'

'Do you like noodles?' Raschid was happy to take whatever came along. This read in his face, so Loretta carried on without him needing to answer. 'I know a place,' she said and pointed; he followed in her wake.

All around him, the streets were full of the baubles and trinkets of the decadent West. The air carried wafts of incense from candles burning on pavement stalls made of upended beer crates with a wooden board atop them. He could hear Elvis fighting to be heard against a booming throbbing wave of sound which seemed to warp and bend as it surged to a metallic crescendo. He could imagine many of his more superstitious comrades, who had barely travelled beyond their own valleys, believing this to be the sound of evil djinns and indeed he had to remind himself it was just music coming from an amplifier and a set of speakers.

As he walked on the beat fought for his attention with the bizarre sights around him. Twenty feet up, the barrel and front tracks of a light tank erupted through the brickwork of an army surplus shop. Elvis Presley's head looked out blankly from above a music store and a ten-foot-long nose with a metal ring through one nostril contended for customers seeking Body Decoration.

All around him swarmed the youth tribes of Europe. He remembered some of the names from the last time he was in England – the ones in the long black coats and embellished motorcycle boots had to be Goths. And over there were punks. Except they weren't scowling at anyone, and the green hair was more carefully groomed: the clothes too were cleaner and more colourful, and he had never seen shoes like that before – the soles were about eight inches thick and made of . . . rubber, was it?

Now he smelt pizza and frying onions. He saw

hotdogs and ham rolls being sold by men he was certain were Muslims. He ignored a thin black man who hissed 'Spliff?' in a whisper as he passed.

And everywhere he saw girls. Girls in tight trousers and dresses with slits and tops that stopped short or started late, revealing flashes of thigh and tattooed cleavages and gold rings through navels. Girls in tight T-shirts with 'Get Your Eyes Off My Tits' in day-glo colours across the chest. Raschid, who was used to seeing a woman's eyes at a distance through the mesh of a yashmak's slit, wondered how any man could live in this place and not go out of his mind.

Raschid, walking behind Loretta, found it weird to be following the woman. Weird, but not unpleasant. He could catch up and walk alongside her, but he was happy to keep a step or two behind so he could look at her, at her long blonde hair which reached almost to her waist, at the narrow band of completely naked flesh where her T-shirt failed to meet the waist band of her hipsters. He could see the shape of her body underneath her clothes. Here were the temptations they had warned him against in the mountains – the decadent fleshpots of the West, the corrupting, degrading power of the Great Satan, luring the unwary from the paths of righteousness with these seductive traps.

Raschid was on his guard, alert, assessing the

dangers around him. He decided he was actually quite keen to be trapped. His senses were giving in one by one. Sight, sound, and smell – all had been seduced so far, he thought. And now they were going to eat which would take care of taste, leaving just the one... As he had this thought, Loretta, still two paces ahead, stopped at the corner and turned towards him.

'It's just down here,' she said.

They were led by a waiter in a green T-shirt and black jeans to places at a long refectory table. Raschid automatically took the seat which allowed him to see the door. They were sitting next to a long, plate-glass wall. Raschid appreciated this; along with uncovered female bodies, buildings containing huge amounts of undamaged glass were something he had not seen much of in recent years.

'So, how do you know Stevie?'

He reached for his green tea and started reading the menu. 'Oh... it's a long story.'

One that he wasn't going to tell willingly, Loretta realised. It made her more curious to know. But she had other priorities.

'This place looks very nice,' Rashid added. He was feeling torn. He couldn't tell her anything but he wanted to tell her everything. He was trying to remember the last time he had sat down alone with a woman. He was trying to remember the last time he had spoken to a woman whose face he could see. This by itself was pretty thrilling. That Loretta's face was a very attractive one shifted the whole thing up a couple of gears. He hadn't been so excited since the first time he threw a grenade down the hatch of a tank. He was fed up with his life. How, for example, would he describe himself in one of those lonely-hearts columns you seemed to find in nearly every British newspaper these days?

'Member of Islamic Fundamentalist Militia, 32, experienced killer and enforcer of Islamic Law, hoping to change careers and lifestyle, wltm Caucasian female for conversation on travel, rock music, motorbikes, poetry . . .'

He must try to concentrate on the Brummie persona. It wasn't going to be easy.

'Have you been in the country long?'

'About eighteen months.'

'I've never been to America.'

'It's insane. But you can get to do your own thing.'

'I'd like to have my own motorcycle repair business. With a roof garden where I could sit in the evenings and listen to music and read poetry.'

'Cool.'

Raschid didn't think it was cool. Raschid was appalled at his indiscretion. Luckily their waiter had arrived, and he nodded without looking up as they ordered, punching the information into some kind of hand-held computer. Raschid was mortified at his outburst. He had never spoken to anyone like that before. He felt he'd gashed himself open, that he would always be vulnerable to Loretta for this knowledge he had surrendered to her, that she could always open the wound and reach inside him. He felt horrified, frightened, and utterly utterly thrilled.

'Do you have a bike?' he found himself asking.

'Not here. Had a couple of Harleys back home. And a boyfriend of mine had this really beautiful old Triumph. It was the same model that Dylan crashed on in sixty-six.'

'Really? So you like bikes?'

'Doesn't everyone?'

'I don't think so.'

'Those people don't count.' Loretta giggled and, as she crunched on a pickled vegetable, emitted a low moan of passion that Raschid found unsettling and very arousing.

She was about to bring the enema kit out of her bag and get down to step one of the official agenda when she decided against it. It was partly because she remembered how a lot of people in this country seemed to find it off-putting to discuss bowel movements directly before eating, especially when equipment was involved, but also because she didn't want to break the mood. She wasn't sure what the mood was but it was there and worth following. This

Raschid guy was interesting to her. He was cute and kind of mean-looking. He was well-built, you got the feeling he'd be able to handle himself in a fight. But at the same time he had this real shy side to him, like he didn't quite belong here . . . Something about the look in his eyes – as if he'd experienced great suffering and had the strength to come through it. This old guy she'd known in San Francisco had always said he could spot a fellow vet from the look in their eyes.

'Were you ever a soldier?' she found herself saying.

Rashid hestitated before he said no. She knew he was lying, but she didn't mind. She knew from the way he paused that he wanted to tell her, but it was too early. 'I'm sorry,' she said. 'I don't know what made me say that.'

'And how about yourself? Ever seen combat?'

She laughed.

'Sure – I was in Vietnam when I was two, then you know, round the place as a mercenary. Retired two years ago, decided I wanted to get in touch with my feminine side, had me a sex change, and here I am.'

Loretta, what on earth are you talking about?

'Well, you certainly found a most skilful surgeon,' said Raschid.

Loretta licked the tip of her finger and shifted slightly in her seat. 'Thank you,' she said.

Raschid blushed. He was finding this very different from relating to Afghani women. But he reckoned he could get used to it.

Their noodles arrived and they chatted more neutrally about food around the world and places they'd been and places they wanted to go . . . Raschid concentrated on his future plans and skilfully sidestepped Loretta's subtly baited questions – 'What's the weirdest thing you've ever eaten? Really? Where was that? When? How come?' – throwing questions back at her about her life and never feeling any pressure to deal quid quo pro on the information revealed.

Somehow Loretta felt he was genuinely interested in her answers. Inevitably she was covering the same ground as with James a few nights before, but the way Raschid followed up showed he'd been listening to how the story affected her, whereas James was more about using it as a link for an anecdote starring him.

After they'd eaten, Loretta suggested they went for a walk in the park and she'd talk him through the enema kit.

They sat in Regent's Park, on a bench in the rose garden, surrounded by hedges which muffled the grinding noise of the traffic almost to zero. There was barely a cloud in the blue, blue sky; the bees played in and out of the blossoms above and around them, which suffused the air with a rich yet gentle scent. Somewhere in the distance someone was playing Edith Piaf singing 'La Vie en Rose'.

Raschid looked at Loretta, who smiled and said: 'OK, so this end of the tube is inserted in the anus, and then you fill the other end with warm soapy water. There's other liquid you can use, but for a first one I would recommend keeping it simple. You need olive oil as a lubricant for the nozzle and the anus. Any olive oil will do . . .'

Raschid listened to her, enthralled by the confidence and simplicity with which she expressed herself, the way she softly bit her lovely lower lip in concentration as she sketched out a little diagram or held up the equipment to demonstrate a detail, the way she looked up with that smile on her face to check Raschid was following, the fact that she was prepared to sacrifice her free time for the well-being of the monstrous Les and his poor twisted lunatic son, the intelligence and vivacity in the rhythm of her speech – Raschid was enchanted. Had he been lying next to her upon a silken divan, in a shaded secret chamber in some palace from the Arabian Nights, eating pomegranates and listening to her recite the Song of Solomon, he could not have been more captivated and seduced than he was sitting here on a park bench, listening to her explain how to administer an enema. He knew he was in love.

'You got all that?' Loretta was saying.

'Yes, I'm pretty sure, thank you. Stevie's father will be very grateful.'

'You want to try one some time?'

'You must be joking!' said Raschid and, to his relief, she burst out laughing. He joined in.

The laughter subsided. For a moment, neither spoke. Raschid said nothing because he could not see any further pretext for remaining and the only alternative was to say goodbye. Loretta said nothing because she was waiting for Raschid to suggest meeting up again. She could tell he wanted to but didn't realise how unused he was to going about it.

'It was really good of you to do this for Stevie,' she said finally.

'For his father.'

'Whatever. I was wondering . . .'

'Yes?' said Raschid, nervously, in a tone that implied he'd agree without reservation to whatever it was she'd been wondering.

'I was wondering if you felt like an ice-cream.'

'An ice-cream?'

'Yeah, there's this fantastic Italian place? It's not far, really . . .' She caught the look of bewilderment on his face. 'I mean, maybe you have plans for this afternoon, but . . .'

Raschid was dealing with all this as fast as he

could but it was new territory. She wanted to spend more time with him, that was clear. This uncovered daughter of the Great Satan, wanted to spend more time with him, an Afghan guerrilla on a mission to assassinate an enemy of the revolution (admittedly not one he wishes to fulfil, but even so . . .) and this girl wanted to eat ice-cream with him. And he, Holy Warrior and Scourge of the Infidel, could think of nothing nicer to do. But would she really want to do this if she knew his true identity? What the hell . . .

'Yes, sure.'

'Great. We can get a bus or walk.'

'I'm in no hurry.'

If he was being watched, his defence would be that consorting with an American female was a great cover story. Who would expect a fundamentalist assassin to do that? Admittedly he did feel a bit odd. It wasn't a terribly manly thing to do, after all – to spend an afternoon walking in parks and eating ice-cream with a woman, one who didn't walk three paces behind him either. Raschid wondered if he should assert his authority somehow, then decided he didn't know how to. What could he do – force her to wear a burqa and then go home? More importantly, he didn't want to. It felt utterly decadent and perverted, walking along with this woman as if she were a complete equal – decadent and perverted and utterly right. He just hoped they didn't run into anyone he had fought with in the mountains, that was all, and then reminded himself it was unlikely any Taliban militia would be living in the area Loretta said was called Primrose Hill.

The ice-creams were magnificent. Raschid noticed there were other couples in the café and didn't feel quite so emasculated. In fact, he felt he could get used to it; perhaps there was more to life than killing enemies of the faith. He suggested they have more ice-cream and felt his stomach clench with disappointment when Loretta declined. Then, by way of explanation, she patted her own stomach – her own flat, smooth, naked midriff – as she urged him to have one anyway and ordered a mineral water for herself.

'There was something else I wanted to ask you,' she said as they strolled slowly out into the street.

'What?'

'You know when we passed the zoo, and you said how you hated to see all those animals locked up?'

Loretta explained about the ostriches, their living conditions, and the plan to liberate them the following Saturday, during the wedding. 'And, well, we need help. To make sure the ostriches run in the right direction, to take out the security cameras, to create a diversion for the security guards . . .'

Raschid knew there was absolutely no way he

could get involved in something like this. What if he were arrested? It wouldn't take very long for the police to find out where he had been for the last ten years – and who knows what kind of clues they'd already picked up from James's flat, courtesy of Stevie's recklessness? On the other hand, how could he possibly refuse Loretta anything? What would she think of him if he said no? If he said yes, it would be because he loved Loretta and if his love for Loretta was right, then Providence would protect him. And if he were caught, then that, too, was what was meant to be.

'Of course I'll help you,' he said softly.

There was something in his tone that melted Loretta, but it also set off alarm bells. She wasn't quite sure what it meant but she had the feeling she was about to start living in interesting times. She smiled.

'That's great. I knew you wouldn't let me down.'

Raschid smiled too. He was recalling the time he had to run across open ground for a hundred metres under Russian fire to break out of an ambush, and telling himself what he was about to do now could not possibly be harder than that.

'I've got something else I want to tell you,' said Loretta.

'You can tell me anything,' Raschid was thrilled to find himself saying, and meaning it.

'Well,' continued Loretta, 'and this is going to sound really weird, but yesterday, when I met you in the pub, I . . . I'd seen you before, in a dream. And the dog pissing, that happened in my dream too. This is insane.'

'I have dreamt of you too, Loretta.'

They exchanged dreams. Raschid was a little unsettled to learn Loretta believed hers to be transmitted by a dolphin rather than the Supreme Being but, what the hell, something was happening.

'Look, Loretta, there's something you should know about me. I mean, I'm not used to this . . .' He wanted to say 'being in love'. '. . . this situation, but—'

He took her hand and groped for a way to tell the woman he wanted to spend the rest of his life with that he was in England to carry out a theocratically sanctioned assassination but a loud crunch of metal hitting something hard in the next street distracted them. Loretta stood perplexed as Raschid's instincts propelled him into an immediate crouch tight up against the nearest wall, alert, his arms protecting his head. He stood up again, smiling sheepishly.

'You *have* been in a war-zone recently, haven't you?' said Loretta, not accusing, just curious.

'Perhaps I should tell you about it another time,' said Raschid. 'Are you doing anything this evening?'

She pulled a face. 'I have to work. But it's kind of on your way home if you want to come up there with me. We'd maybe have time for some coffee first.'

They both smiled. Loretta waited for the kiss, which didn't come. She kind of liked his shyness and as they headed towards the bus stop, took his arm with both of hers, just to make him feel a little nervous, but delighted.

'Can I ask you not to mention this to Stevie, Loretta? You see, he's got a crush on you and, well, I don't know if you've ever seen him lose his temper but—'

'Who needs to know except us?'

'That's great.'

CHAPTER TWENTY-NINE

They decided to separate well before the supermarket, for discretion's sake.

'Well, see you Saturday.' He paused, then added in a timid voice, 'Maybe before?'

'I'd like that.'

'Enjoy your shift.'

'OK, I should be going. Thank you for a very pleasant day.'

'Thank you.'

He was walking away. 'Raschid, you have my mobile number, right?'

He turned and nodded, perfunctorily. Then smiled and blew her a kiss. He watched her walk across the car park, thrilled. A new life was opening up for him. All he had to do was explain that he and Stevie were supposedly accomplices in a murder plot, and find a way of persuading her to disappear with him to somewhere on earth where they could never be traced, to live together happily but with the possibility of a revenge execution hanging over them forever. He headed back down the road and then stopped. He needed some more toothpaste.

Inside the supermarket Raschid was disturbed and impressed by the rows and rows of shelves and the overwhelming attack on his senses – the last time he'd seen so many bright colours he was being mortared by a group of neighbouring tribesmen. In fact, he wasn't sure which was more frightening, being under fire or standing in this... well, supermarket, though it was like no other supermarket he'd ever been in before. The atrium with its fountains and muted, slowly changing spotlights, the crowds of people, the strange, impersonal yet powerfully rhythmic music, the security guards in smart uniforms moving among the shoppers... it reminded him of the villain's lair in some old James Bond film.

Inside, writing yelled at him in so many loud colours he could barely make sense of it all. There was so much of everything... and the amount of *things* was practically supernatural compared to what he'd been used to. He had wanted to catch a secret glimpse of Loretta at work, to see how she moved and walked and did everyday things when he was not there, but it was too much, all this *stuff*. He paid for his toothpaste and left.

Stevie was standing on the walkway above the ostrich

pens, casually chatting to One-Eyed Jack, the head storeman.

'They're dangerous bastards these ostriches you know. Have your guts out with one kick.'

Stevie was impressed. He could think of a few people he wouldn't mind seeing this claim tested out on.

'They let them wander about up in Scotland, in the mountains. Then, you know how they round them up?'

Stevie shrugged. 'Sheepdogs?'

One-Eyed Jack shook his balding head, and lifted a canister from its wall-mounting.

'A fire-extinguisher.'

Jack shook his head again.

'Ain't a fire extinguisher. This is full of sex hormones. *You* can't smell it, *I* can't smell it, but you spray out a little cloud of this, and to a male ostrich it smells just like a female ostrich on heat. They can smell it for miles. Drives them mad, it does, horny as hell. When they get a whiff of this they just come running. If they don't trip over their hard-ons.' He cackled and leered. 'And this other one,' he tapped another canister, 'does the same for the bird birds. Brilliant what they think of, innit?'

'Innit, innit.'

'We keep these ones for if they escape. Like I say, they'd kick a man's guts out just like that.'

'Right.'

'I'm trying to teach this one to talk.' Jack pointed at one of the birds in the male enclosure who was in fact staring at them.

'All right, mate?' called One-Eyed Jack. 'He ain't that quick a learner though.'

'That's what you think,' thought Spartacus.

'I thought you were on the minicabs today, Stevie,' said Loretta when she ran into him in the canteen a few minutes later.

'Car broke down. Then when I got home they rung up 'cos Billy's off sick so I'm covering his shift.' He didn't mention that he'd smashed his car into a bus stop earlier that afternoon when he'd seen Loretta and Raschid holding hands in the street and had accelerated off in a seething jealous rage.

CHAPTER THIRTY

That same evening, Sid was due to meet Stride Boswell for dinner. At lunchtime a dispatch rider delivered a package to her office guaranteed to ensure that neither of them would have any appetite for the magnificent food that would be laid before them at Bibendum, nor the slightest compunction in leaving it undisturbed on their plates. Buying packages like this one was Cressida's way of diverting wealth from the developed world into the pockets of poor South American peasants. She could actually mount this argument with a straight face and also used it as her reason for never giving to Comic Relief.

She opened the package and transferred one of the little plastic envelopes of white powder into a smaller Jiffy Bag and addressed it to Stride Boswell, care of his hotel in Covent Garden, and then asked her assistant to order a bike.

They had arranged to begin their evening in Pristina, the latest members-only club in Soho. According to the owners, the place was 'conceived as a new concept in clubs, keeping the creative elite of the world's hottest city aware of the dark side of the spiritual Zeitgeist of the times even when they're having fun: a crucial synergy of pleasure and *engagement*. Plugged in, even when we're hanging out.' Five pence was donated to UNICEF for every absinthe cocktail sold.

Sid got there ten minutes before the agreed time – which shows exactly how important to her Stride Boswell was. She swiped her smart card (assymetrically designed to represent a piece of shrapnel) through the electronic lock and picked her way carefully down the bare wooden steps into the dimly lit bar, apparently an exact replica of one of the chicest bomb shelters in Sarajevo which had always been plentifully supplied with black-market *palinka* and *slibowiz* even at the height of the siege.

She was staggered to see Stride Boswell already seated at the bar, sipping an Atom Bomb (absinthe and brandy in equal measures) and smoking a large Romeo y Julietta. When he stood up to greet her his head almost touched the bare wooden beams. He was well over six feet and built like a football player. Indeed, he was proud of having played tight end for whichever Ivy League college he had attended – Sid could never remember – and when he embraced her she seemed to disappear, so that he looked like some strange four-limbed alien. This indeed was exactly how he looked at that moment to a young man in the corner who had been drinking absinthe since late afternoon to celebrate having been introduced to Jane Birkin earlier that day by his lunching companion, a television producer who knew everyone who had been anyone since 1968 but didn't look nearly old enough to. The young man looked at the four-limbed alien, turned slightly green, looked at his absinthe, stopped talking about his idea for a novel for the first time in about four hours, and headed to the gents rather too quickly to be cool enough for membership here, as the barman would put it later.

'Sid!' drawled Boswell, 'Great to see you looking great!' He released her. 'I got here early just to see if I was as important to you as I think I am. And I am! Ten minutes early! You flatter me, ha ha ha!'

'Great to see you too, Stride. You're looking fabulous.'

'Yes, I am. I'm feeling very centred these days. Kambucha mushrooms and alfalfa juice. Changed my life. What are you drinking? The Atom Bombs are very good.'

'Sounds good.'

Stride turned to the barman, who, with all the attentiveness and professionalism required of someone working behind the hottest coolest bar in the hottest coolest city in the world had already heard him and pretended not to. Then he felt Sid's gimlet eyes burning into his head and snapped to it, wondering just exactly how she did that.

Sid and Stride skirmished around each other for the first cocktail or two, affecting polite yet interested small talk about mutual acquaintances and projects and product and exactly where various performers and producers were on the thermometer this season. Stride was delighted to be in a city where you could smoke tobacco in public.

Sid was delighted to see Stride in such a good mood. You never knew if you were going to get the affable off-duty man or the dreaded persona that had earned him the nickname The Pink Grizzly. Not that he was ever really off-duty. The casual affability was just an act which he had learnt from watching ordinary humans being casual and affable for real; just a trap to lure out indiscretions or undue familiarity which would be registered and avenged at a later date. Like most show business executives he was an android spy, living amongst men and women to exploit their emotions for profit and power. A spy was never off-guard – the war was always on, and had to be won. He respected Sid because he had never caught her out. She was a replicant too – they could spot each other. But the deadly game went on because, although they were both leeching the humans, that didn't mean they were on the same side, just that they were hunting the same prey. Evidently both thinking these same thoughts, there was a lull in the conversation and they looked into each other's eyes.

'It's good to see you,' they said simultaneously, and then laughed.

The young man who had met Jane Birkin turned his head at the noise and whispered to his companion, asking if it was just his imagination or did the two people at the bar with their mouths wide open really have little vampire fangs? He decided his only hope was to order another absinthe and have the faith it would carry him out the other side of this chilly paranoid flush.

Finally Sid summoned the bill with a deadly glance and they climbed the wooden staircase in search of a cab.

'Wow,' said Stride, as the fresh air hit them. 'I'm bombed... Bombed in Pristina... I get it – hey, that's pretty good!'

Sid reminded herself he was one of the most important comedy producers in the world and laughed just in time.

'So how is Mr James Randall?' asked Boswell once they were in the cab.

'He's fine,' lied Sid. 'Terrific. And very excited

about meeting you. I've arranged a dinner for Saturday night.'

'Perfect.'

'Somewhere intimate.'

'Even more perfect. Oh and thank you for your gift. Perked me up just fine this afternoon.'

'You're very welcome. I think it's rather a good year. In fact I have six bottles set aside for James,' she added, and made a mental note to arrange it first thing in the morning.

'Sounds like it should be a fun party.'

'I hope so,' said Sid.

CHAPTER THIRTY-ONE

Friday night at his mother's and Henry's having a terrible time. They've watched *Countdown* every afternoon, they've drunk tea, they've discussed the most scandalous article in the *Daily Telegraph* and resisted the desire to contest Draconian solutions for every problem facing humanity over boiled eggs and locally-made organic sausages. They have had the *Parish Magazine* decoded to reveal its hidden mysteries about who was flirting with the vicar like a common tart in order to get the most prestigious Sundays to prepare the Church Flowers. They've heard how the retired insurance salesman from the Highlands had always seemed suspicious from the very start and there he was already a senior Sidesman and he's a Jekyll-and-Hyde character he is and then, bingo, if Mrs Mitchell didn't see him taking a drink out of a hip flask at the Under Tens Mass Spice Girls Impersonators' Evening Slide Show.

They have gone to bed at ten-thirty and politely

complied with requests to turn off the film they're watching immediately as the sound travels at this time of night. They have gardened, shopped and ignored comments about how the washing-up liquid was a different size to the one she usually gets. And they have also experienced conversation upon conversation – a monologue would be more accurate – from Henry's mother about James.

'Does he phone you regularly then?' she asked in a tone of surprise and indignation. 'He doesn't have time to talk to me on the phone! He's far too busy. I get it all from the papers. Don't you follow his career?'

'Of course we do. I see him just about every week. It's just that . . .' Henry wanted to say, 'It's me who phones you twice a week and comes up once a month and looks after you, and you've never shown the slightest interest in anything either Elizabeth or I do.'

'What?'

'Never mind.' He was waiting to address the issue on a more gentle tack when his mother said, 'All right then. Let's watch one of his videos.'

Ten minutes later this same reactionary crone was howling with laughter at some of the most risque and confrontational comedy ever to be shown on British television. Material that had offended just about everybody at some point and people like his mother one hundred per cent of the time. And here she was lapping it up, implying a knowledge of the jargon of sexual perversion and drug abuse which suggested either that she had led a radical secret life in her youth, or that she was just laughing ignorantly because everyone else did. Henry was so appalled in so many different ways that he jumped up and said he was going to the pub and that Elizabeth was coming with him.

Henry's mother gave him a knowing sneer. This was the unfeeling and ungrateful boy who lurked beneath the grovelling exterior. She'd been on to him from the very beginning; every little move he'd ever made from the very very beginning – even the way he had come out of her hurt her – had shown that he was trying to make up for the fact he really wanted to kill her. What perverted creature has murder fantasies about his own mother, for heaven's sake? He wasn't even capable of a proper Oedipus Complex. No wonder he and his wife had never conceived. Although they probably wouldn't, just to spite her.

Henry and Elizabeth left, saying they'd be about half an hour. After two large whiskies Henry was really stoked up.

'I can't fucking believe it, Elizabeth . . . it's relentless. Worse than ever. And that little twat gets all the fucking credit. He hasn't been to see her in years.

I'm going to ring him. Give me your phone – come on, Elizabeth, just give it to me. I'm going to phone him now. If he's cried off tomorrow – and I bet he has – another two large whiskies, please – if he's cried off – thank you – if he's cried off, I'll fucking kill him.'

When the phone rang James was lying on the sofa with a big spliff listening to *Blonde on Blonde*, trying to pick out key phrases with which to sweep Loretta off her feet in a whirlwind of romantic seduction and wondering how much it was going to hurt on Saturday night when he furthered his career by submitting to Stride Boswell's lust.

He could tell Henry had been drinking, and tried to remain calm and matter of fact.

'Oh, hi . . . yeah, everything's fine . . . I was going to call you about that . . . Actually I'm afraid I can't make it. I've got to cook dinner for an American producer . . . Well, I'm sorry but it's really important. It could be the big one, the one that's going to change my life forever . . . I'm sorry you feel that way but in this business you have to take your opportunities when they come along . . . I'm *not* happy about it . . . do you think I enjoy sacrificing my private life like this? It's just the way it is . . . There's no need to be like that Henry, I'll make it up to her – is she there? Oh, right. Well, look, I'll call her tomorrow morning . . . You're going to kill me? Join the queue . . . Same to you.'

Henry slammed the phone down and the other customers stared as he swore loudly.

'The little wanker!'

He went to the bar for another whisky and the barman politely suggested he might have had enough. They left quietly, Henry inwardly cursing James for once more causing him grief.

James immediately forgot about his mother and brother and went back to thinking about the raid. He had never actually engaged in anything as dangerous as this before. The limits of his direct action in the past had been student marches, demonstrations and, of course, scathing satirical routines on stages and down camera barrels. He couldn't help thinking that with this, actually doing something unannounced and unsanctioned by the authorities, there was a chance of getting hurt or arrested. He was doing something that wasn't *allowed* and he tried to ignore the fact this was making him nervous and, worse, reluctant.

He reminded himself that even if he were arrested it would only enhance his reputation, and, that night, focused on this thought as a meditation to send him to sleep. He tried to ignore the sneaking suspicion that his whole professional career had been one long attempt to act in denial of who he really was – a self-centred reactionary who wanted a luxurious life and hated himself for it. Nothing he did was for real; it was intended to create an image in the world of the ideal James Randall that he wanted to be. Yet he used this image only to get the things that he wanted to have – fame, money, adulation – things which were much more important than the process by which he attained them.

But what if he got arrested now, just before he made contact with the mighty Stride Boswell? It could screw everything up. Radical credentials were all very well, but not when you were looking to go mainstream and global. So why not just bale out? Did he really want Loretta so badly? It wasn't as if he'd ever have to see her again. She deserved letting down – not only had she said she wasn't going to sleep with him, she'd told him there was someone else. Did that kind of flagrant honesty really deserve to go unpunished?

Then again, James realised he really did want to be the kind of person his audience thought he was, and this was a chance to take some genuine action for once, to set against all the words and posturing. He should do it precisely *because* his meeting with Boswell was so imminent. The degradation he was prepared to put himself through for his career would surely be offset by this final act of his radical phase, an act that would be genuinely unselfish, genuinely risky, genuinely idealistic. Heroic. And – who could say? – he might still win Loretta round. How could she refuse him, for heaven's sake, when he wanted her? If he wanted something he got it, that was the way of the world. Couldn't she see what an incredible person he was? He managed to go to sleep now, holding on to the thought that tomorrow he would be a hero. And comforted by the knowledge that, if the worst came to the worst, he would be able to afford extremely good lawyers.

At the same time, Stevie was working a night shift. He casually examined the locks and code pads for the warehouse doors, satisfying himself he'd be able to open them in the shortest possible time the following morning. Making sure no one was around, he switched on the machine that beamed microwaves into the ostrich pens and left it running. He wasn't sure what the effect would be, but felt sure that irradiated ostriches would, in some way or other, be more dangerous and cause more chaos than non-irradiated ones. And he slipped one of the pheremone canisters into his rucksack.

CHAPTER THIRTY-TWO

Henry woke up on Saturday morning with his brain trying to expand to twice its normal size and his skull determined to crush it to the size of a pea. He knew that when he opened his eyes, the sudden inrush of light would increase the pain, but with his eyes closed he would have no chance of finding his way to the kitchen and a glass of water.

He kept his lids as closed as he could, groped for his faithful faded old dressing-gown and shuffled downstairs.

The clock in the kitchen said ten past six. He fumbled for a glass in the cupboard, relying all the time more on touch and memory than sight – his eyelids stuck together when he tried to open them wider but he lacked sufficient saliva to moisten them. He gulped down four or five glasses from the running tap and then sat thankfully at the kitchen table. He could feel his body slowly being brought back to a life of sorts. He became aware of the birds calling to each other outside in the woods and, as his eyes unstuck themselves, he enjoyed the dawn light in the east-facing window and the stillness.

Blackbird has spoken. Another day. So far so good. Peace and quiet. In a little while I'll make a pot of tea and a bacon sandwich and no one up yet fantastic don't have to talk to anyone for hours just listen to the birds oh no I don't believe it . . .

His stomach had just ambushed him, but somehow, in the split second after the first lurching jump of his guts, he managed to make it to the sink just before the wave of vomit jetted up and out of his mouth. It was bilious, acid. Henry was angry because here he was vomiting and there was nothing in his stomach to emit, save its own juices and two pints of water. It was as he hung exhausted over the sink, tap running, mouth agape, with a long cloying string of saliva endlessly lengthening itself into the gurgling water that – of course – his mother came in to make a cup of tea.

'Good morning,' she said brightly. 'You're up early for once. Oh, I see. How charming.'

He was about to defend himself, or at least beg her not to speak so loudly, when he felt another surge of bile being squeezed cruelly out of his stomach lining. *Why?* he asked himself. *Why so much? And how?* And now his mother nagged at his back.

'I won't make it to the bathroom!'

He bent back to the sink for another spurt of acid

searing up and then down his nose. *What have I done to deserve this?*

He rinsed his face, swilled out the sink.

'What a lovely start to my birthday,' said his mother. 'First you tell me James isn't coming, then you – do this in my kitchen.'

'It's hardly my fault James isn't coming.'

'He's never – done that in my kitchen sink.'

'I doubt he's ever been here to see it let alone *throw up* in it.' He deliberately leant on the verb to challenge her primness. 'And it's not my fault he's not here.'

'I expect he has his reasons. Although if he's had to put up with you for a week getting drunk and . . . being sick in the kitchen sink, I shouldn't wonder he couldn't face being up here at the same time as you.'

Raschid was awoken on the Saturday morning by the sound of Stevie shouting at his father.

Les was lying on the sofa, writhing in pain, red-faced and sweating, a hot water bottle on his stomach, which creaked and rumbled like ice-floes thawing. Every so often a small fart would escape and Stevie would be forced to back away by the foul Stygian stench.

'Why don't you go to the doctor's?'

'I don't need no doctor. He won't do no good. All he ever does is tell me I shouldn't eat nothing and give up me fags. What kind of life is that?'

'But you ain't had a shit for weeks, Dad! He'll give you something for it.'

'Get away from that phone!'

There was the sound of a struggle and the telephone was thrown across the room.

'Fucking hell, Dad, you've broke the fucking phone.'

'You better give me your mobile then, ain't yer.'

'What you mean give you my mobile?'

'How else am I going to order a pizza?'

'There's loads of food in the house.'

'I ain't cooking. I'd have to wash up first. You know I get out of breath.'

'When you get back from work tonight I want this place cleaned up. It's like a fucking pigsty.'

'I'm going out, ain't I?' said Les defiantly.

'You're going out?'

'I'm coming with you. To the wedding. Up the Supermarket.'

'You need a doctor.'

'It ain't fair... I wrote to them and everything, said I could be a lucky wedding mascot.'

'You what?'

'Everybody knows it's good luck to have a fat bloke at your wedding. They're jolly people, fat people are. I'd add to the atmosphere.'

'Yeah, right. Kind of atmosphere you'd add everyone'd be fucking dead.'

Another huge muffled explosion racked Les's insides, but failed to escape. Les moaned in agony as the bubbling sound rose and fell.

'Look, Dad, at least try the enema kit. I took you through it last night and Loretta wrote out the instructions. Here.'

Les snatched the leaflet, crushed it up and slung it on to the floor.

'I ain't sticking nothing up my arse for nobody. I'll have a shit when I'm good and ready.'

'But, Dad, it's been weeks.'

'So? People have different metabolisms.'

There was a long loud fart. 'That's better,' declared Les triumphantly. 'See, nothing wrong with my guts.'

'Fucking hell,' said Stevie, choking. 'I'm going outside to work on me car.'

'Get us an aspirin, will yer?'

'I'll see if Raschid's got some. Raschid, got any aspirin, mate?'

As he opened Raschid's door, the foul air followed him in and fell on Raschid palpably, like a wet invisible methane blanket. Raschid had hoped to have a lie-in but now he rushed to the window, slid the lower frame up and thrust his head out, gasping for fresh air.

'On the chest of drawers,' he said, not even daring to look round. After five or so minutes, he inhaled deeply, held his breath, stepped away from the window to grab some clothes and dressed with his head back out of the window.

Stevie was outside reattaching the front bumper to his car with garden wire and string. 'Need a hand?' said Raschid, sprinting out of the front door.

'Yeah, thanks – you could hold it for me. Sorry about me dad by the way.'

'He's not well, is he?'

'Can say that again. Won't fucking listen though, will he?'

'What time are we meeting at the café?'

'Loretta said she'd be there about ten. You sure you want to get involved? I mean, she's my mate but it's a bit risky for you, innit?'

Raschid knew Stevie was right, but there was no way he could let Loretta down.

'Well, I promised Loretta – you know, the way she described how those birds are being kept, I couldn't say no.' He knew it didn't sound convincing.

'Yeah. Right,' said Stevie, looping wire round the bumper and then back through a rust hole in the wing, not even bothering to hide his sarcasm.

Alan Mason, Aldingtons' store manager, gazed down proudly from the ochre-tinted windows of his office on the third floor. The car park was looking magnificent, for a car park.

Bunting had been strung from lamppost to lamppost, a triumphal arch of plastic orchids (available from the gardening section at £9.99 a bunch) had been erected, spelling out the message 'Congratulations to Amanda and Lawrence from Aldingtons' Superstore.'

Men in T-shirts and workboots swarmed back and forth from large trucks, setting up sound equipment on the ceremonial podium. The air was alive with the persistent hum of a fleet of council street-sweeping buggies. A couple of men in suits scuttled about, beckoning to various members of the workforce, who did their best not to look completely pissed off as they pretended they hadn't already worked out what to do before their bosses told them.

James was trying clothes on in the mirror. He needed to impress Loretta from the off, that was the crucial thing. He needed to look cool, hard, streetwise. He had found an old pair of Henry's Doc Martens, crushed out of shape under a pile of other stuff in the bottom of the wardrobe, which hurt his feet. But they looked good and battered that was the important thing. They gave the impression of having walked every mile of every demo and march that had been held in the last twenty years. He had combat trousers – genuine Army surplus, none of the designer stuff he usually wore – which he had bought the day before and slept in to rough them up a little. Then a hooded fleece and, over that, his favourite well-worn and voluminous denim jacket. It looked good in the mirror. He pulled on his woollen hat and tried to get the same hunch in the shoulders that Daniel Day Lewis had in *My Beautiful Laundrette*. He was disappointed that his stubble was not more obvious, despite having not shaved for two days, but there was nothing he could do about that now.

As usual, he'd got up later than he'd intended, and realised there was no time to do any preparation for the evening's all-important meal. He quickly checked the freezer and saw several plastic boxes of home-made meals all neatly labelled in Elizabeth's immaculate hand. There would be plenty to choose from after the raid. He made a mental note to buy some roll-ups on his way and set out to become a fearless eco-warrior and put things right between him and the gorgeous Loretta. He had to have her now – because he wanted to – and her not feeling the same was a massive insult to his sense of the way the world worked. One more quick session in front of the mirror perfecting his scowling expressions and he was out the door.

Loretta had told James to meet her at a café just down the road from the supermarket. When James walked in she was having a cup of tea with an Asian guy. James immediately felt a hot pulse of adrenalin when he realised the Asian fitted Loretta's description of the man she preferred to him. James suppressed an urge to punch the guy in the face, and told himself it was because he abhorred violence. Actually, it was more to do with his natural cowardice. He grunted out 'Hey, all right?' as nonchalantly and street-credibly as he could, and Loretta introduced the two men. James acknowledged Raschid with a solemn repetitive nodding before offering his hand and saying 'Safe, man' as he sat down.

That's the last thing you are, pal, thought Raschid as he realised in concealed amazement and alarm who this extra reinforcement was. 'Safe?' Wait till Stevie comes out of the toilet. Why couldn't this James guy just piss off out of his life? What was the meaning in the way their fates were constantly intertwined?

When Stevie appeared and saw James, Raschid was extremely impressed at how he registered his presence without the merest flicker of surprise. The Stevie who trashed James's flat would have jumped upon him there and then – obviously Raschid had been successful in impressing on Stevie the need for restraint. Again, Loretta performed the introductions and Stevie actually smiled as he said, 'All right, mate, nice to have you along,' and gave no hint of what was going on in his head, not making the slightest eye contact with Raschid. Who could say, maybe

Stevie would hold himself in check all morning and James would leave with his life? Nonetheless Raschid would have preferred James to go home now.

But how would he explain that to Loretta? This was not the time to blow his cover. He sensed that Loretta might not be overly impressed if she found out he was here as a hit-man. He needed the leisure to break it to her gently. He couldn't think of any plausible pretext for excluding James.

James sat and said nothing, which was a novel experience for him. He rolled a cigarette and said, 'Tea, please' without looking up at the waitress. Stevie asked if he could bum a fag, and would James please roll it for him? James was happy to. He felt he was doing a pretty good impression of a dangerous and experienced radical activist – this weird-looking punk with the metal in his face and the broken teeth clearly accepted him, even if the Asian guy was giving off less friendly vibes. That was cool. James would just give them back, in spades.

Yvette stormed in and crashed down on to one of the seats at the next table. The black-and-white Palestinian kaffiyeh draped round her shoulders swept the sugar shaker off the table as she turned to join the conversation. She didn't acknowledge in any way the sound of smashing glass as it hit the floor.

'I'm really fucking looking forward to this. I can't

wait to see those fucking wankers getting their big fucking day all fucked up.' That pretty much covered the ideological basis of the mission, thought Loretta. Now for the praxis.

'Coffee,' Yvette commanded the waitress when she approached with a dustpan and brush. Loretta tugged at the collar of Yvette's black denim jacket. 'So that's what happened to my coat,' she said, daring to sound a little angry.

'You can have it back. Just went with what I was wearing last night. I didn't think you'd get so fucking uptight about it!'

'It's OK, Yvette,' replied Loretta gently. 'I'm fine with this sweater, I just wish you'd asked, that's all.'

Loretta waited for the waitress to deliver Yvette's coffee and withdraw again, and then pulled them into a huddle to outine the plan.

Stevie would spin a story about having left his watch in his locker and would slip inside to open the ostrich pens and the loading bay exits. Then he'd shoo the birds out. James, Loretta and Raschid would be outside making lots of noise to drive the ostriches in the direction of the wedding podium. After that, they could just retreat in the chaos.

Stevie decided not to mention the pheremone spray; he would delay his gratification until afterwards when everyone would comment with delight on how directly the ostriches had all headed straight for the podium and how ferocious they were when they got there. That's when he would reveal his secret. He would do it modestly, almost casually, and, with any luck, Loretta would then see who was the superior warrior between himself and Raschid... for now he just felt the shape of the canister in the inside pocket of his parka. Then he looked at James and a smile oozed across his face, so broad it made the two bolts in his eyebrows lightly tap against each other.

Loretta looked at her watch.

'Time to go, I guess.'

They filed out. Stevie stood directly behind James while they waited at a pelican crossing. As an articulated lorry changed into third gear almost alongside them, Stevie surreptitiously directed a few short bursts of the pheremone spray on to the back of James's jacket and then peeled away from the others.

'Gonna take the car down. Wanna lift?'

'We'll walk. I think it's better if we arrive separately.'

'All right, can't be too careful. Later, yeah?'

'It's colder than I thought,' said Loretta.

James seized his moment and offered his jacket.

'I've got a fleece on underneath, yeah?'

She accepted with a smile.

❋ ❋ ❋

It only took Stevie two minutes in the car. He parked up and headed towards the stockroom, via the back of the podium, spraying the fabrics and flowers and the banners the whole time as he walked along.

In the stock pens, One-Eyed Jack had just had his coffee and a read of the paper and was pouring the specially blended ostrich feed into the troughs, as ever attempting to engage them in conversation. Then he noticed the geiger counter above the microwave flashing frantically. It took him a few moments to take in what was happening and then he ran to the internal phone.

'Hello, security? Look, you'd better get someone down to the ostrich pens. Tell Mr Mason someone's left the irradiator on all night. The birds are all over the safety level.' Behind him was a mechanical clicking and whirring and clunking. He looked round. 'Fuck me, they're escaping! The ostriches are radioactive and they're getting out!'

It's like this: when Stevie turns the irradiator on, he doesn't know what effect dosing the birds up with radioactivity will have. Essentially, all the extra subatomic particles buzzing about inside them and around them and through them start to play havoc with anything electronic. And they've been biffing and shaking and jostling the electronic locks on the ostrich pens all night. Finally the electronic locks decide they've had enough and malfunction. Then the ostriches are out and so too are the toxic particles. The particles are like a swarm of tiny drunken football fans, looking for anything with an electronic pulse to screw over – mobile phones and bleepers start ringing and buzzing ... *click* go the locks on the outer doors and the ostriches, led by Spartacus, run for the light ... car alarms are going off now and timers and operating systems in cameras ... digital watches start going backwards ...

Standing outside, Raschid, Yvette, James and Loretta are taken by surprise. There's no need for them to do any work as the electronic whoops and whistles are thickened with cries of human anguish and distress as thirty horny ostriches with martial arts skills stampede towards the rostrum, knocking men and women out of the way, latching on to anything warm with a pulse and trying to fuck it.

In accordance with the infinite-monkeys-and-typewriters theory, the electronic announcement board suddenly throws together a random collection of letters so that Mrs Zbigniew Kryzwicki, a Polish lady who has been in Britain for sixty years, is able to read in her native tongue news of her long-lost brother and his fondness for apricot ice-cream and his collection of odour-eaters, along with a new quadratic equation and a telephone number which when she returns home she will call; her brother, whom she last saw in 1939, will answer and there will be a tearful reunion six months later in Lodz, at which Mrs Kryzwicki will arrive bearing gifts of rare odour-eaters and they will sit down to a meal of apricot ice-cream and toast the miraculous announcement board. Fifty years later, the miracle-working electronic noticeboard will be investigated by a Papal Legate with a view to possible beatification but will be pronounced just a noticeboard that went weird once.

Alan Mason looks out over his splendid car park, now transformed into a suitable setting for launching a loving young couple into permanent bonded bliss, not to mention a setting for pushing the profile of the store head, shoulders and hips above that of his competitors. Life is good. Then he sees the crowd lurch back in fright at something he cannot see. He steps closer to the window, looking down. The crowd is running from ostriches. His phone rings and he takes in information with mounting horror.

Even as the raiders begin to mingle with the outer edge of the crowd, they hear screams and confusion from the direction of the podium. As the people in front of them stampede and scatter they can see the ostriches rushing hither and yon.

The raiders' plan is going better than they could have hoped for, and without them even being involved. But Yvette is not to be denied. It is not enough for her that the ostriches are causing chaos, she must be part of it. She sees her immediate section supervisor running for cover and launches a flying kick to his groin. The guests of honour are falling and jumping off the podium, the bride is tearing at her hair (lovingly coiffured in-store by Sharee, the premier stylist, earlier that morning) and the groom is looking for representatives of the company to blame, or punch. Onlookers are falling into flowerbeds, cowering behind cars and running into the store in blind panic.

The pheremone spray has dispersed into the atmosphere and the birds are shooting off in all directions.

Realising there is no need for him to get into the storeroom Stevie runs to the car and drives back amongst the panicking screaming crowd to join up with the others.

An ostrich is running towards them. However they try to evade it, the bird changes direction and comes straight at them – specifically for Loretta. Its beak catches her full in the forehead, she clutches her face, blood spurts through her fingers. Raschid pulls a bucket out of a rubbish bin and hurls it at the creature. James lights his Zippo and waves it at the bird, lights his newspaper and uses this to repulse the next attack. Loretta is picking up and throwing bits of rubbish at the bird as Raschid continues to thrust at it with the bucket and James, inspired by his desire to compete with Raschid for Loretta's affections, is still waving the charred newspaper and the Zippo. But the ostrich is insane and keeps lunging forward until it is hit smack in the body by Stevie in the Nissan. The bird drops down, twitching, with a clearly broken leg, but still lashing out with its beak.

More birds are approaching. Stevie opens the doors, one of which falls off, and yells for everyone to get in. Raschid tries to stop James, but James misinterprets Raschid's intention, thinks it's to do with their rivalry over Loretta and is having none of it. 'She's got my jacket, mate,' is James's retort.

Alan Mason begins to compute the full magnitude of the problem. In a nutshell, it is this: he is the manager of a supermarket which has just allowed thirty radioactive ostriches, highly skilled in Chinese martial arts, to escape into London in full view of the local press. Without thinking, he lights a cigarette directly underneath a smoke sensor which happens to be the only electronic device for miles which is still working normally, and it begins raining in his office.

Doubled up in terrible pain, Les lies on the floor, writhing and twitching. The explosions continue in his bowels, twisting and wrenching his guts, none of the gas managing to escape but, building up pressure, crushing his internal organs, stretching and tearing at his muscles. He is beginning to regret having eaten what he did for a mid-morning snack, but he was hungry and the tins of marrow-fat peas and baked beans were all he could find in the cupboard. Apart from a year-old box of dried figs which he ate anyway. Such is the pain, however, that Les is searching the scraps of paper on the floor for the enema-instruction leaflet.

'My place is nearest, we'll clean her up there,' declares Stevie.

Raschid is tearing his shirt for a temporary bandage. 'We need to stop at a chemist for some first-aid stuff.'

'All right, mate.'

'You let them out a little early. We weren't ready.'

'I never let them out at all. They was doing it themselves – don't ask me how.'

'It worked out pretty good – apart from Loretta's head.'

'What happened to Yvette?'

'She was fighting one of the managers last I saw.'

'At least she's happy then.'

'They trashed the podium.' Loretta is giggling with adrenalised excitement. 'I'm fine, really – it's not that deep, is it, Raschid? Always bleeds a lot, the head, but it's not too serious. I mean, I feel OK.'

'It doesn't look bad now I've cleaned it up a bit.'

'We didn't even have to do a thing to make them go that way!'

'I know, like they were programmed or something.'

'I did have something to do with that,' says Stevie proudly. 'I'll tell you when we get inside.'

CHAPTER THIRTY-THREE

Spartacus has not followed the rest of his comrades towards the smell of the pheremone spray. Just before the doors opened, he had stuck his beak deep into the layer of ostrich dung that lay all over the floor of their cage, using the smell to counteract the alluring sexual perfume. So, while the others run towards the podium and make it a day to remember for the wedding couple in ways they had not expected, Spartacus runs for freedom. He crosses the car park and hits the road at a pelican crossing which, thanks to the renegade electrons he is emitting, immediately turns green. He sees trees and bushes, leaps a small fence and finds himself on a railway track. Thanks to the cost-cutting efficiency of the railway company that owns this stretch, the foliage which runs alongside the line has not been trimmed back for nearly two years. Spartacus disappears into the undergrowth.

The car pulls up outside Stevie's house.

'Well, I'd better be going,' says James, who is beginning to realise he's not going to have time to seduce Loretta today. 'Nice to meet you all.'

'You can't shoot off just like that, mate,' cries Stevie. 'Come in and have a cup of tea, you're a comrade now after all.'

'OK,' says James, mostly to piss off Loretta's Asian boyfriend who is looking well fed up.

You stupid git, thinks Raschid as he follows the rest of them towards the house.

Les hears them coming and is furious. Partly because he doesn't like visitors generally, but also because he's now attempting to put the enema kit into operation. He has warm coffee ready in a bucket, but has been struggling, through a mixture of general physical clumsiness and a more specific inhibition, to get the nozzle of the tube sufficiently far into his anus. Having discovered there is no Vaseline in the medicine cupboard, he is making his way stark naked from the bathroom to the kitchen in search of some cooking oil or margarine when he hears the visitors approach. Moving as fast as he can, he just makes it back into the bathroom before anyone sees him, and sits down on the toilet to recover from his exertions with a quick fag.

'What the fuckin' ell's goin' on you little shitbag? Inviting half the bleedin' street back here when I'm trying to get a tube up me arse, for Christ's sake,' mutters Les to himself. 'Can't a man get a shred of privacy in his own house?'

Stevie turns to Raschid in the hall.

'Right. We gotta get Loretta out of here and get him to stay behind, yeah?'

'We can't do it here, Stevie. Even if Loretta leaves, she'll be able to say she saw him here with us.'

'Well, we can't piss about forever waiting to be sure we don't get caught. I mean, who cares about that? This is holy work we're doing, man – I mean is it a coincidence that the guy gets delivered into our hands? Actually . . . I reckon we're under divine protection. We could probably chop him up in broad daylight in the middle of the street, right, and nothing would happen to us.'

'I am in charge here. So do nothing unless I tell you.'

'I know that.'

Les yells from the bathroom for Stevie to give him a hand.

Raschid dabs at Loretta's forehead with cotton wool, applies a plaster and she kisses him on the nose.

James decides he's beaten, but can't stop having one last try at Loretta anyway. 'If everything's OK then I ought to be going, I got a few things to do. But, Loretta, I was wondering—'

'Just go,' says Raschid.

James is indignant. 'All right, all right, no need to be like that . . . let me get my jacket.'

Loretta hands it to him. 'Thanks for that, James.'

'Go now, James,' says Raschid.

James ignores him and taking his jacket back from Loretta, pulls a notebook from the pocket, and scribbles in it hastily.

'OK. Well, Loretta—'

'James.'

'Look, I'm cooking dinner for a few people next Wednesday,' improvises James, 'here's my address, if you want to come.'

He tears the page from the book and hands it to her.

'James. Go. Your life is in danger.'

Oh well, thinks James, at least I pissed the guy off.

As James turns round, Stevie shoves a gun in his face.

'Yeah. All your fucking lives are in danger. You're not fucking going anywhere, my son. Sit down.'

Raschid shouts, 'Stevie.'

'And you can fucking shut up as well. Betraying the cause, you slag. And you—' pointing the gun again at James, 'thought you could take the piss out the Taliban and get away wiv it, did yer? You fucking toerag! We are everywhere, you scumbag.'

'Look...'

James is in a state of shock, and only beginning to work out what's happening. Someone is pointing a gun at him and talking about 'doing it'... he is gaping like a landed fish... he is about to be murdered... Although he knew it was a serious situation, James can't help but feel the tirade has a slightly surreal quality to it, being threatened by an Islamic fundamentalist villain version of Sid Vicious.

Meanwhile, in the bathroom, Les has finally managed to get the nozzle inserted. He lights his cigarette to celebrate the moment before pressing on.

'Stevie,' Raschid is saying. 'This is wrong.'

'Yeah, might have known you'd say that. What's the matter? Frightened of killing someone in front of your girlfriend? Frightened of her finding out you're an assassin? Moment my back's turned – I ought to do you and all... she was mine.'

James raises his hand. 'Wait a minute, can I just ask something?'

His tone is so calm that Stevie is put off-balance.

'What?' he snarls.

'You're the guy who phoned me with the death threat, yeah?'

'Yeah,' says Stevie. Raschid looks down, avoiding Loretta's appalled reaction. 'Now get on your knees.'

'OK, OK, in a minute; I just want to ask one thing.' There is no fear in James's voice, just an urgent curiosity, which is infectious.

'What?' snaps Stevie again.

'Can I just ask, was it the set I did from the Astoria that brought this on? Where I did the big bit on Afghanistan and the Taliban?'

'I don't fucking know,' said Stevie. He looks inquiringly at Raschid, who nods.

'That's right.'

'Wow, the power of TV!' exclaims James, although what he's really excited about is the power of him on TV.

'So, just let me get this right – it was the Taliban themselves that ordered this, in Afghanistan?'

Raschid nods again. 'They sent me here to do it.'

'They did?' says Loretta, aghast.

'All the way from Afghanistan? To kill me?' The joy in James's voice baffles Stevie into silence. Raschid, seizing the opportunity to play for time, and frustrated that Stevie and his gun stay out of reach, explains the whole story.

'That's really amazing,' says James, slapping his thighs. He's so utterly consumed with evidence of the power of his comedy that it's only when Stevie finally yells out angrily, 'OK, that's enough, it's time!! Shut up!' that James notices the gun pointing at him and remembers that his execution is not an abstract idea, but only moments away.

Raschid is weighing up the options, which are not good, and tensing himself for a desperate leap on to Stevie . . .

Meanwhile, in the bathroom, Les is in bliss. He can feel the warm liquid working its way up his colon, loosening, massaging . . . his first bowel movement for months is only moments away, he can sense it . . . he can feel trapped pockets of gas bubbling through the liquid, can see his abdomen rippling in conjunction with the movement he feels within. He lights another cigarette to mark the moment and a long sustained trumpeting fart – actually more like something from a bassoon or a group of Buddhist monks at prayer – resonates around the bathroom, on and on for ever. Les is ecstatic. Muscles and sections of flesh that have been stretched to breaking point for weeks and weeks are relaxing, the constant burning pain, the knives that have been torturing him constantly are being removed, he is free. He inhales another long drag on his cigarette. As he exhales, the pitch of the impossibly long fart goes up a semitone. Les is floating. He lets the hand holding the cigarette sink down, weightless to his waist, into the cloud of rank methane.

* * *

'You got a choice, Loretta. Either you come and live with me and my dad and help him out with his enemas, or I blow you away with the rest of them.'

Not only Loretta, but also Raschid and James are aware this is a very tough choice. But before Loretta can make a decision, there is an explosion. At first James thinks it is the gun going off. His life rushes before his eyes. He finds himself imagining the obituaries and thinking how cool it is that he has been executed as a martyr to free speech. Such is the monstrous size of his ego that fear is relegated to a little blip of thought anticipating the possibility of pain as the bullet enters the brain. There's no fear of life ending, no fear of what lies beyond – then he thinks, *Wait a minute, this can't be happening. I'm meeting Stride Boswell tonight. My career in America's taking off – you can't kill me now*!

But, as it turns out, the noise is not the gun going off, but an explosion from the bathroom, where the cigarette has ignited the methane cloud and, *boom*, blown Les into pieces which splatter in all directions and burst through the weakest part of the wall, knocking Stevie over, covering him in blood and flesh and shit, the larger part of the mighty corpse pinning Stevie to the floor.

The others run for it as the immobilised Stevie yells threats of revenge. Stevie's gun hand is trapped and the pistol too – he can't get a shot off.

'I'll fucking have you, you traitor. You scumbag! Dad, Dad! Call an ambulance! Dad... urrgh—' Stevie is silenced by a large section of his father's midriff — which has been stuck to the ceiling by the force of the blast and now crashes downwards on to Stevie's head, knocking him unconscious and threatening to suffocate him in its gelatinous mass.

Raschid rushes into his bedroom to pick up his suitcase which, as always, is packed ready for a quick exit. Loretta notices with regret that he is not concerned with Stevie beyond knowing he is silent and immobile. Raschid sees the disappointment in her eyes. 'Loretta, please, I can explain but we must get out of here first. Please trust me.'

CHAPTER THIRTY-FOUR

Raschid peeks through the window. People are starting to come out of their houses to see what the noise was.

'Look, I've really got to go,' says James.

'The back way,' says Raschid. 'We can get on to the railway line – less chance of anyone seeing us.'

They follow him through the kitchen, across the back lawn and through the hedge on to the path by the railway. Raschid does not stop until they reach the footbridge which takes them into Finsbury Park. Only now, once they have found a place to sit and look much like any other group of people does he start talking.

'I tried to warn you,' says Raschid to James, 'but you were too concerned about trying to impress Loretta.'

Loretta is sitting close to Raschid. Still keeping to his own set of priorities, James can tell he has no chance, which makes him even keener to go. There is nothing for him here – no physical gratification or boost to his ego. 'And believe me, I didn't know he had a gun.'

'Sure, I believe you. And you're really not going to kill me?'

'Like I said, it was just my ticket out.'

'And they really got that offended by my set?'

'Yes. They wanted to kill you, didn't they?'

James feels a flush of pride after all. 'Yeah. I guess so.' This is going to make such a fantastic chapter in the autobiography, James thinks. 'But, when all's said and done, that's just part of the job. You know, if you're saying the unsayable, it's the kind of risk you have to be prepared to take.' He says all this looking down at the ground, in an attempt to seem self-effacing and heroic. 'And what did you think of it?'

'What do you mean, what did I think of it?'

'My set – did you find it funny? Did you get all the jokes? Did it ring true? Because, you know, it's very important to me to try and capture a certain authenticity, even in the most knockabout sections ... I mean, getting the laugh is important, but there has to be a reason for the laugh beyond just laughter, in my opinion – does that make sense? I mean, if you compare say ...' he looks at Loretta, 'Richard Pryor and Dick Gregory ...'

Raschid and Loretta look at James in amazement. They are no longer listening to him because the content is irrelevant – they are just staggered that within five minutes of having his life saved by the chance intervention of a man exploding in a bizarre enema accident, James is talking in impenetrable detail about the philosophy of comedy and his career.

'Well, anyway,' says James, after what seems like a good while, 'I really have got to go. Thanks for everything and –' he can't help looking more at Loretta than Raschid '– if you ever fancy a drink some time, you know where to find me, yeah? OK. Thanks for everything.'

They watch him walk across the park, getting on with his life as if nothing has happened.

James calculates that, as no one has seen them leave and it's doubtful anyone paid much attention to them on the way in, the chances of him being caught are remote. And even if he should be, he has done nothing. Besides, as he reasoned earlier, the fact that he's due to meet Stride Boswell that evening and put his career into the outer reaches of the stratosphere, demonstrates that he's untouchable. Has he not just survived an attempt on his life? Not only survived for the moment but for good, his two assassins having both become deactivated – one through choice and the other through death. That's what happens if you dare to interfere with the glorious destiny of James Randall!

The only thing that can ruin his life now is getting

cold feet before – he finds himself trying to banish the image of what he must do – before he and Boswell – he trembles at the prospect – consummate their relationship. It occurs to him, But it's all in a good cause. James Randall, first British comedian in space!

CHAPTER THIRTY-FIVE

Loretta and Raschid sit silently in the park for a little while. 'I wanted to tell you all this,' says Raschid, 'and yet I was afraid to because I didn't want . . . to lose you.'

'You're not going to lose me,' says Loretta calmly. 'I love you.'

Loretta and Raschid look at each other and then kiss. It's a sunny day now in the park. It's perfect.

Loretta pulls away from the embrace.

'We have to decide what we're going to do now.'

'I've been thinking about that. We should leave the country. But all I have is three hundred pounds and a return ticket to Karachi.'

'You know what I'd like to do? Check into a nice hotel, have a hot bath, chill out, use room service, sleep, get on a plane to somewhere they could use a good motorcycle mechanic, and have lots of babies.'

Raschid laughs and lies back down on the grass.

'Come on, this is no time to go to sleep. It's three o'clock; we have things to do.' She pulls him to his feet and leads him off across the park towards the tube.

CHAPTER THIRTY-SIX

James gets home, ignores as usual all Henry's pedantic instructions for which alarms and sensors to reactivate once he is inside the building, throws his clothes into a pile in the corner of the bathroom, starts running a bath and sits down on the toilet with a copy of *Mojo* in one hand and a banana in the other.

Meanwhile, Stevie is regaining consciousness and crawling out from under the sticky bulk of his father's mutilated body parts. Covered in blood and mucus he blinks at the world anew, with one thing on his mind – vengeance. If only he knew where to find James . . . and then, like a big light switching on . . . of course!

When he picked the guy up the other day – when Providence had delivered the enemy into his hands – he'd been at that house in Barnsbury . . . what's the address? He tries to picture the road. It's not easy, but he'll find it. He remembers two big lions on the gateposts and a hi-tech burglar alarm on the wall . . . Barnsbury isn't that big . . . he can already narrow it down – north of Copenhagen, south of Mackenzie, and obviously between Upper Street and the Cally. It won't take him that long and if the people who live there know where James is hiding out, they'll tell him. He has the gun.

CHAPTER THIRTY-SEVEN

Loretta and Raschid get off the tube at Oxford Circus. They stop off to buy a couple of cheap holdalls in John Lewis and all the while she refuses to tell him where they are going, just leads him by the hand with an enigmatic smile on her face. They go into Selfridges, where Loretta asks to be taken to the safe deposit boxes. She produces identification, is given her key and takes her box to the private cubicle where she opens it and Raschid's eyes bulge with astonishment.

'A hundred thousand pounds.' She looks at Raschid, suddenly realising they're in the movies and adds with a dastardly laugh: 'And it's all mine.'

'How?'

'Not here. Later.' She grabs a couple of wads, puts the rest back in the box. 'Come on, we're going shopping. If we're going to stay somewhere cool, we need to look a little more upscale.'

They spend an hour or two in Bond Street and Savile Row and emerge transformed into a well-to-do cosmopolitan couple with the world at their feet. Raschid chooses – or rather Loretta chooses for him, in an act so foreign to his nature that Raschid is both turned on by it and liberated by his submission – some casuals from Timberland and a suit from Nicole Farhi. Loretta gets some stuff in Nicole Farhi and a little brooch from Tiffany – 'Just because it's so disgusting.' They go back and collect the rest of the money from the safe deposit and take a suite in a smart hotel in Covent Garden. The moment they're through the door, Loretta turns on the TV and channel hops.

Raschid is now insistent to know what's going on.

'It's pretty simple,' Loretta says, casually undressing and flitting in and out of the bathroom with fewer and fewer clothes on each time, perching on the edge of the bed just in a white towelling dressing-gown, channel-hopping with the sound down as she begins to tell the story of –

'Wait a minute,' says Raschid, 'let me just get the football results, see how the Villa have done – look, those are ostriches on the news!' They flick on the sound. A concerned-looking reporter is addressing the camera while behind him policemen wander around purposefully putting up tape.

They turn up the sound, but unfortunately the item ends and cuts to the rugby union results.

They would have learnt that the ostriches at Aldingtons' supermarket had escaped due to a freak failure in the security system and ruined the wedding day of two loyal Aldingtons' customers who would now reschedule their marriage ceremony for the day after they returned from their hastily extended honeymoon. They would also have heard Alan Mason assure the public that, while the ostriches were indeed dangerous and had tragically killed a member of staff who was bravely trying to restrain them, all had been recaptured.

Spartacus, his nostrils clearing of ostrich dung as he lurks along the cover beside the railway line, would have laughed. But he has not seen the broadcast and is preoccupied – for he is beginning to pick up faint traces of female ostrich scent.

Loretta continues with her story, tells how through a friend of a friend she made a few trips smuggling LSD crystals into the UK when she first arrived and was well paid for it.

'That's one of the advantages of growing up amidst the Beverly Hills international kleptocracy – you're never far away from someone you can mule for in style. I'm ready for my shower now but you still have all your clothes on.'

She turns round, kisses him, forces him down on to the bed, pulls off his shirt and gently bites his nipples, opens her gown and presses her breasts against his stomach. Raschid kisses her back, then tenderly pushes her away and sits up.

'First I have to pray.'

'Pray? What do you mean, pray?'

'I haven't prayed yet today. Give me ten minutes, OK?'

'OK. But if you get anyone telling you you shouldn't be making love to a Christian girl, ignore them, OK?'

'OK.'

'Promise?'

Loretta wraps her left leg over his shoulder.

'I promise.'

On this occasion, Raschid gets on with his prayers very quickly.

Later, as Raschid and Loretta lie in bed together doing all those things that lovers do when they're recovering from time-stoppingly good sex, like feeding each other chocolate from the mini-bar, staring blissfully at the ceiling, trying not to fart and planning their future, Loretta's mobile rings. She swears and debates whether to answer it or not.

CHAPTER THIRTY-EIGHT

Lunch at Henry's mother's was a tense affair. He was still reeling from the embarrassment and anger of the morning, and she was still making references to it. Finally she said something that made him snap.

'OK, fine. I tell you what we'll do.' The anger cured him. He could stand upright, open his eyes fully, talk without feeling every word stabbing him in the temples. 'We'll go back down to London and pick James up, I'll drive him back here and the pair of you can celebrate your birthday without me or Elizabeth to get in the way and make your life a misery by in taking you shopping, chopping the logs, mending the guttering, repainting the windows or digging the garden. OK? It'll just be you and the good son. How does that sound?'

Mrs Randall frowned. 'He has an important business meeting. We mustn't disturb him.'

'An important business meeting which he cancelled seeing his mother on her birthday for.'

'Oh don't split hairs.'

'Split hairs? Where are there any split hairs in that? What do you mean split hairs?'

'Don't shout. How dare you be so inconsiderate. James had his flat broken into. You should have taken care of him, and instead you left him to fend for himself alone in London. Of course he refused your suggestion that he come up here with you – it was clear you wanted to abandon him. He's a sensitive artist. And I hope you're going to scrub that sink with disinfectant before you go home. What a lovely way to treat your mother on her birthday.'

And the day had begun so well.

Elizabeth had been reflecting all week on the horror of her life. She realised that she could see herself turning into Henry's mother. She also realised that that is what she wanted – someone like Henry to control and boss around – and began to hate herself for wanting so little in life except domination of a willing complicitor. She had chosen Henry she realised now because, though he was talented and capable, he was not confident. And he had not come up to her expectations. She had believed that she could give him the confidence to make full use of his undoubted potential. He should have been a senior partner by now, because she had told him he was capable of it. That should have been enough. But he had not obeyed her instructions. He had messed up her plans by failing to believe in himself. It was an insult to her and undermined her power. Elizabeth was greatly agitated. It was the end of the road for the two of them, unless something changed very soon.

Loretta disliked screening calls, so finally she pulled herself half out of bed, scrambled around in her tote bag and answered the call. The voice ranted without introduction.

'I thought your boyfriend might like to know I will be carrying out the mission tonight. And if I ever manage to catch up with you two I'll kill you and all – understand?'

When Raschid heard this and declared he was going back to save James from Stevie, Loretta flipped and said, 'What is this? "A man's gotta do what a man's gotta do?" This is life, not a movie. You're not John Wayne.'

'No, I'm not John Wayne,' said Raschid. 'And I also resent the implication that honourable behaviour is the sole preserve of Hollywood movie heroes.'

'You talk funny for a mid-eastern guy.'

'That's because the only ones you've ever seen are in Hollywood movies, gibbering and being blown up by Arnold Schwarzenegger,' retorted Raschid tartly. 'And I'm not from the Middle East. I'm from Birmingham.'

'Whatever. We should get out of here. Have you ever been to Costa Rica? I know a few people who have set up there real easy. They have motorbikes. It would be a quiet life and we could start tomorrow.'

'I have to stop Stevie.'

'What do you mean, you have to stop Stevie?'

'He's going to kill James. I can't let that happen.'

'But it's too much of a risk. I don't want to lose you the moment I've found you.'

'I've been in worse situations.'

'And one day your luck will run out. I'm not going to let you go. They're both arseholes.'

'That's not the point, is it?'

'But . . .'

'You can't stop me. It's a question of honour.'

'Shit.' She followed him out of the room.

CHAPTER THIRTY-NINE

Spartacus struts purposefully along a quiet Islington side-street, keeping close to the hedges and front gardens, taking full advantage of the large number of street-lights that aren't working. In his radioactive wake, car after car starts flashing and beeping. Fortunately for him, everyone inside adopts the customary reaction to car alarms – they swear and assume they have been triggered accidentally. No one thinks to check what is going on outside.

Stevie has finally found the house where he picked James up the previous Saturday night. If God is willing, Stevie thinks, James will be inside.

And James *is* inside, running around nervously, defrosting *boeuf bourgignon* in the microwave, raiding the wine cellar (a few racks in the cupboard under the stairs) and selecting six bottles of Krug and three dust-covered red Burgundies which Henry had laid down for a special occasion.

The house itself is looking reasonably good.

He is amazed at the chaos he has managed to create in less than a week. Just about every coffee cup and mug in the place has been used. Take-away cartons colonise most of the remaining horizontal space. He does not usually do a lot of cleaning as it interrupts his creative flow – unless he's actually meant to be writing, when it becomes crucially important. Given that not only is he not working on anything but that he's also acutely aware it isn't his house, there has been no incentive to clean up all week. Now he reminds himself it is actually work of a very important kind; if the evening goes well and he manages to impress Stride Boswell, the world will be his for the taking.

James tries not to think too much about what is actually going to happen to him after dinner. Whether it will be painful. Whether they will have to kiss. Whether he will get through it without throwing up. And whether – perhaps this is his greatest fear – whether he might enjoy it. It's all for a good cause – that's where he must keep his focus. If this evening goes right he could be well on the way to the *Tonight Show* and his face fifty feet high on Sunset Boulevard. Imagine it – being the first comedian in space.

After his bath, James cleans and washes up with an energy he hasn't mustered since college and the yearly ritual of getting the rented house back into decent enough shape for the landlord to return the deposit. Of course, the thought crosses James's mind that perhaps Boswell will not honour his part of the bargain after he has got what he wants, but that is a chance James has to take. Well, he doesn't *have* to take it but, given that he is a vacuous egomaniac whose sole *raison d'être* is fame and recognition, then he has no alternative. He is tired of being just a well-known and respected comedian in Britain, he wants the world.

It had also occurred to Sid that Boswell might try to renege on the deal, which is why she called an old friend, Donald, a cunning paparazzo with great skill in concealment techniques, acquired during his time in command of the reconnaissance section of the Scots Guards, who is even now quietly appraising the back garden of Henry and Elizabeth's house seeking the best position to lie in wait with his camera. Donald was discharged from the Army under a cloud – something to do with misuse of the diplomatic pouch when he was a military attaché somewhere in Central America. It's a long story but, essentially, his family have disowned him and cut him off from his huge inheritance until such time as he can demonstrate penance for dragging the family's good name through the mire. His somewhat eccentric father has ordained the penance: Donald must stay awake continuously for two weeks. There is no easy way of proving this of course; his father says simply that when Donald appears at the house and gives his word he has not slept for fourteen nights he will be believed, because he is still a gentleman with a sense of honour.

The purpose of the two sleepless weeks is for Donald to contemplate in awful depth the terrible effects of narcotic abuse. Sadly, Donald, while having the sense of honour his father predicts, does not have the strength of will nor body to carry out the penance unaided. As a result he is living on a sink estate in Harlesden, trying to break the fourteen-day barrier, snorting vast quantities of speed and cocaine, and generally passing out at somewhere around the one-and-a-half week mark, at which point he detoxes (comparatively) for a few weeks before trying again. Consequently he is always looking for money and high-grade stimulants. Sid has offered both. She has also told him she will do her best to leave curtains and doors unclosed, but he will have to be prepared to improvise.

Spartacus sniffs the air and follows the scent. It is getting grey and dusky now and, thanks to the drizzling rain and the fact that the lottery draw is imminent on TV, there are no people on the streets to see him advance cautiously from hiding place to hiding place, in doorways and behind hedges, as he is drawn by the faint but ever-strengthening odour.

A couple of people notice him, but Spartacus has another trick in his locker – he has learnt a phrase of human speech, the one phrase that his captor the Cyclops would use over and over each time he tipped feed into the troughs: 'All right mate?' He repeats this phrase to the passers-by so that they either think they are hallucinating, or are disbelieved as time-wasting hoaxers when they call the police.

James gets out of his bath, dresses – casual but classy. A pair of tight French designer trousers and a brightly patterned silk shirt from somewhere in Mayfair which is two years old but, according to an article in one of the Sunday supplements, is 'iconic of a period undergoing intense retro-chic admiration'.

The food is all ready.

Sid has suggested caterers, but James is reluctant to hire them for two reasons: he does not want any unnecessary witnesses, and he's a tight-fisted git. He is willing to be buggered in the furtherance of his career, but he is buggered if he's going to pay more for the privilege than he absolutely has to.

'The caterers can be long gone before the guests arrive, love,' Sid explains. 'It just means the place looks impressive.'

'I can do that on my own without forking out an arm and a leg.'

The doorbell rings.

James gets up to answer it – walking towards the door knowing that his future lies on the other side. He opens it. There is a beaming Sid and a beaming Boswell.

'Well, hello, Mr James! My, let me look at you. Agnès B and . . . Equipment? Right? Exquisite. The future of British comedy is looking very good to me. Great to see you again.'

Boswell embraces James. They have met twice before. Boswell stands back to let Sid in for one of her clinical pecks. James sees Boswell's reflection in the Art Nouveau mirror that hangs in the hallway and, while he is comforted to know that Boswell does indeed have a reflection, the look on his face makes James feel like a chicken being surveyed by a chicken hawk.

'Do come in,' he says, forcing his voice a little louder than usual to try and overcome the tremble in it.

'Nice place you have here,' says the Pink Grizzly.

'Thank you. Let me fix you a drink.' James opens one of the bottles of Krug.

'Krug!' exclaims Boswell. 'Are we celebrating?' And everyone laughs.

'I hope so!' says James. And everyone laughs again without anyone wanting to go into details.

All three of them affect a brightness to accompany

the froth and fizz of the champagne, but it's plain from Boswell's eyes there's only one thing on his mind – and it's clearly not food. Sid is happy just to observe and facilitate. James is trying to convince himself that somehow he will still have some self-respect when the sun rises tomorrow.

'So Sid has been getting me up to speed with the dazzling path of your career. Congratulations! That last series sounded so . . . out there.'

'Thank you.'

'I saw the tape of the one where you do that tirade at New Labour? The way you feel so betrayed? The way you expose how Tony Blair will do anything, abandon any principle for the sake of his own self-interest? It was so moving I really didn't know whether to laugh or cry.'

'Thanks. I guess it came straight from the heart – that kind of political hypocrisy really fires me up, you know . . .'

Sid cuts in, 'Now now, Jimmy, no need to get quite so serious – you're among friends here now you know – it's not the Lynn Barber interview. I'm ready for another glass of champers. And do you have a little mirror we might be able to put out flat on the table?'

Sid stands.

'I must say you're looking good, Jimmy. Have you been working out?'

'Not really, but thank you. Just you know, bit of walking . . . and how about yourself?'

'Well, work is good, I think I have a couple of projects we ought to discuss at least informally . . . and I'm having a fabulous time here in London with Sid as I always do, mixing business and pleasure which is always my favourite way of doing things . . .'

'Here we are!' Sid rescues both men from their awkward conversation with six large lines of cocaine on the glass of a delicate Italian portrait of a lady with her spaniel, one of Elizabeth's prize possessions.

'Terrific! I've got to say, Sid, you get the best cocaine I've ever had in London. I don't know how you do it. You are amazing.'

'Thank you, Stride. Enjoy.'

He does, hoovering two enormous lines off the glass so expertly you might have doubted they were ever there.

James takes the straw and does his lines, half at a time. It has been a while since he's done any coke – perhaps nearly a fortnight. He notices immediately, however, that it is far better coke than Cressida has ever laid out for him before – even on that first night in Edinburgh.

The cocaine is a good thing. Suddenly everyone can talk and feel they're being entertaining because no one really listens, just waits for their turn to be the one making a noise through the mouth. Of course, at the same time they are all playing a little game, waiting to see whose guard will drop the furthest and most permanently, who will give away something that the others can exploit.

Sid is waiting for the moment she can leave and let the evening develop under its own steam. If possible, she will get some kind of comment out of Boswell committing James to the space-gig project, and then leave the front door on the latch for Donald to get in for close-ups – for insurance purposes – later on.

Stride is looking at himself with absolute disbelief. He cannot believe the way he behaves sometimes – he is *so* free of the moral and material restraints that most people submit to. He *is* a genuine *Ubermensch*. And so *decadent* – hedonistic is a better word. Here he is, in London, just about to get his rocks off with this boy. James is so right as the comparative unknown in the space station gig – the Tracy Chapman figure as someone has put it. There's so much buzz about him in LA that Stride has had to concoct a phoney business trip to get here ahead of the competition so he can make Sid think that the ... casting-couch situation is necessary. (The way he's put it to Sid is that he might, just might be able to squeeze in a dinner with her and James if his major meetings haven't overrun too badly.) And it looks like he's done it, done it again – got what he wants no matter how much it costs. Hey – it's all on expenses. What's life for, if not to enjoy?

Sid meanwhile has managed – completely by chance of course – to run into a couple of the people Boswell has been seeing and they've both given her the impression the meetings have been low-key courtesy encounters booked because Stride happens to be in London. From this – and a few transatlantic social phone calls – she has worked out how high James's stock is in certain quarters and has guessed Boswell's strategy. It had occurred to her to cancel Donald but, in the end, she decided to let it run. The photo could still be useful. It also amuses her to see James forced to become the image he has so ruthlessly exploited. And she's fascinated to see how fully he is prepared to abandon any sense of who he really is, in order to become his own perfect media-conquering fame-seeking reinvented doppelgänger. He is so willing to sacrifice himself it is thrilling. The idea of letting himself be buggered for global stardom turns her on so much . . . she must give him another blow-job sometime. In fact, she's tempted to stay around and make it a foxy threesome, but for the fact there's so much long-term extortion potential if Donald gets the right snaps of the boys.

Suddenly James leaps up from the happy group of worshippers kneeling to their god.

'I'm going to do a starter.'

The cocaine reveals to James that a long and detailed account of his culinary expertise will be fascinating and he begins to explain: 'I only know how to do one starter. But, though I say it myself, I'm fucking good at it – corn on the cob. Sounds mundane I know, but trust me. I'm an expert.'

The others are staring at him and he can't work out if they are captivated by the exciting nature of his story, or stunned into silence by its pointless banality. Best to keep going. Never apologise, never explain . . . 'Yeah, when I was at college there was this guy I shared a house with . . .' James envisages the end of the sentence in his mind's eye – 'This guy's dad used to give us loads of corn on the cob that he grew in a greenhouse so we used to do all sorts . . .' *Change it*. 'This guy I shared a house with used to have this weird habit . . . of doing hold-ups from greengrocers, you know, (*yeah, this is better*) and, like, one of the things he always used to go for was corn on the cob . . . and so we always had loads of it in the house . . .'

They are looking at him with half-smiles. Sid is thinking, 'How long before I can go?' Boswell is thinking, 'I want to fuck this boy.'

'Anyway,' James is now fixed on his mission to prepare corn on the cob. 'If you'll excuse me . . .'

He waltzes around the coffee table and refills the champagne glasses. Suddenly he is feeling nervous. *Am I really going to do this? What if it hurts?*

* * *

'This is a new experience for me. To be having dinner in someone's home on a Saturday night?' says Boswell confidentially as James goes into the kitchen. 'I hope it's going to be worth missing a night on the town for.'

'I'm sure it will be, Stride,' says Sid in her most Gushingly Certain voice, resonating from deep in the diaphragm for added sincerity, and she flips out three more big lines with a few deft flicks of her solid-silver titanium-edged razor blade.

'Normally, I like to be out and being seen, you know? I miss that buzz of people pointing me out to their friends . . . I have to be sure of getting something back, you know. I *need* attention. Damn, this *is* good coke.'

It ought to be, thinks Sid, smiling humbly in gracious recognition of the compliment and reminding herself that, in the circumstances, it's a legitimate expense.

'I'm sure it will be worth your while, just as I'm sure it will be worth mine and James's.'

'Corn on the cob,' announces James, appearing at the mention of his name and placing a tray on a low table.

'We were just saying, Jimmy, that you'd be perfect for this space-station fundraiser that Stride is organising. Isn't that right, Stride?'

'Well, naturally, there's a lot of people keen to do

it, but I have a feeling you could be great.'

'It would be nice.' James is doing his best to keep an even, understated tone. 'I think my satirical stuff is very global – unlike a lot of the other Brits who, of course, I admire but, if we're talking honestly, I think I have the edge.'

Certainly in terms of arrogant self-belief, thinks Sid, nodding enthusiastically the while.

'I mean, there's probably quite a lot of material I could use that you've never seen.'

'I'm sure there's lots of you I haven't seen,' drawls the Pink Grizzly, homing in on another line. 'The thing is,' he continues, rising from the snort, dancing his fingers round his nose, 'and I have no doubts about your ability. The thing is, I like to know that the people I work with, that there's the right chemistry between us – especially on this project which is very special to me. Very close to my heart. We're going to be earning a lot of money for a lot of very good causes – famine relief, AIDS charities, addiction programmes' – sniff – 'so the chemistry is important to me. I have to know that my personnel are all totally one hundred per cent committed to the ethos of the project, not just what they get out of it. That's the important thing, you know?'

'Sure. And, I'm going to sound self-serving here – you know, immodest, and I apologise for that – but what you're looking for, it's exactly what I do.

Commitment is what I do.'

Sid looks at the two of them and has only admiration for how deeply they believe their own delusions.

'That corn on the cob looks great,' enthuses Sid, purely in order to break the slightly charged silence, and she takes a piece by the little forks that are already inserted in them.

'There's different butters,' James says, distributing the contents of the tray. 'Dill, garlic, chilli. And extra-virgin olive oil, black pepper.'

Boswell leers. 'Extra-virgin? My favourite.'

James takes a piece of corn. Boswell watches him eat. 'You do that so very well.' And there's a nervous smile from James followed by silence while they all slurp and nibble for a mouthful or two. James notices halfway through his second mouthful that his mouth is so numb he has bitten deeply into the cob. Resisting the urge to spit it back out immediately, he swills it down instead with Krug and then gets up once more to fetch another bottle from the fridge, hoping he can stifle the unstoppable belch by getting to the door as it escapes. Then as the allusion in Boswell's remark sinks fully in, James pulls up short, horrified. Would doing *that* be part of the transaction? He put another bottle of Krug in the fridge. Just in case. He hears laughter from upstairs.

When he returns this time, Sid is getting her things together.

'You leaving?' The distress in James's voice is undisguised.

'Yes, darling. I'm really not hungry any more for some reason and I need an early night.'

'OK. I'll call you a cab.'

'No need – I had the car wait – just in case.'

'Oh right.'

The moment of truth is approaching. Just think of the rewards. James wishes he had a quaalude or something.

'Don't worry,' says Boswell in a voice like poisoned honey. 'I'll look after you.'

James laughs, doing an impression of the nonchalant Englishman. Sid is already heading for the door. James walks with her. Everything is suddenly happening very fast.

'Do you have to go?'

Sid's smile is so artificial but so real. There is nothing human in it save ruthless ambition. So this is what it's all about. 'Come on, it's what you've always wanted. Now go in there and do the business for the business. You're playing with the big boys now, James. You're going to the top, if you dare.'

'You're sure it's going to happen if—'

'I'm sure – the gig is going to happen – it's yours as long as Mr Boswell goes home happy tonight.'

She might have added it would happen even if he didn't but that would take all the fun out of life.

Besides, James owed her one for that first evening in Edinburgh.

'There's half a gram and a couple of quaaludes on the table. Good luck.' And she's gone without him remembering opening and closing the door.

CHAPTER FORTY

James stands there for a second. It's more of an issue for him than he wants to believe. Then he asks himself what he really wants in life, in his career – which amounts to the same thing and he walks back into the room. Boswell has put some music on.

'So, Mr James, I hope we can seal this deal this evening.'

James recognises the music. It's a Leonard Cohen cover from *I'm Your Fan* – 'Don't Go Home With Your Hard On'. Boswell does not look up from his coke-chopping.

'Does your kitchen have a big table, Mr James?'
'Yeah.'
'That's good. And it's downstairs?'
'Yes.'

'You know what I'd like you to do? I'd like you to go upstairs and put on something a little more... sweaty and unwashed... Then I'd like you to go down into the kitchen, lean over that table and wait for me. And then we can seal this deal and put you into outer space. How does that sound?'

So this is it then. Think of the rewards. 'Yes,' says James meekly. 'I mean it sounds great.'

Now Boswell looks up.

'Say it like you mean it, you naughty little boy. How does that sound?'

James swallows but his mouth is dry. *Think of the rewards.* 'That sounds fantastic. I can't wait.'

'Good. I can though. Here—'

He offers the straw to James, who kneels down and inhales greedily. Boswell rubs the back of his neck roughly.

'My, what an appetite you have. Now take this quaalude and run along.'

James goes upstairs without another word. *Think of the rewards. You're not the only one who's ever done this. Posterity only remembers the glory.*

In the bathroom he digs out the jeans and T-shirt he was wearing that morning, and the denim jacket he lent to Loretta, soaked with ostrich pheremone.

CHAPTER FORTY-ONE

Leaning over the kitchen table, James hears footsteps coming down the stairs. In the window he sees Boswell's reflection. He is carrying a briefcase James did not notice when he arrived.

'Face down on the table please, Mr James. I must have obedience from those who work with me. And you do want to go into space, don't you?'

James's answer is 'yes', but for the first time he's beginning to wonder. 'Can we close the blind please? Just in case,' he adds. There is five yards of front lawn and a hedge between them and the pavement, but you never know.

'If you wanted it closed, you'd already have closed it, wouldn't you? You *are* a risk-taker, aren't you? Just like it says in your notices.' But Boswell does kill the lights. In the bushes, Donald curses to himself. For him it's already like coitus interruptus – happily shooting away, he has been anticipating a whole roll of film that will make the earth move for him and now he can see virtually nothing; there is just a feeble light seeping in from the stairs, offering a very indistinct silhouette. He reloads with his fastest film, deciding to give it a go anyway, and wonders about risking a flash. He should have plenty of time to get away, but he must wait until he's sure the main event is in full swing. Thrust would be a better word, he thinks.

James feels Boswell's body weight slowly press against him. *Think of the benefits*. A velvet blindfold is slipped over his eyes.

'Arms out to the side.'

James obeys and feels ropes tied round his wrists. The rope is tightened under the table, then looped round his ankles and tightened again. The time for choice is over. He feels sick and shuts his eyes. Boswell forces a pill into his mouth which James can tell from the shape is another quaalude. He is grateful, hopes it will deaden the pain. Absurdly and blasphemously, but it shows you how James sees himself, James is reminded of Christ receiving vinegar on the cross and decides he is in the process of making a similar sacrifice for the sake of his art.

Boswell fumbles at James's trousers. Pulls them down. Emits an urgent sigh. James feels a greasy hand forced in between his naked buttocks and can feel burning . . . chilli. It's chilli butter. He feels nauseous and tries to think of millions of people seeing him perform. Donald is thinking the same thing – via *Paris Match* and a big pay-day – and is wondering if it's time to risk the flash.

James braces himself but then hears footsteps – Boswell is going upstairs. James waits.

Spartacus knows he is close now. He can feel his penis engorging as he marches more briskly now. He hears footsteps behind him. Close. He realises he has no option but to try the classic ostrich-invisibility technique. He doesn't try to bury his head in the sand; rather, he lies flat, stretching his neck out along the ground hoping that, at distance and in the right light, he will be mistaken for a small scrubby bush.

Stevie doesn't even cast an eye towards him. If he's registered the dark lump in his peripheral vision at all, he's taken it for a bin-liner.

Donald too hears footsteps and shrinks tighter into the hedge. A man is coming up the path, on tip-toe and unsteady. He crouches low and moves into the garden, stands not more than a yard from Donald, and reaches into his pocket. He pulls out what Donald recognises immediately as a Browning automatic pistol with apparent difficulty. The man cocks it and replaces it in his pocket.

Donald is amazed. Is he about to witness an armed

robbery – or even a murder? What should he do? Donald thinks hard. These could be great pictures – he could pay off his debts, get clean, get his life back – but how could he explain being present at a crime without intervening in any way? And, leaving aside the legal implications, there is a moral side to square with his conscience. Then he remembers he is a paparazzo and decides to stick around. There will surely be a way of telling the tale to make it clear there was nothing he could do until it was too late. He notices the unsteady figure is covered in blood.

Stevie circles the house, looking for an open window. Standing now in the back garden, close to the house, he can see nothing to his advantage.

James's heart is beating fast, despite the quaaludes beginning to kick in. Stride Boswell's pulse is also racing, as he has just taken another line, and two Viagra tablets washed down with a little hint of Krug. He sprawls back on the sofa, rubbing his groin imperiously. As always he enjoys this preparatory moment, countering his own desire with delight at the agonised anticipation James must be feeling downstairs. It makes it all the more thrilling that Sid has tipped him off that James's professed sexual orientation has been nothing but a publicity-gaining charade all along. My God, that woman knew how to turn a man on. Maybe he and she should get it together some time? Isn't that a kinky concept? 'Time to go,' he says out loud. 'Bathroom first, I think.'

If Boswell is fired up and ready to go, and Stevie is throbbing at the prospect of imminent violent vengeance, and Donald is tingling with the thought of financial salvation, then Spartacus is off the scale. The smell of seasoned-up female ostrich is getting stronger and stronger in his nostrils, he homes in on it, breaks cover and sprints for its source.

Donald is creeping closer to the house when he hears a furious scuttling behind him, but before he can turn is smashed over the head and falls unconscious to the ground.

Spartacus moves into the darkness at the sound of an approaching car and flattens himself on the lawn, waiting to assess the danger.

CHAPTER FORTY-TWO

Raschid lets the taxi go past the house they are seeking before telling it to stop. He hands the driver a note and leaps out, telling him to keep the change. Loretta follows angrily, catching him up just as Raschid goes through Henry and Elizabeth's front gate. He gestures for Loretta to stop and waves her back. She shakes her head slowly, telling him that if it's his problem, it's hers as well. Raschid is secretly delighted but merely shrugs and they creep towards the house.

Through the basement window they can make out the silhouette of a half-naked man stretched across the table. Raschid wonders if he's too late, when suddenly, metal spikes are digging into his neck, cutting into the flesh. He wriggles and twists, feels the cuts getting deeper, until there is a massive thump and the grip releases.

Stevie is staggering as Loretta hits him again with the dustbin. He manages to keep his feet, throws a punch at Loretta that sends her flying and, like a drowning man clutching at anything that will keep him afloat, produces a pistol which he clumsily tries to level at Raschid.

Raschid dives to his left, trying to find darkness near the fence which separates the front and back gardens, but Stevie tracks Raschid's move, smiles and steadies himself. He's about to shoot when a giant avian leg appears through the gateway and smashes down on his head. This time Stevie goes down, blood spurting and does not stir. The ostrich hurtles past the prostrate Raschid, smashes the door open with a fierce snap-kick and charges into the house.

Spartacus circles the living room, defecating in his frenzy of desire.

Boswell comes out of the bathroom, where he has been emptying himself to prolong the session that awaits, descends the stairs, and is surprised to see a large bird advancing down the hall. He faints, hitting his head on the wall as he falls.

James hears footsteps coming down the kitchen stairs and bravely prepares himself for his great sacrifice. After all, commitment is what he does . . .

He screws his eyes tight shut and tells himself it will be like going to the dentist – you just have to put your mind in another place. He decides

Boswell smells curiously animal-like and feels body weight and feathers. Then, after a certain desperate, inaccurate thrusting, he is penetrated.

As they drive past the house seeking a parking place, Henry sees that the front door is open. He throws the car hastily into a space, leaving it halfway from the kerb, and leaps out.

Loretta recovers, pulls Raschid to his feet.

'OK, Rambo. Now it's my call. Stevie's dead. It's not our responsibility any more.' They hear car doors slamming and the sound of voices and footsteps heading in their direction. 'There's someone coming. We're out of here.'

Raschid does not argue and they shin the fence, clearing it just as the voices and footsteps turn into the path . . .

Stride Boswell also hears the slam of car doors as he regains consciousness, and the sound of people maybe walking towards the house. He tries to keep cool. Although he's been in various tight spots in his life, this one takes some beating. Somehow he rises to his feet and is walking out of the front door, almost at the gate, as he passes three astonished people, an old lady and a thirty-something couple. He says with admirable aplomb: 'Hello, great party, but my cab's here now. Goodnight.' He keeps walking calmly until he reaches the corner, then he runs.

'Party? He's having a party?' screams Henry, then sees Stevie's body inert and prostrate on his threshold.

'This one's completely pissed!' He runs in, furious. He spins round as Elizabeth and his mother join him, horrified.

'We must call the police,' insists Elizabeth. But Henry is not listening. His worst fear – the violation of his home – has taken place and he is too angry to think. He advances downstairs, snaps on the kitchen light, and stands speechless at the spectacle of his brother being buggered by an ostrich.

He recovers.

'It's OK,' calls Henry triumphantly to Elizabeth and his mother. 'You can come down.'

Spartacus is too busy sating his lust to react, but James recognises his brother's voice, then hears a gasp which probably comes from Elizabeth then feels the heavy weight lift and move away.

'Look, Mother, this is what your favourite son gets up to instead of visiting you on your birthday.'

James computes this information and hopes it's all a bad dream. Someone removes his blindfold. He sees Henry, Elizabeth and his mother staring at him in amazement. Then, in the other corner, he spies Spartacus.

'What the hell is an ostrich doing in your kitchen?'

'You tell me, James,' replies Henry, calmly. 'You were the one having sex with it.'

'Not on purpose!'

Like Zeus and Leda, he says to himself in a grandiose attempt to preserve his dignity – not to mention his sanity.

Raschid and Loretta clear two more fences, creep stealthily through a back garden or two, and finally reach a street, trying to walk at an innocent pace. Turning on to Caledonian Road, they flag down a cab. Raschid pulls his jacket up around his neck to conceal his wounds.

'Don't ever call me Rambo again,' he says smiling, as they climb in, and he kisses her.

Elizabeth surveys the devastation in what was once her kitchen. At first she's calm. Then she has a revelation. Suddenly she realises what she has secretly always known and sought to deny – that the universe cannot be controlled. Her efforts to build mansions of certainty to live in are doomed because their foundations are built on sand and always will be. She is nothing, and there's no longer any way to ignore it.

Then she begins to shake and tremble. Her long high-pitched whine grows into a huge scream.

She seizes a vase of dried flowers and smashes them against a wall. Runs the length of the table, sweeping everything off it with her arm: crockery and assorted cutlery crash and clang on the slates. She tears drawers from their runners, hurling them at pictures, people, light fittings – anything that appears to be looking at her. The kettle goes flying into a framed collection of snapshots. The Alessi fish-kettle into the Heal's wall clock. The Le Creuset casserole dishes dent as they crack the floor tiles with a dull clang.

Henry, his mother, and Spartacus all take cover as best they can, and avoid each other's gaze for fear of causing embarrassment.

A bloodstained figure comes running into the kitchen. It's Stevie, back again from the dead, saved by the metal plate in his skull. He's waving his hands around wildly and, in his left, he holds a pistol. Elizabeth throws herself upon him, screaming, yelling and scratching. Stevie too is howling and they fall to the floor, rolling over and over.

Henry is reminded of the frenzied dancing he has seen in a documentary on witch doctors and orgiastic dance cults.

Stevie's sense of rightness has also been torn away from him, by Loretta's and Raschid's treachery, by his father's death, by the failure of Divine Providence. Somehow, as the two of them fight on the floor, they identify with each other's feral expression of rage and form a common bond which recognises their mutual frustration. Suddenly sexually aroused, they continue to tear at each other's clothes and bodies but with an entirely different purpose. And now they are copulating in an ecstatic mindless frenzy like amphetamine-crazed rattlesnakes, united in their desire to disengage from the terrors and injustices of existence.

'I always said you should never have married her,' says Henry's mother simply.

Henry is too shocked to move. At first he has the sense of time going backwards as he watches Stevie and Elizabeth turn into uncontrolled balls of libidinous energy in front of his eyes. His whole world is collapsing. Is he not partly to blame – in that he has not assisted in the release of Elizabeth's sexual energy as he should have done, prevented from doing so through his own selfish fears? Is all this in a way not caused by his narcissistic refusal to accept his own unimportance? To witness this is a penance without which he cannot hope for absolution. This thought does not last long. It dissolves into fascination and he is transfixed by this staggering release of primal energy. He is affected by the same kind of muted reverence he feels visiting a church. It is as if a ritual is being conducted which, even though he does not understand it, means so much to the participants that it would be grossly taboo to intervene. Henry is beguiled. He needs to know what will happen if he does nothing to change the nature of this rip in the fabric of civilised normality.

At last the frenzied lovers emit a simultaneous climactic howl, collapse limp and whimpering and then, as if regaining their previous selves, burst apart with a cry of shock and anguish. Elizabeth curls into a ball, crying and sobbing, while Stevie, his leg clearly badly injured, limps towards the open French windows, expecting Henry to leap upon him at any moment. But Henry just watches as Stevie makes his slow escape into the garden.

As Henry surveys the wreckage of the room, his broken, sobbing wife amongst the debris, he feels unusually calm. What else can possibly happen to him now that is worse than this?

He looks at James and then at Stevie whose shadowy form he can make out, frantically trying to climb over the back fence.

The sense of his anxiety lifting becomes even stronger for Henry. However many homicidal lunatics there are out there, he now knows for sure that at least one of them does not have Henry's name at the top of his list.

'Aren't you going to untie me?' says James.

Henry doesn't really hear.

'Henry, for God's sake . . . where's Boswell?'

'Boswell?'
'A big American guy, bald . . .'
'Oh, him.'
'You've seen him?'
'Yes.'
'Is he OK?'
'He's gone.'
'Gone? Did he leave a message? Did he seem happy? Henry, untie me, I've got to call my agent.'

Henry moves towards James and now notices Spartacus again still standing quietly in the corner. Henry backs away, not out of fear but rather, with a malicious contempt at his brother's one-track mind, keen to see if the ostrich is ready for a second helping. Then Henry decides that if a man can be raped by an ostrich in front of his family and learn nothing, as James clearly has, then it is unlikely that a second session will make any difference.

He turns politely to Spartacus to shoo him away, but the ostrich is himself intent upon leaving. Now that he is able to process the scene visually, rather than just by smell, he realises he has not been making love to a particularly fertile and attractive female ostrich, but to a human. He feels decidedly uncomfortable and, with a polite nod at Henry, he disappears into the garden.

There is a faint yell and a crash to indicate Stevie has finally cleared the fence.

'Look, I'm sorry about this, Henry,' says James. 'It was a dinner party and it got a bit out of hand.'

'You were having sex with an ostrich.'

'That was not my fault.'

'Over my kitchen table.'

'I can explain. I'll pay for all the damage, apart from – even the things that Elizabeth threw.'

'Take that look off your face, Henry. Creative people are always a little eccentric,' says Henry's mother. 'You might at least put the kettle on, Elizabeth.' Elizabeth remains sobbing on the floor.

'Aren't you going to untie me?' repeats James.

'Not yet,' says Henry. 'I want you to stay there and realise what you've done first.'

'Oh for God's sake, Henry. Get out of the way.' Mrs Randall approaches the table with a carving knife.

'Just leave him there for five minutes, Mother!'

Henry tries to pull her away. She turns round and lashes out with the knife arm. She catches Henry in the jugular, which spurts and gushes. As he falls to the floor, dying, Henry feels totally relaxed. All his paranoid anxieties, his terror at the random, unfathomable cruelty of the universe, have left him.

'Killed by my own mother?' he thinks. 'That kind of makes sense.'

He dies with a smile on his face.

* * *

Donald is able to carry out his father's decree, unable to sleep on account of having come round and seen a man being fucked by an ostrich.

Three days after his death, a letter arrives for Les from a daytime talk show saying they would be interested in meeting him with a view to him coming on the show.

For a few weeks afterwards, James feels a tingling sensation in his nether regions and finally goes to see a doctor. When he gets the result of his tests, the consultant wears a grim expression.

'You have a very strange condition, Mr Randall. It seems you have radiation burns in your rectum. Do you have any idea how this might have occurred?'

'Not really,' James replies. 'Although I used to sit on the worktop in my kitchen in front of a microwave. Perhaps that's it.'

'Yes. Well, it's mixed with another condition which, I have to tell you, we've never seen before in this country.'

'Oh?'

'It's called Third-Policeman Syndrome. The only other recorded case occurred in Ireland. A policeman spent so much time on his bicycle on bumpy roads that he experienced a molecular transference and became part bicycle.'

'And I've got that?'

'Sort of. We've analysed your tissue samples and, well, you appear to have undergone some genetic modification. Your DNA bears traces of ostrich DNA.'

'Ostrich DNA?'

'Yes. You wouldn't be able to recall any... intimate physical experience you've had with an ostrich recently? That involved a certain amount of... vigorous movement?'

'Well, no.' It didn't seem an unreasonable claim.

'And you haven't noticed any strange behavioural traits? You see, it is possible that you may, in minor ways, begin behaving like an ostrich.'

'I'm sure I'd have noticed that,' says James, smiling and stretching one leg out in front of him for no reason.

'Hmm. Well, we'll run some more tests. In the meantime, this cream will help with the radiation burns. They're not too serious.'

'Thank you,' says James, inclining his neck in a long and languid bow.

He leaves the hospital urgently seeking a cab. He is due to visit Elizabeth in the psychiatric wing of a private hospital in Richmond where she was admitted on the night of her mother-in-law's birthday and has remained in a catatonic state ever since. James is going to be filmed visiting her for a programme on traumatic suffering that Sid has sold to ITV. He has already shot the scene where he sends his mother for a long convalescent holiday in Switzerland, and the reconstruction of his description to the police of the body-pierced punk who callously cut his brother's throat before his eyes (and who was found, dead from loss of blood, in the next garden a few days later).

Seeing a cab on the other side of the road, James steps out carelessly into the oncoming traffic. He sees the articulated lorry as it blows its horn, but instead of darting back on to the pavement, he decides the best way to avoid this predator is to disguise himself as a bush and he lays his head and neck flat on the ground and sticks his bottom up in the air. He is killed instantly.

His tearful agent is later quoted as saying his death is a tragic loss to British comedy, and that she will be issuing his last series on video as a tribute.

Loretta and Raschid fly to Costa Rica where they buy some land, build a house and live in happiness, raising children, mending motorbikes and farming the rainforest in an environmentally friendly way for the good of the planet. One of them gives thanks for his bounteous rewards to Allah, while the other attributes her good fortune to a dolphin.

Raschid wishes he could show his old comrades

how he has found a way to live without killing and without oppressing women, but he suspects they would not understand. At night he sits on his verandah, marvelling as the western sky glows a thousand shades of red and pink and wonders at the events which have brought him here. Though of course he believes it is the bounteous mercy of his God, he cannot help asking himself what would have happened if James Randall had not been quite so cocky about the Taliban and about his chances with Loretta; if Commander Omer's nephew had known how to set a video correctly; if Les had not decided to eat himself to death; if Stevie had not been so angry at the world; even if Stevie had understood there was a little more to Islam than blowing up off-licences.

But what of his dreams of Loretta, and hers of him? Was it all preordained? Or just a random collision of events? Raschid understands only that it is beyond his understanding and goes inside to embrace his beautiful wife, who believes she found him with the help of a dolphin. He is content.

And Spartacus? Who knows? Some say a strange long-legged creature, feathered and rapacious, roams Hampstead Heath at night, alone and pining for a partner. But then again, when was this ever not the case?

ACKNOWLEDGEMENTS

Thanks are due to Bill, Mark, Donna Hamilton, Charlotte Cox, Scappa, Simon Cartwright, Dan Docherty, Lionel, Vivienne, Sammy, and, of course, Muriel. Also to Peter Grahame and Huw Thomas, and to Sean, for knowing when what I really needed was a big tequila.

Icebox

Mark Bastable

Here's the deal.

Give Gabriel Todd your brain, and you'll live forever. Gabe'll freeze your head in a flask – and three hundred years from now, you'll be reborn in a new, perfect body. You will be immortal.

Unity Siddorn wants in. She has her own plans to save the world – with genetically pumped tomatoes, as you ask – but she's already thirty-bloody-one years old. In actuarial terms, her life is 41.3% over. She'll do anything – ANYTHING – for more time.

Don, her squeeze, is less keen. A pack of smokes and a gambler's shot at seventy years – he can live with that.

Suddenly, Gabe's theories are about to be put to the test – though circumstances are admittedly less than ideal. The police tend to take a professional interest in a freshly severed head. It's not something you can easily hide . . .

0 7472 6839 8

HEADLINE

MITCHELL SYMONS
All In

Steve Ross has had enough. Of gambling. Of losing. Of feeling bad about losing. Of worrying about what he's going to do when he's lost it all (the money, that is, followed by the wife and kids).

So naturally enough he makes a bet with himself. If his gambling account is in the black at the end of the year, he'll carry on. If it isn't, he'll top himself and leave Maggie to cop the insurance. That way, at least the kids are looked after, and he can escape the hell his life is fast becoming.

With Steve's luck it could go either way. But one thing's a dead cert. For the next twelve months he's going to experience the thrill of the ultimate high-stakes games . . .

Set in the twilight world of all-night poker games, betting shop coups and spread-betting mania, Mitchell Symons' debut novel is the darkly funny diary of one man dicing with death.

0 7472 7316 2

BEN RICHARDS

The Silver River

Nick Jordan is a young journalist who yearns for the big story.

Orlando Menoni is a cleaner from Uruguay who thinks back to the disappeared, and tries to come to terms with terrible loss.

This story of two very different men provides a moving and wholly original vision of the city in which the silver river takes on many meanings . . .

'Ben Richards's third book is all about the people who care, the people who don't yet, and the people who never will . . . Richards writes luminously about the grime and the glitter of London' *Independent*

'As suggestive and lyrical as it is pacy and slick' *Esquire*

'Refreshingly, Richards weaves his knowing sketches of London into a romantic South American tale of past revolution and lost love' *The Face*

'An intelligent, fast-paced read' *Mail on Sunday*

0 7472 5966 6

Slaphead

Georgina Wroe

Terry Small wants a woman. And he's seen a catalogue full of them. They're in Moscow, employed by REDS IN YOUR BEDS marriage agency. Armed with his best Calvin Klein underpants and his new abdominiser, Terry, the most dynamic conservatory salesman in Basingstoke, is on his way.

Awaiting him in Moscow is Katya, the agency's Russian representative. The only mate Katya cares about is her delinquent six-year-old, Sasha – and Terry, probably her most unprepossessing customer ever, isn't going to pose a problem for a woman who's already despatched a redundant husband to Siberia.

But Katya hasn't bargained for the intervention of Fate. Not to mention Moscow's latest entrepreneur, Professor Modin, formerly Lenin's embalmer, now specialising in providing a mounting pile of dead Mafia bosses with the flashy, unforgettable funeral they so richly deserve...

Fast, confident and fantastically funny, *Slaphead* introduces a writer of anarchic brilliance to the fiction-writing scene.

'A female Carl Hiassen' *The Times*

0 7472 6203 9

HEADLINE

Now you can buy any of these other bestselling Headline books from your bookshop or *direct from the publisher.*

FREE P&P AND UK DELIVERY
(Overseas and Ireland £3.50 per book)

Backpack	Emily Barr	£5.99
Icebox	Mark Bastable	£5.99
Killing Helen	Sarah Challis	£6.99
Broken	Martina Cole	£6.99
Redemption Blues	Tim Griggs	£5.99
Relative Strangers	Val Hopkirk	£5.99
Homegrown	Gareth Joseph	£5.99
Everything is not Enough	Bernardine Kennedy	£5.99
High on a Cliff	Colin Shindler	£5.99
Winning Through	Marcia Willett	£5.99

TO ORDER SIMPLY CALL THIS NUMBER

01235 400 414

or e-mail <u>orders@bookpoint.co.uk</u>

...ilability subject to change without notice.